THE
LEGEND
OF THE
PAINTED
HORSE

Also by Harry Combs

BRULES
THE SCOUT

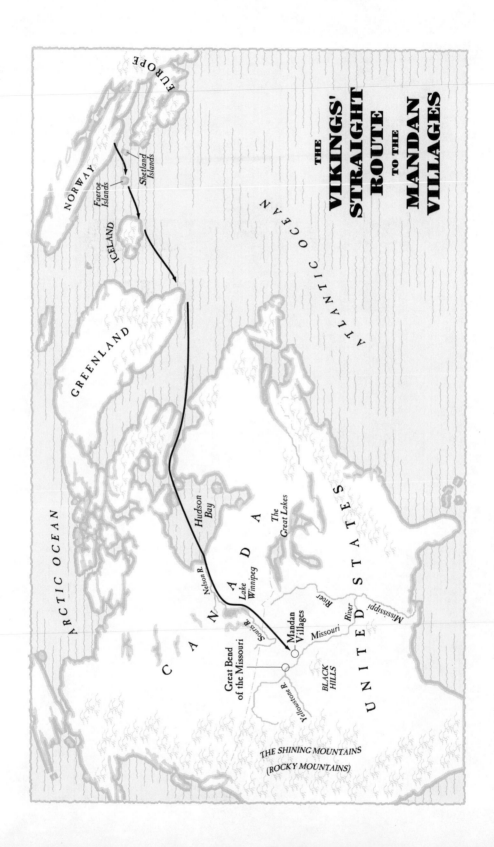

THE

VIKINGS'
STRAIGHT
ROUTE
TO THE
MANDAN
VILLAGES

EUROPE

NORWAY

Faeroe Islands

Shetland Islands

ICELAND

ATLANTIC OCEAN

GREENLAND

ARCTIC OCEAN

Hudson Bay

The Great Lakes

C A N A D A

Nelson R.

Lake Winnipeg

Souris R.

Mandan Villages

Great Bend of the Missouri

Missouri River

River

Mississippi

U N I T E D   S T A T E S

BLACK HILLS

Yellowstone R.

THE SHINING MOUNTAINS

(ROCKY MOUNTAINS)

THE
LEGEND
OF THE
PAINTED
HORSE

HARRY
COMBS

Delacorte Press

Published by
Delacorte Press
Bantam Doubleday Dell Publishing Group, Inc.
1540 Broadway
New York, New York 10036

Library of Congress Cataloging in Publication Data

Combs, Harry.
    The legend of the painted horse / by Harry Combs.
        p.   cm.
    ISBN 0-385-31201-6
    I. Title.
    PS3553.O4789L44   1996
    813'.54—dc20   96-7780
                                                                                CIP

Manufactured in the United States of America

Published simultaneously in Canada

October 1996

10 9 8 7 6 5 4 3 2 1

BVG

To my Ginney

ACKNOWLEDGMENTS

I wish to acknowledge the help of many fine people who worked with me on this book. I am most grateful to:

First, Lee Hayes, whom I must thank for her endless typing;

Next, Erin Porter, who did such a classical job of research on the Viking sagas;

Linda Rank, for her literary contribution;

Later, Mary Dow, who typed endlessly and made well chosen suggestions.

I want to thank my old friend, Corbin Douglas, who provided so much information and lore of the South Pacific.

And then last, but by no means least, Joyce Shaw, who virtually lived with this work for a year and saw it through endless editing and contributed so much to its literary style.

All fine people, I thank you.

THE
LEGEND
OF THE
PAINTED
HORSE

SUMMER OF 1950

Steven Cartwright poked the embers of the campfire and glanced at the young woman sitting on the log beside him. A pale shaft of moonlight penetrated the gently swaying tops of the mountain pines, bathing her in silver light. Somehow her loveliness stirred him. He rose and walked around the fire, nudging the ashes with his boot, then turned and looked out from the high mountainside at the moonlit valley below.

His mind drifted back to his youth, when life was bright and full of promise.

He had been born on this ranch in southwestern Colorado in 1898, almost the turn of the century. It was the last decade of the Old West. Even as a boy, he was well aware that the Indians had been gone from his part of the country fifteen years before he was born. There were no more colorful processions of the tribes, wandering through their hunting grounds. And far over the continental divide to the east, out on the great plains, the thundering sound of buffalo herds had been silenced forever. How he loved the West and its rich colorful history.

He thought back to when he was a kid and rode the high country slopes of Lone Cone Peak, looking for stray cattle. He remembered how he used to pretend, as he came around each shoulder of the mountain, that he would see a band of hunting Utes or perhaps a fearsome war party of Arapahoe in their color-ful beaded shirts and feathered war bonnets.

He would look out across the vast distances to the south-west desert and try to imagine what lay beyond those buttes and mountain ranges a hundred miles away. Someday, he vowed, he would find out. Those were the thoughts he had as a boy, long, long ago, when all things seemed bright and clear.

But now he took a little different view of the world. The Old West was long gone, faded into the past. It would never be quite the same again. But there were many things about this beautiful land, he told himself, that were still the same. The snow-capped peaks, the green, green grasses of the upper ranges in the spring, the gold of the quaking aspens in the fall, the mighty towering blue spruce trees that gave the high country a character of its own. They were the same, and so, too, were the big mule-deer bucks who stealthily eased their way through the oak brush. And of course, above all, there was that wild bugle call of a bull elk far off up on the mountainside on a September morning. These things were, even now, just as they had been in the Old West.

Now, so many years later, he could still vividly recall his childhood fantasies. He remembered growing up on this won-derful land, learning the ways of the cattlemen, horses, firearms, saddle gear, and long dusty cattle drives. He recalled the sad songs of his cowboy friends, who seemed to know so much about life when the West was young.

He remembered his youth with his mother, that stately and beautiful lady with the flashing black eyes who had taught him so much. He smiled as he thought of her now, gray-haired and noble, still ruling the ranch from the ample headquarters in the green hay meadows far below at the foot of the mountain.

Then there was Brules, the wild mountain man with the catlike eyes and the lithe stride of a panther, who lived far up on the southwestern side of Lone Cone Peak. In the old days, those who knew him—the buffalo hunters, the cavalrymen, the Indian scouts, the frontiersmen—called him Cat Brules. But that breed of man was long gone, and by 1900, the local ranchers called him "that damned outlaw."

Steven first heard of Brules on his ninth birthday. He was strictly admonished by his mother never to go near him under any circumstances.

His father called him a mountain man, but his mother used more uncomplimentary terms. When he asked why, she simply said, "Steven, I forbid you to ever go near that man."

"But why, Ma? He's just an old mountain man."

"Steven, that man is a thief and a murderer. He has a terrible criminal record and lives like a savage. I don't want you to go anywhere near him."

"But Ma, was he ever in jail? If he's so bad, why wasn't he hung?"

"Hanged, Steven. All I know is what I've heard. People say he was a very bad man when he was young and committed all sorts of crimes. I don't know if he was ever in jail. Perhaps he was too wild to be caught, but the stories about him can't all be fiction; there has to be some basis for them."

After hearing all this, Steven, of course, decided that the one place he really wanted to go was up on the mountain to see old Brules.

When he was eleven years old, he finally had his chance. After all the calves had been branded at the fall roundup held high up on the mountain, the cowboys from neighboring ranches rode off on their separate ways. Steven then mounted his pony and loped around the side of the Lone Cone until he came to the southwestern slope. There, just as he had been told, was a small cabin, and running along a few yards to the south was a little stream. Beside it knelt an old man panning for gold. It was Brules.

Steven was so excited, he forgot his manners and spoke before he was spoken to. "What ya' doing, mister?"

Brules looked up in anger and let it be known that he liked peace and quiet and didn't appreciate a young scamp blasting into his privacy. "I'm a mindin' my own business."

Steven rode away with mixed emotions. On the one hand, he was excited about having discovered Brules's home, and on the other, he was chagrined at having been so gruffly dismissed. Still, he decided to try again. Over the years, he stopped to see old Brules whenever he could, and gradually a deep friendship sprang up between the old man and the young boy.

Brules taught Steven many things: how to braid a rawhide lariat, how to build a figure-four bear trap, how to bore sight a rifle, how to start a fire with fire steel, and many other things that a right-minded mountain boy should know.

Once when Brules was sixty-three, he put on an exhibition

of shooting at his cabin site, just to show Steven what he could do.

At that time he had a shock of beard and a rather distinguished head of white hair that he partially contained under a black sombrero of unique character. The hat was old but obviously treasured, and it spoke of many things. It said, Here is the plainsman, the Indian fighter, the mountain man, the hunter. Even at his age his eyes were keen as fire, and he moved with the speed and grace of a cat. His face, although weathered, was still handsome, and he stood tall and straight.

Steven had been around men with guns all his life, both before and since, and had seen all kinds of shooting, both good and bad, but he'd never seen anything like Brules that afternoon. Brules fired many times at still or moving targets, with both pistol and rifle, and never missed.

He had an old 1873 lever-action Winchester. The stock at one time had evidently been badly cracked just back of the pistol grip, for it was bound tightly with shrunken buckskin so hard-used it appeared to be part of the wood. The stock itself was old and scratched in places, but the barrel was clean and bright, and the lever action was slick and sound. His old .38 Smith & Wesson revolver was the same—worn with age and use but still smooth and clean in action.

Not only was Brules's shooting unsurpassed, but the speed with which he fired his weapons was unbelievable. He was so fast, it was difficult for the eye to follow his movements. He complained that his reflexes had slowed and his eyesight had dimmed since his youth. That may have been so, but Steven had never seen any shooting comparable to what Brules showed him that afternoon. He was convinced Brules was the best gunman who ever lived.

Once when Steven was about twelve, he let a word slip out to his mother about his visits on the mountain. She saw to it that when his father returned that evening, Steven got a painful lesson in the woodshed. After that, his visits with Brules were always very carefully guarded secrets.

Now, almost forty years later, on this late lovely summer evening, high up on the mountain, Steven felt strangely disturbed in the presence of this beautiful woman as he watched her walk gracefully toward him. He trembled when she untied her hair and the firelight played on the long auburn waves.

Damn, he said to himself, damn me. I'm letting her make a fool of me. What the hell do I think I'm doing? Here I am, getting all upset about a woman who is really just a girl. She's only twenty-four years old, and I'm an old man of fifty-two. I'm thinking things that I have no business thinking about.

The truth is that I don't feel old. I can ride, shoot, and fly just as I always could. And God knows, I feel the same way about a woman as I did when I was a kid. On the other hand, in those days I wasn't mooning over somebody who was twenty-eight years younger than me. I must be crazy! I've got to stay away from this girl, or she's liable to make even more of a fool of me than she's already done.

Steven busied himself by spreading out the bedrolls and covering the packsaddles with canvas tarps in case of rain. Then he went out and gathered some more firewood—any damn thing to keep his mind off his rising feelings for this girl.

That afternoon they had come up the mountain trail, just as they had done several times earlier in the summer. This afternoon was no different. They always had a pack string with them if they were going to camp out for a day or two looking for strays.

As always, he was in the lead, and she was following be-hind, herding the four mules and the two extra saddle horses. She'd been around the ranch long enough to be good at that sort of thing. He kept telling her that she was the best "hand" in the whole outfit. She would laugh and retort, "Now, there you go again, just trying to get more work out of me."

In a few minutes, he came back into the ring of firelight, knelt down, and drew out an ember to his pipe. Becky watched him intently, her gray-green eyes sparkling. Despite his age, he seemed to move with catlike grace.

What an amazing man he is! she thought. His weather-beaten features testified to his rugged outdoor life, yet he was so educated and well-bred. True, he was older, fifty perhaps, but she told herself that he had the body of a much younger man, a man about thirty-five, she judged.

She had known him almost since she could first remember, and he always looked the same. From the time she was a little girl, he had constantly fascinated her with tales of far-off times and places. It was as if she had known him in another life—a thousand years ago. She was never tired or bored in his com-pany. He was always telling her something new and amazing.

Steven was so knowledgeable about all sorts of fascinating things about the world: history, geography, wars, and especially airplanes and horses. Yes, that was another thing that she liked so much about him—the ease with which he handled horses, the way they responded to him, nudged up to him, and obeyed all his commands. Right now she wanted to hear what he had to say about the wild horse herd they had seen earlier.

She looked toward him. "Oh, Steven, weren't those wild horses beautiful today! Especially that painted stallion! Where do you suppose they all came from?"

He looked up at her and grinned. She liked his grin. She always felt warm when he did that.

"Well," he said, "my grandmother brought them here from Wyoming."

"Your grandmother!" she said.

"Yes, my maternal grandmother. You'll understand when I tell you the story. It is in many ways the story of my life."

She stood up for a minute and brushed a fire ash from her jeans, a slender graceful figure, a young woman in full bloom.

His heart began to pound. Oh, God, he groaned to himself, just look at her.

"Do you remember when we first met?" he asked.

"Indeed I do," she said.

"What do you remember about it?"

"Well, I remember that you had been with Pan American Airways doing something out in the Pacific. You had to come home suddenly."

"Yes, that was in the summer of 1938, when Father was dying," he said. "Mother sent me a wire, and I caught the next Clipper Ship out of Wake Island, where I was checking on a seaplane base we had constructed two years earlier. Transportation was very poor back then, and it was no easy feat to get from a remote island in the Pacific to a ranch in southwestern Colorado.

When I got to the ranch, I found my father weak and dying, trying to convey a few last words to my mother. Mother was as stately and beautiful as I had always remembered.

I turned my attention to my father. That great oak of a man, whose power and character had dominated me for so long, now lay on his deathbed.

The lump grew in my throat as I held my father's hand. My

mother, her black eyes shining with tears, watched her husband, who had been the pillar of her life, passing away into the great beyond.

My father died later that same day. His last few words directed at me expressed the wisdom of a great cattle rancher: 'Remember, son, don't push the summer range too soon. Work the south side of the mountain first. Later, you can swing the herd around to the north. The north face of the mountain is our best summer range. Now, take care of your mother.' He said that last sentence twice, then turned his face to the wall and died.

I left the room fighting back the tears. I walked out of the ranch house and down the long lane that led to the gate from which I could look up at Lone Cone Peak and across the pleasant irrigated meadows that were so green on that summer day. It was there that I first saw you: the gangly little twelve-year-old girl my parents had taken in four years before. You were sitting on the top rail of the gate to the corral with your long braids hanging out from under a cowboy hat. You were chewing on something, and I was hoping it was licorice."

"I remember meeting you," she said, wide-eyed, "In your Pan Am captain's uniform, you were the handsomest man I'd ever seen."

He laughed. "I reckon that uniform was pretty crumpled by then, but I didn't have time to worry about clothes. I just worried about getting here before Father died, and I just made it. You were a freckle-faced skinny kid. I wasn't surprised to see you there. Mother had written me about you."

"Yes," she said. "I'm sure she told you the whole thing. I was only eight when I came to the ranch with my mother and father in 1934."

"Yes," he said, "I remember something about that. They

were archaeologists. Weren't they looking for cliff dwellings and studying the Anasazi people?"

"Yes. They had done a lot of work at Mesa Verde and down on the Navajo Reservation at Chinlee and Betatikan, as well as in southern Arizona. They had often heard that there were wonderful cliff dwellings down around the 'goose necks' of the San Juan River. Even at that time, it was very wild country."

"I know it well. It was a damn wild area. I was a rod and chain man on a survey team down there in the summer of 1916."

"Were you really, Steven? Then you do know. Your dad's ranch was the only decent dwelling place in southwestern Colorado back in those days. Still, it was a hundred miles away from the San Juan. But Mom and Dad had a Dodge power wagon, and although the roads were only dirt, they could still move around pretty well. It wasn't like riding horseback."

"No," he said, laughing, "that's absolutely true. I did it on horseback in 1916. It took two days of hard riding to get home."

She nodded. "Anyway, my dad and mom made a deal with your mother and father. They stayed at your ranch and drove the old dirt roads down to the San Juan when they were ready to go on their explorations. During the wintertime, of course, we'd go back to Massachusetts. That arrangement worked just fine. We lived on your ranch during the summer months from 1934 to 1938. That was when you were gone with Pan Am. Many times I was left alone in the care of Aunt Rose. I grew to love her, and I think she also cared for me. I never got to go with my parents on the river because they said the trip was too rough and dangerous. I'm sure they were right because, as you know, Daddy and Mother were lost on their last trip."

"Yes, I know," he said gently.

"It had always been their plan to raft in with all of their supplies and walk out when their work was done, but unfortunately that didn't happen in the summer of 'thirty-eight," she said, her voice cracking slightly.

"I remember the story. Didn't they send out several search parties to look for your parents? It seems to me that they did finally find the raft."

"Yes, they found the raft, but they didn't find any trace of Mom or Dad." She turned away and said nothing more.

Steven could see that it was time to drop the subject. A few minutes later he said, "I remember you vividly. You certainly were some gal. You had a lot of pep and were always mischievous as the dickens. You'd rather ride a horse than eat."

"I certainly would," she said. "I loved the ranch then and always have. I had nowhere to go, and that's why Aunt Rose adopted me."

"Oh, you had a place to go, all right. You worked your way into Mother's heart, and she wouldn't have dreamed of having you go anywhere else. As a matter of fact, when Mom wrote me about it, I thought it was a great idea too.

When I got to know you, I discovered you would do some of the damnedest things. You weren't afraid to ride any of those unbroken broncs. I had a lot of admiration for you. I remember thinking, She's either got lots of guts or no brains."

She laughed. "Yes, I guess I did ride quite a few."

"I know you did. Did you ever get hurt at all?"

"Well, once I got my leg jammed against a corral post by a big stallion that had his head down and was bucking like mad. He crashed into the barrier, and I limped around for a few days, but aside from that I never had any problems."

"Well," he said, "I've watched you coming up these trails

many times now. You're a wonderful rider. You have great hands and a real way with horses."

"Coming from you, that's a real compliment."

"I mean it to be. You're about as good a horsewoman as I've ever seen. I'm really proud of you. You have done awfully well at the ranch. Of course, you have had the best of training," he finished, tongue in cheek.

"Yes," she said. "I remember a little about that training."

"What do you remember in particular?"

"Well, there was the time I left the gate open to the alfalfa pasture."

"Yes, I remember that too." He laughed.

She blushed and stuck her tongue out at him.

"You know, that was pretty serious business," he said. "You know damn well that cattle can't be allowed to get into fresh alfalfa. They will bloat and die. We lost eight good mother cows because a little girl didn't bother closing the gate! Especially when she'd been told to do so time and again."

"Yes, I remember that."

"I'm sure you do. They were prime young cows—a loss of some four thousand dollars."

"Yes, but you didn't have to spank that hard."

"I didn't realize that it was any harder than ordinary. I just used my hand. Heck! I used to catch it with a paddle or a switch."

"I don't care how you caught it. You delivered it damn hard, and it stung like the dickens," she said.

"Rebecca Stuart," he said slowly, "it's good business for little girls, when they disobey, to have a first-class, A-number-one bare-bottom spanking."

"Well, you certainly gave it to me, and I guess I deserved it, but I was pretty upset and angry for a long time."

"Have you gotten over it?" he asked.

"Almost," she answered, "but don't call me Rebecca. It always makes me think of it."

He looked at her and grinned. "I know one thing, Becky," he said. "You never left that gate open again."

"No, never!" she said. "Never, ever."

"Well, if that's what it took, to my way of thinking, it turned out very satisfactorily."

She laughed. "Okay, Mr. Smart Aleck, it may take a long time to get even with you, but I will sometime."

He looked at her for quite a while and thought, Lady, you don't know, you have long since gotten even with me. What I gave you was nothing to what you're putting me through now. I have a heartache for which there is no medicant. Here you are, the most beautiful thing I've ever seen, and I can't even touch you.

He wanted to take her in his arms, he wanted to kiss her desperately, he wanted to hold her, but he couldn't touch her— not because she was too young, but because people would think he was too old.

He thought, Hell, I'm not really old. I'm still youthful and strong in many ways, but I'll be perceived as too old for her. I am too old by custom, by tradition, by convention, and so I must stand aside and see someone else take her away. When that happens, as it surely will, it's going to kill me. Maybe I'll shoot the son of a bitch before he gets off the ranch with her.

His mood was dark, and there seemed to be nothing he could say to break the silence.

Finally, Becky sat down beside him, and he immediately

felt comfortable. "Steven, why don't you tell me the story that you promised to tell me when I was younger?"

"What one was that?" he asked.

"The one about the wild horses. Remember? It was the second time you came back from all your flying. I think it was about 1943, during World War II. You were all handsome in your naval aviator's uniform. It was even more dashing than the Pan Am outfit from five years before. Steven, that was seven years ago. Don't you think it's about time you told me the story?" She paused and looked at him intently. "Please stop worrying about things that neither you nor I can do anything about."

There was something in her voice and in her demeanor that he couldn't decipher. Did she have an inkling of how he felt?

He instinctively put his arm around her and gave her a hug. It was the same kind of hug that he'd given her for many years when they were out together or kidding around at the corral. It was a hug that said, "I'm fond of you, you're one of the family, I love you, you're a good little girl." He would have liked to make something else of it, but since that was impossible, he forced himself to think of other things.

"What do you mean about wild horses?" he asked.

"Don't you remember? We were standing on the porch of the ranch house watching some wild horses on the mountain through field glasses? I was just seventeen then, and you said to me, 'Someday when we have time, I'll tell you the story about wild horses, where they came from, and how they got to be the way they are.' You told me, 'It is a very strange and beautiful story that most people didn't know much about.' That was seven years ago."

There was a moment of silence between them.

"Why don't you tell me now, please? I am still interested," she said.

Again, he looked at her for a long moment, "All right, young lady, now that you are the venerable age of twenty-four, I will tell you the story."

She smiled and snuggled close to him.

"Millions of years ago," he began, "the original wild horses ran loose across the great stretches first of North America and then on to the steppes of Asia. This was long, long before man existed. For some unknown reason, the horse died out here in North America. Later, when man came on the scene in the Old World—this would have been about six thousand years ago—he started domesticating the wild horse. That's when our story really begins."

Becky looked at him with those beautiful gray-green eyes.

"Less than a thousand years ago, horses were brought back to the New World and were caught and tamed by the Indians. Now, just look at the North American Indian and what the horse meant to him. To Indians, horses meant everything. They were the sign of wealth, a medium of exchange in trade. In short, they were a power to be worshiped. The Indian knew in his heart they had been sent to him by the Great Spirit to enrich his life. For that reason, somehow, in his mind they had mystical powers, strange and inexplicable, but nevertheless real."

"Mystical powers?" Becky asked. "All kinds of horses?"

"No, to be honest, not all of them. Although all horses were, to Indians, a manifestation of the Great Spirit's blessing, one breed of horse was particularly dear to their hearts, the painted ones.

Just imagine what a dramatic sight it must have been. The Indian mounted on his pinto, with his war bonnet, long-feathered lance, war paint, and evil-eyed buffalo-hide shield. Somehow the pinto, in his brilliance and natural pageantry, seemed to embody the free spirit of the Plains Indian. The pinto set a perfect background for the savage's own colorful costume and made him stand out like some sort of god. Indeed, while he rode his horse, perhaps he believed himself to be just that.

When he rode, didn't he have the speed of a bird? Didn't he stand ten feet tall in the saddle? Yes indeed, it was the painted horse that held a special place in his heart.

True, there were blacks and bays and duns and whites. Some of them had great speed and endurance, obedience and intelligence that were not to be scorned. But the paint stood above them all in the Indian's mind.

He felt that the painted horse was somehow endowed with mystical powers. He could carry his rider through battle without harm and almost bear his master up into the sky to the arms of the Great Spirit. He was the Indian's link with the supernatural, a handhold on the toga of the Great Spirit. The paint was special that way and was treated as such by the Indian.

Now, here is a strange, strange matter. For four hundred years, we have been told that the first horses came to the New World with the Spanish, and that the descendants of their runaways became the wild mustangs that the Indians caught and tamed. I don't think the painted horses came that way, though. Really, I don't. I have a different idea about where they came from."

"You mean someone else brought the paints to America, perhaps by another route?"

He nodded. "Definitely by another route."

"Steven Cartwright, that is the craziest thing I've ever heard. Everyone knows the Spanish introduced horses into the New World."

"Well, Becky, now just how do you know that? Can you prove it?" asked Steven. "Think of this. From the mouth of the Columbia River in the west, all the way across the northern part of the North American continent to Nova Scotia, the distance is three thousand six hundred miles. It's full of forests, rivers, lakes, prairies, and mountains. A hell of a big territory. Just tell me, who was in that wilderness a thousand years ago to say whether or not Indians had horses in that part of the continent before the Spanish came? No one knows! People might say that you cannot prove they did, but by the same token, you cannot say they didn't."

"Now, Steven," she said, "that's just going around in circles. It's a bit ridiculous."

"No, my dear, I don't think it is, because I think that I can prove that horses were there, at least in part of that vast country."

She looked at him steadily as he began again.

"How is it that in 1805, when the Lewis and Clark expedition entered the valley of the Columbia, they found so many beautiful painted horses owned by tribes like the Kutenai, Shoshones, Flatheads, and Blackfeet? Lewis was so impressed, he wrote in his diary, 'It is not uncommon for one warrior to own two hundred head.'

Why were the painted horses all gathered there? Why weren't they found farther to the south? Why did the Comanche tribes along the Mexican border have to trade with the Shoshones (the only northern Indians who spoke their language) for painted horses? Why didn't they have any of their own?

The truth of the matter is that the painted horse didn't come with the Spaniards."

"Steven," she said, "how can you possibly say that!"

"One reason I'm sure is that the Spanish horsemen had no use for paints. Let's take just a moment and look at the Spanish horses.

The original horses of Spain were of Iberian stock, similar to European saddle horses, bays or blacks, sorrels, white, grays, or duns. Sometime during the early eighth century the Islamic culture spread into Spain. It was at this time that the Arabs brought their famous horses into Spain and superimposed the Arab stock on the Iberian horse.

The Arabs, it must be remembered, had no use for painted horses either. Traditionally they destroyed painted foals at birth.

Curiously, the first introduction of paints into Spain came as a result of the subjugation of the Spanish Netherlands in the War of the Spanish Succession. The importance of this is that the Spanish Netherlands was close to Friesland and the Scandinavian countries, which had many painted horses.

The painted horses were introduced into Spain from the north. In fact, the first artist's pictures we have of them date from 1650 (160 years after the Spanish had entered the New World). So as you can see, the paints were never included in the first Spanish horse shipments to Mexico, or to Central and South America.

The Spanish, like the Arabs, always ridiculed the paint and continued to do so, even after their introduction. We see this in the story of Don Quixote, whose painted steed, Rocinante, reflected his master's comical air.

Yet mysteriously the Indian, particularly the northern mountain Indians, had paints in considerable numbers."

Becky could contain herself no longer. "Now wait a minute, Steven, let me ask the obvious. If the northern Indian tribes had so many paints, where did they come from? Where, when, and how?"

"My dear lady, that's just the question. The mysterious source of the beautiful painted horse of the northern Indian tribes is a secret of history and a legend. It's a beautiful legend and very, very old."

"How old?" she asked.

"Oh, perhaps as old as thirty thousand years."

"You mean thirty thousand years ago they came to this country?"

"No, no. I mean thirty thousand years ago is more like the beginning of the painted horse in the world."

"Well, where did that happen?" she asked, raising her eyebrows.

"I believe the first traces of the painted horse can be found in the brown, rocky, snow-flecked Khingan Mountains of northeastern China. This would have been during the last glacial age of the Pleistocene. Its legend runs like a rainbow curve westward across the mountain ranges of the Mongolian Altai to the Tibetan Himalayas and Carpathians, the Urals, and into the mountains of Scandinavia—even across the Norwegian Sea to Iceland and the fjords of Greenland, on to the western shores of Hudson Bay, and finally to the open prairies and what were once called the Shining Mountains of northwestern America.

The migration ends approximately eight hundred years ago in a blaze of beautiful painted horses. It ends in the hollow of a basin—the basin of the great Columbia River.

THE SNOW LINE

Before I tell you how and when painted horses appeared in America," Steven continued, "let me tell you how I got interested in researching it."

"My, it sounds as if you've made quite a project out of this."

"I guess I have. I started working on it a long time ago. You know, my first year at Yale was a bit discouraging."

"Tell me about it," she said tenderly.

"It was back in 1916, when I was eighteen. I was just a country boy from a remote ranch in southwestern Colorado. Old Brules had a fit when I told him I was going back east to college. He allowed as how I was a western boy and ought to go to college in the West. In a way, he was probably right. But Mom and Dad wanted me to go east for an education in the worst way, and so I finally went. I had a few eastern contacts but very little knowledge of eastern customs. Sure, I made the freshman football team without any trouble and got acquainted with a lot of fellows that way, but it took a long time to make firm, fast friends."

Becky looked at him for a long minute. "You missed old Brules, didn't you, Steven?"

"I sure did," he replied. "But you know, I spent three wonderful days with him up at his cabin on the mountain before I left. I'll never forget it because that was when he started telling me the story of his life, which I had so desperately wanted to know."

"Oh, Steven," she said, "How wonderful! I never have known very much about Brules. Tell me about him first."

"Well, back in October 1867, when Brules was eighteen, he was driving cattle up the Chisolm Trail to the railhead at Hays City, Kansas. That's where he met and fell in love with a beautiful dance-hall girl. He killed his bullying trail boss in a gunfight over her, and they escaped on horseback in the middle of the night. In a desperate effort to throw off the pursuing posse, they crossed the Arkansas River and headed for the head-waters of the Cimarron. It was a very dangerous route to take since it led right through Quahadi Comanche territory. After several days without any sign of the posse or Indians, they began to relax. They spent two exciting, happy weeks together. But then one terrifying night, they were captured by the Coman-ches. The girl met a torturous death by fire. Brules was to be next, but he managed a last-minute escape. After recovering his rifle and killing half the pursuing Comanche party, he climbed over the high Sangre de Cristo Mountains and dropped down into the valley of the San Luis in Spanish America.

In Taos, he organized a buffalo hunt with his best friend, a

Mexican named Pedro "Silver Pete" Gonzales, so named because he always regaled himself in silver trappings.

The two young men ventured out onto the wild plains east
of the Sandia Mountains and hunted all the way to the Canadian River. After a tremendously successful hunt, they had a
huge stockpile of buffalo hides. It was more than they could
carry back in one trip. They decided that Pedro should drive a
wagonload back to the Santa Fe Trail, where the hides could be
sold or stored, then come back for Brules and the rest. Pedro
never returned from that first trip.

After waiting for weeks, Brules, with his keen hunter's
sense, was still able to follow the faded tracks of Pedro's mule
team. Eventually, he found the wreckage of the wagon, surrounded by dead mules feathered with arrows and a few rotted
buffalo hides. A little farther on, he discovered, to his horror,
that Pedro had been dragged to death from a horse and that his
shattered body had been left for the coyotes.

In a deep rage, Brules declared a one-man war against the
Comanche nation. For four years, he stalked the Indians and left
his sign—the sign of a cat—at the scene of every fight and
ambush. The Comanches began to believe he was an evil spirit,
for he stalked them with the greatest skill and was a dead shot
with his rifle. He so terrorized them and inflicted such incredible
losses on the tribe that they left that part of the country.

Brules, satisfied that he had avenged his friend, traveled
west again to the border of Utah and the La Sal Mountains.
There he happily engaged in the dangerous business of hunting
grizzly bears. On one such hunt, he was badly mauled by a giant
grizzly. Somehow he managed to crawl down the mountain to a
stream. He was found there by a Shoshone girl, named Wild
Rose, who nursed him back to health.

In 1875, he married that beautiful Shoshone girl from the Wind River country of Wyoming and brought her back to his cabin on Lone Cone Peak. After a short idyllic time together, Wild Rose had a terrible accident. She was crushed under her falling horse in the last month of her pregnancy. After a painful struggle, she died in Brules's arms just three weeks after her baby was born. She had named the child Morning Star.

Brules, devastated and heartbroken, found himself in a terrible quandary. There he was all alone high up on a mountain with a dead wife and a hungry baby and no way to feed the child. He realized he had to get to a wet nurse.

He wrapped Wild Rose's body up in blankets, as for an Indian burial. Then with ropes he drew her up to the ceiling of the cabin, where she would be well protected from bears and other animals.

He took little Morning Star, naked as she was, and tied her back of his left shoulder next to his bare skin and pulled a long bear-hide coat over both for warmth.

He barred the cabin door as best he could and headed out for Medicine Hat, on the Navajo reservation. He chose the strongest stallion from his remuda and made a remarkable ride to Medicine Hat, a distance of 124 miles, in twenty-four hours. There among the squaws he found a wet nurse for his little baby girl.

Accompanied by the wet nurse and her warrior, he took the baby back up to the Shoshone reservation at Lander, Wyoming, and left her with her aunt. He paid off the Navajo couple with some of the prized painted horses that had been part of Wild Rose's dowry.

Brules was heartsick and did not want to return to his home. His good friend, Wesha, the son of the Shoshone chief, convinced him that a good war would ease his pain. So they and eighty other warriors went off to join General Crook at Cloud Peak Camp in fighting against their blood enemies, the deadly Sioux. They were with Crook at the Battle of the Rosebud. Later, Brules carried a message from Crook to General Custer through Indian-infested country and became a scout for Custer at the Battle of the Little Bighorn. Some time after that, he was asked to join Crook in the Apache wars against Geronimo.

Brules finally returned to his cabin in the late 1880s or early 1890. It was about twenty years later that I first met him.

Yes, Becky, I did miss him during that first year at Yale. After football season was over, I was frequently lonely and homesick. I would often go for long walks to try to shake my mood.

When you're a young man who has come from the West, where the distances are vast and spread out under the great canopy of the blue sky, it's difficult to adjust to the narrow confines of the New England countryside and the ghastly weather.

Anyway, on one of my afternoon walks, I wandered into Yale's Peabody Museum and found it absolutely fascinating!"

"The Peabody Museum!" she said. "Oh, yes. I've heard about it."

"George Peabody was a great scientist of the mid-1800s, and he established the museum. It had all sorts of wonderful exhibits and I visited it regularly. One of the things that really stimulated my curiosity was the eohippus."

"Say that again."

"The eohippus, the 'dawn horse.' "

"What is it?"

"My dear, that is the earliest known ancestor of the horse.

Strangely enough, it was only the size of a dog, and it was found by Peabody right here in North America.

It seems that almost all of the great prehistoric discoveries and geological changes come from the Old World rather than the New. But here was something that absolutely came from the New World—the eohippus, the little horse of millions of years ago."

"Fascinating," she said. "What became of it?"

"It was like this," Steven said. "Long, long ago, the continent of North America was the birthplace of the horse. As I have said, the earliest ancestor was called eohippus. It ran across the open plains of the Missouri Basin. Its fossil bones, along with the bones of several branches of its descendants, have been found and studied by paleontologists and have given us clues to the evolution of the modern horse, which we call the Equus caballus.

Down through the geological ages, all of the various ancestors of the modern horse died out—all but Equus caballus. Although it became extinct in the Americas, it ended up on the vast steppelands in Asia—the only equine survivor.

In fact, a branch of Equus caballus, Przewalski's horse, was still living in a wild state on the plains of Mongolia a hundred years ago. We now know that Przewalski's horse had a different chromosome count from all other horses and therefore was not the original source of the modern horse, but rather a sort of offshoot.

We also know that except for Przewalski's horse, all breeds of horses have been utilized by man in one fashion or another. Their domestication has continued for a period of at least six thousand years.

Another thing we know is that nature has a subtle genetic

coding for all living things. It is the means by which organisms adapt to a changing environment and enhance their odds for survival. Why a black or a bay horse developed might be difficult but not impossible to explain. When it comes to a painted horse, the puzzle would seem to be even more complex, until we really look into the matter.

Actually, the camouflage of the painted horse gives us a clue to its origins and how it developed.

The painted horse consists of two color types and two pattern types. The color combinations are either black and white or brown and white. The pattern types are either Tobiano or Overo. In addition to the painted horse, there is also the appaloosa, which has a different set of colorings but might have developed its qualities and characterisitics for the same reason as the paint.

When we look at these horses with their effective coloration, our immediate question is, under what circumstances could such a kaleidoscope of patterns and colors be used for camouflage? Wouldn't its colors make a paint stand out more clearly than if it were a solid color?

The answer is simply that under most circumstances it would.

Perhaps this is one of the reasons why the Arabs were not too keen on the painted horse. It might have been too conspicuous in a desert environment. A dun-colored horse would be a much better camouflage in the desert. In fact, dun is close to the coloration of the elk and the red stag, and it has served as excellent camouflage in forest environments. The painted horse, on the other hand, would stand out like a sore thumb in the areas where those animals range.

Even if the painted horse were out in the open grassland

prairies, its coloration would make it extraordinarily conspicuous and, therefore, easy prey for the saber-toothed tiger, the bear, or the most deadly hunter of all—man himself. In the desert, the forest, or on the grassland, the painted horse was not very well camouflaged. So we must look for a condition under which the painted pattern would be advantageous and assume that its camouflage was developed to accommodate it to those surroundings.

Under what conditions would a horse become painted, either brown and white or black and white? If we apply our imaginations, it is not too difficult to see. The picture emerges very plainly, like the answer to a puzzle, once we get the pieces in place.

Let us examine the world environment at the time the painted horse developed its characteristics. It would have been during the last glacial age, which lasted from roughly 25,000 B.C. to about 9,000 B.C., a long enough period of time for natural selection to do its work.

During the last glacial age, three great glaciers existed simultaneously. The Laurentian glacier was in the Laurentian Shield area of Canada and the northern United States; the Scandinavian glacier covered all of the Scandinavian countries and part of northern Russia on the east side of the Baltic, and it extended as far south as Germany and the Balkans. The third was the Siberian glacier, which stretched out over the middle and eastern part of the Asiatic continent, embracing that area which we more or less define as Siberia.

When these glaciers were at their maximum, they were anywhere from three to seven thousand feet in depth. As they spread out over vast areas they locked in enormous quantities of water.

As a result, sea levels were greatly reduced, and large tracts of land on the continental shelves emerged, to become either forests or grasslands. Certainly they were habitats adequate to sustain animals and men.

One of the most notable of these newly formed tracts was a land bridge across the Bering Strait from Alaska to Siberia. This was the very bridge which allowed the modern horse, Equus caballus, to travel from the New World to the Old.

The horses, like all the other animals of the Pleistocene Age, must have grazed along the edges of the glaciers. The mois- ture in those areas produced fine grassland, particularly in the spring of the year. As a matter of fact, the best hunting grounds for northern game are still found along the edges of glaciers.

Thousands of years went by, and then the glaciers began to melt. They receded in slow progression toward the highest and coolest points of land, the great mountain ranges of Europe, Asia, and America. When the ice retreated, the sea levels rose and the land bridges disappeared. The herds of Equus caballus in the Old World were isolated in the process.

No one seems to know why the early horses died out in North America, but I believe that along the four-thousand-mile snow line of the Siberian glacier, a certain type of horse, with the subtle capacity of nature's genetic coding, gradually changed its coloration to become the painted horse.

As the snows receded from the desert mountains, the brown and white painted horse blended perfectly with the brown rocks and white snow patches of the desert mountain- sides.

Where the slopes of the mountains were volcanic and the rocks were black against the white snow, the black and white horse blended beautifully. In some other areas there may have been other factors or some combination of those already mentioned, but wherever they were, the hides of the horses eventually began to blend in with the environment.

It is easy to see how even the appaloosa, with its spectacularly spotted rump, could be disguised on the snowbanks of a mountain, especially when it had its head down to feed uphill. Its rump blended in perfectly with the snow patches, and what's more, no horse feeds facing downhill.

This, then, was the snowline horse, the horse of the North, the horse that followed the ebbing glaciers to their mountain fastnesses. It became painted in accordance with the genetic code that operates to protect all animals from their enemies.

Later, as descendants of this horse met warmer conditions or as they drifted south of the snow line to warmer pastures, nature's camouflaging processes took over again, and those horses changed to other colors—blacks, bays, duns, whites—colors that served to protect them in their environments. But all of them came from the snowline horse long, long ago."

There was a chill in the night air, and the wind whispered softly through the tall pines. Steven stood up and threw another log on the flickering fire.

Becky watched him for a moment, then spoke.

"I'm beginning to understand a little about your theory of the painted horse, and I can see how its descendants could have eventually drifted toward the south, developing different solid colors as they went. But"—she paused—"it's still just a theory."

She looked up at him quizzically, then shook her head and smiled. "Yet I must admit, it's amazingly logical. But now I'm wondering: If the horses died out in North America, who brought the painted horse back here?"

Steven drew a deep breath. "I believe that the painted

horse arrived back on this continent in the hands of men—not Spanish men but northern men who came here five hundred years before the Spaniards.

The Spanish horses that were brought to Mexico by the conquistadores were direct descendants of the cross between the Arab horses of the plain of Andalusia and the European saddle horses of the medieval knights.

After the conquest of Mexico, great horse ranches sprang up in the north, particularly around Chihuahua. During their early days, the rancheros took extensive measures to keep the horses out of the hands of the Indians. On foot, the Indians were powerless and confined to small villages. However, if *los Indios* were to acquire horses and learn to use them, they could become a real menace. The Spaniards might find the conquest of the plains north of the Rio Grande very difficult.

So whenever the ranchers lost horses to raiding bands of Indians, they would follow them across the Rio Grande and hundreds of miles up into Texas. Their efforts to recapture the horses were sustained through the late fifteen hundreds; but finally it became a hopeless situation.

The horses had multiplied by great numbers in the wonderful grasslands of Chihuahua. Their increased population roamed wild in bands, each led by one stallion who had fought his way to supremacy over his rivals. Often he stood aloof from the herd on some high promontory, his watchful eye guarding against all enemies. At the slightest sign of danger, his shrill whinny and pounding hooves propelled his band of mares and colts into a dash for safety. The stallion followed in the rear. With their manes and tails flowing in the wind, a band of wild horses in flight was the very symbol of freedom—all grace and speed, endurance and energy.

The runaway horses were described by some writers as 'thundering out of the Southwest.' They flashed in a kaleido-scope of colors through the desert mesquite amid clouds of dust, and they raced over the grassy plains with drumming hooves.

It is little wonder that those horses delighted the Indians. Perhaps in them, they saw their own freedom, their own wings, and somehow mystically, their own bridge to life in the spirit world.

Eventually the mustangs—or the *mestengos,* as the Span-iards called 'the wild ones'—were caught, trained, and bred by the Indians. The horse expanded the horizons of nation after nation of North American natives, and in their savage hands it served as a formidable barrier to the westward advancement of the American pioneer.

But it was the painted horse that was the major symbol for all Indian nations. Just as Pegasus, the winged horse of Greek mythology, ruled the imagination of the classical ancients, so did the painted horse appear everywhere in the lore of Ameri-can Indians.

So revered was the painted horse that those warriors who rode on whites, blacks, or other tones would often paint symbols on the sides of their horses with vermilion clay to give them the semblance of the paint.

Paints were only occasionally found among the Indians of the south. They were far more prevalent among the northern tribes for the simple reason that they had gotten there first from farther north."

"From farther north?" asked Becky.

"Yes, you know the cavalrymen who moved through the lonely military posts of the American frontier some three hun-dred and fifty years after the arrival of the Spanish horse remarked on the stamina, endurance, and hardy qualities of the strange painted horse of the Indians.

No cavalry unit, mounted on straight descendants of the domesticated European horse, could begin to compare to the endurance of the Indian and his wild pony.

In the course of many arduous campaigns, cavalry horses experienced great difficulty in surviving solely on the grass feed available to them during their short camp rests. It was necessary to supplement their diet with grain, which had to be laboriously carried in the wagons, or by the pack trains that followed the troops.

In addition, every large cavalry detachment was accompanied by a blacksmith, as the sore-footed animals of European stock constantly needed reshoeing.

The Indian pony, on the other hand, never saw a shoe from the time he was a colt until he finally collapsed on his last, long hard ride. If he was shod, it was with a leather shoe made from a twisted buffalo hide, whose purpose was to muffle his footsteps as much as to protect his hooves.

The capacity of that horse, the mustang, to endure the frigid storms of the winter and the heat of the southern deserts was legendary. It seemed almost impossible that the horse herds could survive some of the winter storms on the western plains, where temperatures could drop to forty below.

How any animal could sustain life under those conditions is difficult to imagine, yet the horses that did were incredibly tough and became even tougher as they moved north and came in contact with a whole new breed.

For it was up in the Dakotas and Montana, in Saskatchewan and Manitoba, that the mustangs, 'the wild ones from Mexico,' first met the small bands of painted horses that had been running wild on the prairies for hundreds of years before the Spanish mustang came up from the south.

These paints were a different breed, born in the north and inured to its hardships. When they mated with the mustangs, you had the hardiest horses in the world."

Becky suddenly exploded. "Steven Cartwright, are you saying that all over the plains of the northwestern United States there were vast bands of a different breed of horse, the painted horse? That they had been there for a long time before the Spaniards came to Mexico and before the mustang wandered that far north? You really don't expect anyone to believe that, do you? I bet you can't find one historian, one archaeologist, or one paleontologist who will go along with you. It's crazy as hell!"

He turned and looked straight at her. This time there was no grin. His color rose, and his blue-gray eyes flashed a spark of steel.

Oh, God, she thought, I've gone too far. I've hurt his feelings.

She hung her head, then slowly looked up at him, her eyes filled with tears.

It was then that she saw his grin. He was looking at her with warmth and understanding.

"Steven, I'm sorry, please forgive me. I was very rude."

"Think nothing of it, my dear girl, I know how you feel. When somebody brings out a far-fetched idea, it appears as if they are trying to pull the wool over your eyes. You have never been one to take that, and rightly so. But come to think of it, that's my fault. I haven't been as attentive to your education as I should have been these last few years. You are still swearing as badly as you did when you were a little girl, and that comes from a lack of discipline."

She stuck her tongue out at him, and they both burst into laughter.

"All right," she said, "I'll be good. But you really do have to explain a little more about your startling proposal."

"Thank you for putting it so delicately," Steven said. "We're making progress, but to set the matter straight, I did not say that there were vast bands of painted horses running in those areas of the north. Quite the contrary, there were only a few bands, and they were isolated and concentrated in a very few locations, but they were there."

"But please explain again. Where did these painted horses of the north come?"

"From the north," he said, smiling.

"Well, someone must have brought them here."

"They sure did."

"You mean they didn't come from the East Coast or from the West Coast, but straight from the north?"

"Yes, that's right. That is what I'm saying."

"You mean from up around the Hudson Bay country?"

"Even farther north than that," Steven said.

"That's a pretty exciting concept," she said. "Maybe you had better develop it a little."

"I will in time, but first I want to be sure you understand that these painted horses were not spread out all over the northern prairies but were tucked away in small herds.

In 1805, when the Lewis and Clark expedition penetrated the vastness of the great basin of the Columbia River, they found hundreds and hundreds of painted horses. In discovering these wonderful horses, which had been bred and cherished by the Flathead, Nez Percé, Shoshone, and Kutenai tribes among others, they had, without knowing it, stumbled onto the traces of one of the world's great hidden stories."

Becky looked at him with shining eyes, her mind racing ahead. "Explain," she said.

Stephen grinned.

3

THE GREAT ADVENTURE

"As you know, when Thomas Jefferson became President of the United States in 1801, the western boundary of the country was the Mississippi River.

The Napoleonic wars were raging in Europe. In 1802 Napoleon's star was still on the rise, and the demands made on the French treasury for his military expenditures were enormous. It required vast amounts of money to feed, clothe, and field an army to support his dreams of world conquest, and the French treasury was being quickly depleted.

Napoleon cast around desperately for other sources of revenue. He was assisted by his unscrupulous minister of state, Talleyrand.

The satanic partners in crime concluded that France should dispose of her holdings in the New World—holdings that had been obtained by the bravery and sacrifice of French explorers for more than two hundred years.

There was a great deal of conspiracy, plotting and counterplotting involved in the transaction, but thanks to Jefferson's skill and statesmanship, the Louisiana Purchase was completed on April 3, 1803. Fifteen million dollars was transferred from the United States treasury to France via Talleyrand, who promptly pocketed five million of it. He generously and faithfully gave the other ten million to the French treasury to finance the military ambitions of the bold young Emperor Napoleon.

Although some narrow-minded individuals criticized Jefferson for making the extravagant Louisiana Purchase, the average American citizen was thrilled with the acquisition. Excitement ran rampant as men recognized the possibilities of the new frontier. They longed to know what lay beyond the Mississippi in the vast land that was now theirs.

Jefferson himself looked forward to western expansion and dreamed of great things to come. Particularly dear to his heart was the concept of a northwest passage.

What if an easy route to the Pacific could be found! Then all the hopes of the great explorers would indeed become reality. The northwest passage, the fabulous sea route that would link Europe to the Orient, had only been a dream to men like John Cabot, Martin Frobisher, and John Davis, each of whom had striven mightily to discover it two hundred years earlier.

Now, an overland route up the Missouri and down the Columbia—rivers unknown to these earlier explorers—appeared a reality to Jefferson. It would somehow link together a nation, and that link would make it the richest nation on earth.

It was Jefferson's firm belief that the breadth of the land between the headwaters of the Missouri and the navigable waters of the Columbia would be less than 'half a day's portage.' The great possibilities made him burst with impatience to discover the real nature of this vast tract of land. To that end, he commissioned an expedition.

As you can imagine, the scope of the expedition was enormous. To ensure its success, Jefferson selected his trusted friend and secretary, Meriwether Lewis, to lead it.

Lewis was to journey up the Missouri to its headwaters, cross the Cordillera Barrier, the great ranges of the Rockies that at that time were known only as the Shining Mountains. From there, he was to descend to the headwaters of the Columbia and follow the river to its mouth on the shores of the great blue Pacific.

In his famous directive to Lewis, dated June 1803, Jefferson specified what he expected of his trusted subordinate and reinforced his implicit faith in him.

Lewis was no less excited than his chief. He set about energetically organizing one of the greatest expeditions in the history of pioneering. As co-commander, he selected his old friend and military comrade, Captain William Clark.

When Lewis took leave of Jefferson's beautiful Monticello on July 4, 1803, he crossed the Blue Ridge Mountains of Virginia and entered into the Ohio wilderness. He traveled down that river to its junction with the Mississippi, and from there he headed for St. Louis, where he met Clark.

The young men selected to join them on their great adventure were sons of Kentucky riflemen, born and bred to the frontier and to hardship. They were capable, resourceful, and brave, good hunters and trackers, crack shots, skinners, fishermen, and campers, who shared their leaders' enthusiasm for exploration. Lewis and Clark also wisely engaged experienced French river men to handle the pirogues, boats that would be laboriously poled or rowed up the Missouri.

It was many long tedious months later that they reached the 'Great Bend country,' where the Missouri River flows from the west rather than the north. At this point, the expedition came upon a very interesting tribe known as the Mandans.

Both Lewis and Clark were startled by the appearance of these people, who were strikingly different from the tribes that they had passed downriver. Some of the Mandans were blond-haired and blue-eyed. Though they professed never to have had any contact with the white man, their physiognomy was evidence of a different racial heritage. Lewis wrote in his diary, 'These are not Indians.'

The Mandans were such hospitable people that Lewis and Clark decided to settle in their vicinity for the winter. During their stay in the severe winter of 1804–1805, the expedition had many opportunities to study the habits of these people, and they wrote quite extensively about them.

Certain things that they observed about the Mandans—their dwellings, personal habits, bull-hide boats, saunas, ceremonies, and death customs—were very different from any other type of Indians and have a very special significance to our story."

"Saunas?" Becky asked.

"Yes, saunas. And all of this is part of the legend of the painted horse's coming to America.

Lewis and Clark had learned from the Mandans that far to the west, near the headwaters of the Missouri, there was a range of towering mountains covered with snow. These were the so-called Shining Mountains.

The two captains began to think that perhaps the portage

from the headwaters of the Missouri to the headwaters of the Columbia might be far longer than Jefferson's estimate of 'one half a day.' If a longer portage were involved, horses would, of course, be needed.

Further questioning of the Mandans revealed that a tribe of horse Indians lived in the Shining Mountains. These were the Shoshone, the tribe to which Sacajawea, a squaw who had been captured a few years before by the neighboring Minnetarees belonged. She had subsequently been sold to Charbonneau, a French half-breed trapper.

Lewis and Clark, with their instinct for doing the right thing at the right time, decided that Sacajawea would be of great value when they reached the headwaters of the Missouri and needed to trade for horses to transport their goods to the headwaters of the Columbia. They first tried unsuccessfully to buy Sacajawea and finally agreed to hire her owner, Charbonneau, as interpreter.

During the four months the expedition poled its slow way up the Missouri, Sacajawea, who carried her little papoose on her back, was a listless and indifferent slave.

When they finally reached the point where the Missouri River divides into three branches (the famous Three Forks of the Missouri now known as the Jefferson, the Madison, and the Gallatin), Sacajawea grew animated. She was back in the area from which she had been stolen as a child, in what is today western Montana.

Her excitement rose as they approached the Beaver Fork of the Jefferson. Here Lewis left the expedition on foot. Taking only two experienced men, Shields and Drewyer, with him, he planned to cross over the continental divide into the totally unexplored country of the Lemhi River.

On the way to the divide, Lewis saw the first Indian since they had left the Mandan villages three months before. As Lewis was walking up the long broad valley of the headwaters, the Indian appeared out of the pines. He was riding what Lewis described as an 'elegant' horse, probably a paint.

The Indian was about a mile away, but Lewis was able to discern through his eyeglass that he was a Shoshone. Lewis realized that this was a heaven-sent chance to make contact.

Lewis called to the Indian, *'Ta-ba-bone!'* meaning 'white man' in Shoshone. But the Indian seemed reluctant to be approached by more than one man. He gave the quirt to his horse and disappeared into the bush. Lewis's chance to make easy contact with the Shoshone tribe had passed.

When Lewis finally reached the headwaters of the Missouri, he courageously decided to proceed alone. A short passage of a few miles took him over the continental divide at Lemhi Pass and down into the steep-sided valley of the Lemhi River.

On the afternoon of the second day, Lewis came quite suddenly upon two Shoshone squaws and a child. Expecting instant death, they bowed their heads in fear, but Lewis spoke kindly to them and gave them some beads as a token of friendship. They were fascinated with his gifts and greatly relieved to have found not an enemy but a friend.

They conducted Lewis to their camp, and it was there that Lewis saw for the first time a great band of painted horses. He saw immediately that these horses could be used for the expedition's portage to the Columbia.

Lewis wanted the Shoshone chief to cross back over the divide with him into hostile territory, to rejoin the rest of the expedition. But persuading him was no easy feat. The Shoshones were terrified of journeying any distance down the

Missouri drainage basin. Many, many years before, they had been driven out of those fabulous hunting grounds by the fierce Blackfeet and the Sioux, who had acquired guns from the white man.

In fact, being forced out of the lush plains and up into the barren mountain fastnesses had been a tribal catastrophe. When Lewis came upon them, the Shoshones were nearly starving to death—yet they refused to eat any of their magnificent horses.

With great diplomacy, Lewis finally convinced the Shoshone chief, Cameahwait, to accompany him to the expedition's camp at the head of Beaver Fork. A powwow was called when they arrived, and Sacajawea was brought in to interpret. At once, she recognized Cameahwait as her brother. She threw her arms around him and wept for joy. Cameahwait was obviously moved, but being a warrior, he refrained from any extravagant demonstration of emotion.

Lewis and Clark, as well as other members of the expedition, were touched by the scene and overjoyed at the results. For with the favored Sacajawea acting as interpreter, the success of the expedition seemed assured. Still, it was not a simple matter to barter with the Shoshones for their precious horses. And once they had secured the horses, most of which were paints, the journey over Lemhi Pass and down the Lolo Trail to the Clearwater River took forty-four arduous days.

At the junction of the Snake and the Clearwater, Lewis and Clark encountered the Flathead Indians. This meeting was immortalized in a stirring scene painted by Charles Russell some eighty years later. In it, the Flatheads were portrayed dashing about the expedition's camp on their beautiful paints.

Farther along, they came upon the Nez Percé, a tribe that dwelled in the valley of the Palouse River. Instead of paints, the

Nez Perce depended on a breed of horse that had a peculiar speckled rump. They were dubbed *appaloosas* because they thrived in the Palouse River valley.

Later on, I'll tell you about the significance of these particular discoveries and their bearing on the legend of the painted horse in America.

The Lewis and Clark expedition opened up a new era, the likes of which the world had never seen. It was a vivid and colorful era that in many ways captured the essence of the human spirit.

It was the era of the mountain man, the trapper, the prospector, the buffalo hunter, the scout, the Indian fighter, the cavalryman, the bullwacker, the stage driver, the express rider, the sodbuster, and the railroad builder. It was a time of hope and fear, of nobility and villainy. It ran the gamut of human emotions, giving expression to the very depths and heights of man's possibilities. It was marked by bitter trails and sad fire-songs.

In time it passed, as all things pass, leaving its echoes on the whisper of the prairie wind."

Looking into the fire, Steven continued in a low voice . . .

"Listen to the voices of the prairie wind.
They tell of towering castle clouds, all gold with sun.
Of the Horseman passing in the west,
Of drifting veils of dust,
And the creak and groan of long-gone wagon wheels.
They speak the murmur of the wandering streams,
And hum the sad fire-songs of men who went with dreams."

THE ARTISTS

As they sat, warmed by the now-crackling fire, Becky asked, "Whatever became of Lewis and Clark? Did they return to the lands they explored and live happily ever after?"

"I'm afraid that Lewis died in a mysterious manner, the victim of murder or suicide on the Natchez Trace, the horse trail between Natchez and the Shenandoah Valley. So only one of our heroes had a proper fairy-tale ending.

In 1813 President Madison named William Clark governor of the Missouri Territory. He held that position until 1821, when Missouri became a state.

The Indians knew that Clark could be trusted—that he never broke his word or spoke with a forked tongue. He was admired, liked, and respected by white and red men alike.

Six years before Clark's death in 1838, a young man named George Catlin came to St. Louis to seek his advice.

Catlin was an artist who had decided to devote his considerable talents to recording the fading culture of the American Indian. He wanted to paint the red man in his natural state, in all his splendor and squalor, nobility and savagery—to paint him as he really was.

Clark was a keen judge of men. He recognized Catlin's passion and genius. He knew that the artist had not only the talent to portray what he saw but also the courage to face the hardships of the wilderness. As soon as he realized that the young man could enhance the white man's knowledge of Indian culture, Clark decided to assist him. In 1832 he procured passage up the Missouri for Catlin on the steamer *Yellowstone*.

More important, he suggested that young Catlin stop near the Great Bend of the Missouri to visit, observe, and paint what Clark called 'the gentle Mandans.' "

Becky's eyes lit up. "Yes, you told me not to forget the Mandans, because they are an important part of the legend."

"That's right. Let me tell you why.

It was many months before Catlin made his way to the Mandan village, but he remembered Clark's urging and determined to stay there for a month to paint all phases of their tribal life.

It wasn't long before Catlin realized why Clark had urged him to pay special attention to these amazing people. Not only did these Indians possess many painted horses, but they were physically different from other natives.

Catlin was in the habit of writing down his observations and forwarding them to the *New York Commercial Advertiser*. In one of the letters he wrote from the Mandan village in the late summer of 1832, Catlin remarked that these Indians appeared so different from all others that a visitor would be inclined to say that these are not Indians. Many had hazel, gray, or blue eyes—in contrast to the usual black or brown. He also remarked that the women were especially beautiful.

Catlin could not explain these unexpected characteristics, nor could the Mandans themselves. They claimed they had had no contact with the white man until the Lewis and Clark expedition, some twenty-eight years earlier. Yet they had the same range in hair, eye, and skin color as the white population had.

The Mandans were naturally fascinated with Catlin's ability to portray lifelike images of their tribe members using brushes, pigments, oils, and canvas. Many of them began to call him 'the Great White Medicine Man'—a title of considerable distinction. But some skeptical and superstitious tribesmen believed that if Catlin painted them, they would not be able to close their eyes or rest in peace at death. Catlin cleverly allayed most of their fears and went on to complete many famous paintings.

One depicts the strange earthen lodges of the Mandans, with their almost turtlelike appearance. These dwellings were substantial, spacious structures, circular in form—they looked like overturned bowls. They were between forty and sixty feet in diameter and housed anywhere from twenty to forty Mandans.

To build these superstructures, the Mandans would excavate about two feet into the ground and then smooth out the earth to make a floor. They would then plant enough upright six-foot timbers until a solid wall was formed all around. On top of this wall, they placed timbers that were much longer, tilting their small ends inward to the center of the lodge at a forty-five-degree angle. At the very top of the dwelling, they left a hole that served both as skylight and as chimney.

Wet earth was solidly packed around the outside of the structure to hold it together, and inside the ceiling was supported by large posts embedded into the floor and ceiling beams. A canopy of willow boughs was placed on top and then covered with a two- or three-foot layer of earth. When the clay dried, the entire structure was impervious to water.

Perhaps one of Catlin's most significant paintings was that of the inside of a Mandan lodge. It showed the arrangement of stalls and booths. Target shields and buffalo-horn headdresses hung on partitions between them. Long benches surrounded the entire structure, except at the doors. The benches divided the booths for each family and were covered by curtains to insure privacy.

The Mandans bathed regularly in the waters of the Missouri, and the interiors of the houses were kept spotless. The floors were hard-packed and polished from constant cleaning.

Strangely enough, the Mandans, unlike other Indians, kept their horses inside their houses during the deadly cold Dakota winters. Another thing to remember is that the Mandans used round bull-hide boats, as opposed to canoes, the classic Indian craft. As you will see, these practices were unique to their tribe and have special significance in our story.

The Mandan houses were grouped together around a central court, where community cooking was done over an open fire and where dances and ceremonies were held. In the summer, Mandans often observed these ceremonies from the clay roofs of the houses surrounding the courtyard.

Encircling the village was a stout stockade, one side of which bordered the high bluff of the river. The great grasslands of North Dakota stretched out from the village. They were ideal for grazing ponies and attractive to the buffalo herds that occasionally appeared. When buffalo came into sight, the Mandans would run for their painted ponies and, with much shouting and excitement, slay as many as possible to obtain their meat and hides.

The Mandans were not a numerous race. Only about two thousand were living in the upper and lower villages at the time of Catlin's visit. For this reason, they did not venture far out onto the plains, fearing that they would be outnumbered by their enemy, the powerful Sioux.

Catlin learned a good deal about these interesting people, the Mandans. And he immortalized them for all times in the now-famous paintings that he brought back to civilization

Only five years later, in 1837, a river steamer bearing a crewman stricken with smallpox anchored alongside the Mandan village. The Mandans lacked resistance to the white man's disease, which spread like wildfire among the light-skinned people. Within a few short days, there were fewer than three dozen Mandans left alive.

The destruction of the Mandan race was a terrible catastrophe. The few remaining survivors became the slaves of the Arikaras, who took over the Mandan village. Later, these two tribes joined the Hidatsa and became known as the Three Affiliated Tribes. Their alliance meant that the customs and languages unique to each tribe became intertwined. In the process of assimilation each lost some of its original identity.

Had this anthropological tragedy not occurred, we might understand more today about the mystery surrounding the fair-skinned, blond-haired, blue-eyed Mandans. But the beautiful, gentle Mandans passed away on the whisper of the prairie wind."

Steven looked off into the darkness for a moment, then turned toward Becky. She was staring at him with tears streaming down her cheeks.

"What's the matter?" he asked.

"You've just told me a beautiful story. Steven, you were born in the West, and you understand what this wonderful country is all about. That's why your feelings about the Lewis and Clark expedition are so strong. You are so passionate about the significance and adventure of opening up the whole West. And because you feel it so deeply you can tell its story in a way that no one else could."

WINGS

"Steven," Becky said, drawing closer, "you have always seemed so inquisitive about life, so self-assured and confident. Have you ever felt otherwise?"

"Oh, hell, yes," he replied. "You should have seen me during my first semester at Yale. During the final weeks of the fall term, I realized that I wasn't going to be spending the Christmas holidays with my family. In 1916, taking a train back and forth would have meant two weeks of travel, which was preposterous since I had only a three-week vacation.

I either had to arrange to stay at the college during the vacation or else visit some friends in the East. I hadn't been at school long enough to make many friends, and I missed the ranch terribly. One afternoon when I was feeling particularly homesick and gloomy, I decided to wander down to the harbor.

It was there that I saw an airplane for the first time. It was a

Curtiss flying boat taking off out of the smooth waters of New Haven Harbor. I'll never forget that sight as long as I live.

It was late afternoon. I was looking east, and the sun was at my back. Out of the corner of my eye, I saw a white plume moving rapidly along the surface of the water.

Then I heard the roar. At first I thought it was some kind of very fast speedboat. I had never seen anything go across the water so fast.

I stood transfixed, and then suddenly the white plume disappeared. To my utter amazement, the boat lifted out of the water and climbed into the air. The invisible air!

It was as if I were hallucinating. It was a miracle! I had never seen an airplane before. Oh, I had seen pictures, but I'd never seen one fly. It turned west and finally disappeared in the setting sun. I watched it until the thunder of its engine faded into the distance, taking a part of me with it. It was one of the turning points of my life.

That night while eating dinner at the freshman commons, I told a friend that I'd seen an airplane flying out of New Haven Harbor.

'Oh, yes,' he said. 'That flying boat belongs to the Yale Naval Aviation Unit. Trubee Davidson started it.'

'Trubee Davidson—who is he?'

'He is a sophomore, but he is also a big man around campus. His old man is a partner of the J. P. Morgan Company.'

'J. P. Morgan?'

'Yeah, you've never heard of him?'

'No.'

My friend looked surprised. 'Well, you will.'"

A red log in the fire suddenly burst, and hot pieces of charcoal fell off the side of the fire. Steven stood up and pushed the flaming pieces back into the fire with his boot. Then he sat down again.

Becky looked up at him. "Oh, Steven, for heaven's sake. Of course, you'd heard of J. P. Morgan!"

"Oh, no, I hadn't! I was such a country hick, stuck way back in the four corners country of Colorado, I didn't know anything about financiers in New York. Of course, I found out plenty about them later.

Right then and there I told my friend I was very interested in flying and how I could get to meet Davidson.

'Maybe I can fix that up,' he said.

Freshmen didn't mix very readily with sophomores, but my friend told me his older brother was a sophomore and roomed with Davidson. I thought that was a pretty good connection, and a week or so later, we were invited to his brother's room to meet Trubee.

Davidson turned out to be a very, very nice guy. He had none of the standoffishness that I expected from a stuffy New York or Boston student, especially toward a western cowboy. In fact, he seemed to like me and to be interested in my freshman football career. I'd been fortunate enough to make some good touchdown runs, and apparently Davidson had read about them in the *Yale News*.

A little later Trubee looked at his watch and said, 'Say, are you fellows going to eat dinner pretty soon?'

'Yes,' I said, 'we'd planned to go over to the Freshmen Commons.'

'Why don't you come with me to my eating club?'

At that time, Yale had eating clubs all over the campus. They were very much like fraternities. This was about twenty years before they started the system in which the students eat in the dining rooms of their residential colleges. The eating clubs were a good idea because they permitted you to make social contacts that were beneficial and often lasted a lifetime. It was the one-of-a-kind benefit of a school like Yale.

Trubee graciously saw to it that we were seated together and started asking me all sorts of questions about Colorado.

When I told him I lived down in the four corners country, he said that he'd read a lot about that area. He asked if it was close to the cliff dwellings of Mesa Verde.

'Yes,' I said, 'it's very near there.' Then I went on to tell him a bit about ranch life.

'That sounds great,' he said warmly. 'I'd really love to see that part of the country.'

'Why don't you come visit me sometime next summer?'

'Thank you,' he said. 'I might just do that. But right now I'm pretty involved in the Yale Naval Aviation Unit, and I'm very excited about it.'

That's when he started telling me how he had set it up and what work he had already done. In the summer of 1915, a year and a half earlier, he had gone with his father to France. As a partner of J. P. Morgan, his father was engaged in the international financing of the British and French war effort. While Trubee was there, he spent some time during the summer driving an ambulance for the American Ambulance Corps. He saw quite a lot of fighting and developed strong opinions about the hideous trench warfare and the mud, slime, stench, boredom, and terror that went with it.

After observing some aerial combats in the skies over France, he concluded that the future of warfare was in the air.

He believed that air warfare had vast possibilities. He was also quite excited about what appeared to be the chivalry between the opposing air forces. He felt that men with spirit and daring could express themselves here. It was certainly far better than being a doughboy cringing in the mud while heavy artillery pounded your position and blew off the arms and legs of your comrades.

He told me something that I'll never forget. He said that the morale of troops who had been subjected to an artillery barrage was consistently low. As the barrage crept forward yard by yard, it pounded to death everything in its course. One could not maintain morale under those conditions. Those poor fellows had no defense. The shells kept crashing around them, and they could not fight back. The only thing they could do was burrow in the mud and pray.

It was after a barrage, of course, that the opposing force launched its attack and usually swept the positions with very little resistance.

Trubee made it very clear that ground combat and trench warfare was a hideous business. True, you could meet death very quickly in the air, but it would be a sudden and clean end.

I listened very carefully. I thought war was a bad situation no matter what the hell branch you were in. The days of the gunfighter, like Brules, were over. Now warfare was a matter of monstrous machinery, tanks, and heavy artillery pounding each other to pieces. That didn't appeal to me. I wasn't eager to be a doughboy with a bayonet. But flying seemed a lot like being an Indian scout.

Brules had always said I would have made a fearless scout. It seemed to me that a flyer would have to have the same qualities as Brules. He would have to be willing to take chances, to be adventurous and self-reliant, and to adapt to different situations. He would also have to think fast enough to get himself out of jams.

I thought your chances for survival as a pilot in a war were about fifty-fifty, but that was a chance I was willing to take. As I listened to Trubee, the thought of flying excited me. I wanted to be a pilot.

Trubee's enthusiasm for flying had been bolstered when he'd met Robert Bacon in Paris. Bacon had taken a very active interest in forming the American flying unit that would later join the French air force in the war against Germany. The unit evolved over a period of several months. It was financially supported by wealthy Americans living in Paris.

The notion was to form a squadron of French-built airplanes that would be purchased and flown by Americans. It would fly under French command as a freedom-loving American group called the Lafayette Escadrille.

During the American Revolution, General Lafayette and some other Frenchmen were largely responsible for the Americans' victory at Yorktown, and now a hundred fifty years later, American troops were going back to France to help Lafayette's kinsmen.

It was a beautiful concept and an important piece of propaganda in promoting America's entry into the war.

I have always admired Trubee for what he did that summer of 1916. Originally, he had planned to go back to Europe as an ambulance driver with several of his Yale friends, but during the spring he'd talked to his close friend Bob Lovett, stroke of the Yale crew, about the possibilities of an American squadron. They reached the conclusion that there was no reason to go back as ambulance drivers, and that they might better spend their time putting together a flying unit over here.

In any case, a privately financed Naval Aviation unit struck Trubee as something that could be formed in this country. Lovett agreed.

With that in mind, Trubee approached his father. At first, Mr. Davidson would have no part of it, but eventually he came around and agreed to help finance the enterprise.

Trubee's plan was aided and abetted by the fact that the *Lusitania* had been sunk in the summer of 1915 with the loss of more than one hundred American lives. This infuriated the country, so that even though America had not yet entered the war, there was strong anti-German feeling everywhere. Plenty of moneyed people admired Trubee's and Lovett's enthusiasm, courage, and determination to participate in the great war against the Kaiser's military domination.

Even while his father was still mulling over financing the Yale Naval Aviation Unit, Trubee did not remain idle. He had been flying in a Curtiss flying boat, nicely named the *Mary Ann*, with an instructor pilot named McCulloch. McCulloch was an experienced aviator and had spent some time flying with the Italian forces. He had come to the United States and was working for the Greater Ocean Company, a business created by Sam Wanamaker to enter the field of aviation with flying boats. Wanamaker envisioned flying boats so big, strong, and fast that someday they would fly across the ocean.

After old Mr. Davidson and others in the J. P. Morgan group finally agreed to support the effort, a deal was made to buy a small hangar at Port Washington, on Long Island, along with the lovely *Mary Ann*. Ten Yale men showed up for the first training lessons.

They ranged from the halfback on the football team and the stroke of the crew, to the pitcher on the baseball team and the editor of the *Yale News*. All were leaders of their class, highly idealistic, and came from some of the best families in the country. A good group to have if you're going to start such an adventurous new project.

I urged Trubee, as much as I could within reasonable bounds, to work me into the scheme. He told me what he was up against.

'This unit is composed mostly of seniors,' he said. 'There are only three sophomores—myself and two of my friends. The only other non-senior is my kid brother Henry, who is a freshman like you. I got Henry in because I formed the squadron and because my old man is the principal backer. We've turned down many requests from sophomores and even juniors because at this stage, we have many more applicants than we can handle. Maybe later on, there will be a possibility.'

He expressed these things in a very kindly manner, but I felt a terrible disappointment.

But when we broke up later that evening, he held out some hope. 'Cowboy, I don't know what we can do with you since you're a freshman and so many other applicants are coming in. But let me see—there's got to be something. I want to think it over for a while.'

The nickname Cowboy, by the way, was to stick with me all through my college and war years.

Trubee apparently liked me, and it seemed as if we were good friends right from the very beginning, which seldom happens in the East.

A few days later I found a message from him in my mailbox inviting me down to his home at Peacock Point for the weekend. I ran over to his room and accepted immediately. 'Would there be any chance while we're there that we could drive up to

Port Washington and see the flying boats, hangars, and the whole setup?' I asked.

'You bet, if you're interested.'

'I'm about ready to die with interest,' I said, laughing.

On Friday afternoon, we went down to Bridgeport in his car, took the ferry over to Port Jefferson, Long Island, and drove down to Peacock Point.

PEACOCK POINT

Peacock Point, Trubee's home, was the most impressive mansion I'd ever seen. It had a beautiful view of Long Island Sound, and the beach wasn't more than a hundred fifty yards from the house, which was surrounded by beautiful lawns and trees. The inside of the house was marvelously furnished and filled with lovely old paintings that must have cost a fortune.

The house was well staffed with a butler, an upstairs maid and her helper, a chef, and of course, uniformed waitresses to serve in the dining room.

Henry Davidson, Trubee's younger brother, was there too. I hadn't seen much of him at Yale, but he greeted me very warmly. He said he had gotten a big kick out of watching me in the Harvard-Yale freshman football game that year. It was a terrific game, and I'd managed to run back a kickoff for a touchdown.

'Boy,' he said, 'there was a lot of cheering.'

Henry was also interested in hearing my stories about the West.

Trubee had a couple of older sisters who seemed nice. But the loveliest person was his mother. Mrs. Davidson was just as kind and gracious as she could be. As her guest, I was made to feel very special, and she extended every courtesy to me.

I was glad that my mother had drilled good manners into me, because I was able to get by all right, even though I felt a little country awkward.

There was one other person there whom I remember distinctly. She wasn't very old, probably in her fifties. I thought she was absolutely beautiful for a fifty-year-old woman. I'd never seen anyone like her. She had a beautiful figure and a lovely complexion.

I sat and talked with her for quite a while after dinner on Sunday. She seemed to be so interested in all the boys and what they were doing. She thought the Yale Naval Aviation Unit was very exciting. She was extremely complimentary about Trubee and his initiative in getting the unit going. There wasn't a doubt in her mind that eventually we'd get drawn into that terrible European war.

She asked me where I came from, and I told her Colorado.

'What part of Colorado?' she asked, brightening.

'The four corners country.'

'Oh, is that so!' She seemed excited. 'I came from that part of the world too. I was born on a ranch out in Utah.'

She began questioning me in more detail. I told her that our ranch wasn't near any big town but was about fifty miles southwest of Telluride. 'We're at the foot of a beautiful thirteen-thousand-foot mountain. It's the westernmost mountain of the Colorado Rockies. It's called Lone Cone Peak.'

'Lone Cone! That's a beautiful mountain! That's absolutely the most beautiful country in the world!' Her eyes were shining.

'Yes, you're right. Of course, where we are, there weren't any other ranchers close by, but when I was a young boy, I found some of our old cowhands fascinating. And one of my best friends was a mountain man, an outlaw, and a gunman. He lived in a cabin high up on Lone Cone. I was clearly told that I wasn't to go anywhere near that fellow. But of course, being a kid, that's just what I did.'

'Of course,' she said. 'When you are told you shouldn't do something, that's exactly what you want to do.'

'Yes, and I got into real trouble for it.'

'I bet you did. I bet you got yourself a trip to the woodshed, didn't you?'

'Yes, I certainly did.'

She laughed. 'Tell me about your old friend. What was his name?'

'Brules,' I said. 'His name was Cat Brules. He had eyes like a cat. God, he was a dead shot. I was just thrilled by him. He lived on Lone Cone there on his ranch, and I'd go up the mountain to see him every chance I had. He taught me so many things. He was a wonderful man!'

Just then, Trubee Davidson came up to me and said, 'You know, Steven, I've got an early morning class that I just can't skip, which means I've got to leave now to catch the last ferry out of Port Jefferson. If you'd like to stay on, go ahead. If you care to come with me—'

'Of course I'm coming with you, Trubee. I'll be ready in five minutes.'

'Okay, I'll meet you out at the front door.'

I turned back to say good-bye to the lady I had been talking to, but she was gone. I inquired about her from someone who was sitting nearby.

'Oh, you mean Sandy?' one of the girls said. 'She did leave suddenly, didn't she. I guess she wasn't feeling very well.'

'She was looking awfully pale. I don't understand,' one of the others remarked.

Thinking no more about it, I ran up to my room, packed my belongings, and met Trubee at the door. I didn't have the heart to remind him that we had not gone down to Port Washington to see the *Mary Ann*. I didn't want to make him feel bad when I was trying to make such a good impression. On the way back to New Haven, he said to me, 'You know, Cartwright, you certainly made a hit with Mother.'

'Oh, is that so?'

'Yes, she said that she had seldom seen a more gentlemanly fellow and that you must come from a fine family. She said that western people were very polite, and that if there was an aristocracy in the West, you'd be part of it.'

'That's a really nice thing for her to have said, but I'm afraid where I lived was too far out in the boondocks for me to have much social life of any kind. But my mother was really pretty tough on me about my manners when I was a kid. Not only table manners, but social etiquette of all kinds. I guess it made a difference.'

When we got back to the campus that night, I felt as if Trubee and I were genuinely friends.

About a week later, I received a most cordial letter from

Mrs. Davidson. 'Trubee suggested that I write you,' it read. 'We would love to have you come for the Christmas vacation and stay with us here at Peacock Point. There will be many parties, lots of visitors coming and going, and we always have a large Christmas tree. We would be delighted if you were able to join us. I'm sure that a popular young man like you has a number of invitations, and if that is the case, you could perhaps arrange to visit us for at least part of the time. We would be so pleased to have you.'

When I received that letter, I almost bawled. Of course, I had no other place to go, and I didn't waste any time accepting their heaven-sent invitation.

Then I shared the wonderful news with my mother. I told her all about the Davidson family and what a marvelous opportunity it was.

By return mail, my mother wrote how pleased and delighted she was for me. Then, of course, there were the inevitable long lists of instructions as to what I should do—keep my shirts clean, change my socks every day, and keep my suits pressed. She admonished me to be polite and not to 'hog' the conversation, reiterating all the things that she had been telling me all my life. I got a big laugh out of it, but I knew that I should pay attention.

So it was that two or three days after classes ended, I went to the Davidsons'. It was five days before Christmas.

When I arrived at the house, Mrs. Davidson treated me like a long-lost son. She hugged me and then led me into the sitting room. She told me that she had received the nicest letter from my mother.

Oh boy, I thought, Mom turned on the charm, and I bet she had a lot to say.

'Steven,' Mrs. Davidson said, 'I knew you came from a fine family. The letter from your mother only confirms it. She has a beautiful hand and wrote the most engaging letter. I can see now where you get your fine manners. She told me a little about your ranch, and it sounds absolutely wonderful. She spoke so warmly about your father and what your life has been like on the ranch. She said you have been raised to be resourceful, strong, and firm in purpose, and that you are, of course, the joy of her life.

Now, let's see,' she said, after pausing for a moment. 'You should be upstairs in the green bedroom. Henry is next to you, and Trubee is down the hall. I think that you will find it comfortable.'

'I'm sure I will, Mrs. Davidson. I'll take my bags up now, and please tell me, what time is dinner?'

'We usually meet for a small cocktail hour here about a quarter of seven. Then at seven fifteen, we will be going into the dining room. There will be several guests here tonight, nearby neighbors, and I think you will find them very interesting people.'

'Shall I dress for dinner?' I asked.

I was nervous and wanted to make a good impression. I absolutely couldn't make a mistake.

'Oh my, no. No black ties or anything like that. Just a jacket and tie.'

Dinner was elegantly served by a butler and several maids. Mrs. Davidson was a wonderful hostess who saw that everyone was included in the conversation. The whole meal was absolutely charming.

After dinner, the men went into the den, which was furnished with large leather chairs and a small bar. We all had an after-dinner liqueur while the ladies went upstairs to Mrs. Davidson's quarters.

Mr. Davidson, Henry, Trubee, and I immediately started talking about the Yale Naval Aviation Unit. No one could really discuss anything else.

'Of course, you know by now that everyone at J. P. Morgan Company is pushing hard for you fellows,' Mr. Davidson remarked. 'We want to see this thing go. We want to make sure that we have built a unit of which we can be proud, and one that the military will find useful when the time comes to turn it over.'

'Yes, Father, I understand exactly,' Trubee said. 'But what are we going to do about college?'

'Son, I think the time is going to come when you are not going to have to concern yourself very much with Yale University. That war in Europe is a terrible, terrible thing. We really haven't thought much about it in this country except for selling war materials to the Allies.

But there's been an awful lot of bleeding and dying over there. It's a contortion that is not going to end easily. I think we'll be at war in a very few months. The more training you have, the better off you boys are going to be.'

'Father, I can't quarrel with that a bit.'

Mr. Davidson then said, 'Trubee, I think it is becoming self-evident that the unit needs some sort of central control, someone to pull all the details together and do the management job, while you boys perfect your flying techniques and maintain your aircraft.'

'Do you have any ideas, Father?'

'Yes, I have an old friend, Colonel Thompson, who lives in Georgia, who I believe would be ideal. He is a great fellow, and I think all of you would like him. A man like him could be in-valuable. I suggest that after Christmas, you and I make a quick trip to Georgia and discuss the possibilities with him.'

'Gee, that would be wonderful, Father. I'd like to do that.'

'Then consider the matter settled.'

I stayed around for Christmas and had a wonderful time. There were several parties at the country club and at other people's homes. I met a lot of nice attractive girls. I loved to dance and had a natural rhythm and grace that they seemed to appreciate.

Dancing was great fun. It was a lot different from today. Dancing was a good way to find out what a girl was like. After holding her in your arms for a minute, you could see what kind of rhythm she had. She, of course, was sizing you up the same way, so it was one of our favorite pastimes. Everything was strictly above board and there was no monkey business like there is nowadays. Sometimes it was a real test of character. Nevertheless, that was the way we were all brought up, and that's the way the girls acted. If a girl didn't act properly, she simply wasn't accepted.

Throughout my stay, I continued talking to Trubee about flying. 'You know the last time we were here, we didn't have time to go to Port Washington and see that favorite flying boat of yours. I wondered if we could go during the holidays.'

'Oh, yeah, the *Mary Ann*,' he said. 'Listen, we ought to do some flying. I'll tell you what—I'll take you for a ride.'

'Wonderful! Wow! I'd love that!'

THE *Mary Ann*

We went to Port Washington the next morning. Even though it was during the holidays, there was a lot of activity going on. That's when I met the great McCulloch for the first time. He was a very, very able guy. A hell of a flyer. I couldn't understand just how he could have a name like McCulloch and be an Italian instructor.

There were more flying boats than I expected. I had only heard Trubee talk about the *Mary Ann*.

Anyway, I finally got to see the *Mary Ann* close up. She was a nice little Curtiss flying boat with an OX5 water-cooled engine—about ninety horsepower. That was a lot in those days.

I'll never forget the smell of the salt sea and the sight of those gossamer wings. The wing was covered with Irish linen, sixty-six strands per square inch. You could put your hand under it and see your fingers right through the fabric. The wing would drum and sing when touched, it was so light and so delicate. The wood on those beautiful little planes reminded me of an eight-oared shell. The workmanship was so exquisite. Everything from the spars to the interplane struts, the longerons, the propellers, and the boat hull itself were beautifully crafted of the finest spruce.

When we got in, I put on a helmet and goggles for the first time. Then I was shown how to buckle down. The center post of the control column was between Trubee and me. It branched out into wheel controls for each of us. Each of us had rudder pedals that worked off the same system. With my hand on the wheel and my feet pushing on the rudder pedals, I felt as though I were mounting a flying horse and going off to slay the dragon. Trubee instructed me on how the ailerons and elevators worked when you pulled the wheel back and forth. There were wires that went through some pulleys to the tail, and a few instruments on the instrument panel. I looked at them carefully. There was an altimeter, an oil pressure gauge, an oil temperature gauge, an air speed indicator, a gas gauge, and a propeller revolution counter—called an RPM indicator—which told you how much power you were using. That's about all—remember, this was 1916.

A mechanic, by pulling the propeller through, kicked the engine over while we were still on the slip. It had a hell of a roar even though it was only ninety horsepower. I was sitting just forward of the engine and hoped it wouldn't fall on my back.

Incidentally, that was one of the dangers of those little planes. With the engine overhead and back of you, you didn't have much chance of survival if it hit you in a crash.

We taxied out onto the water and ran along slowly to get the engine warm. The oil temperature came up on the gauge.

We were nodding to one another since we couldn't hear over the roar. Smiling, Trubee pointed to the different instruments, showing me what they were.

It was a beautiful cold crisp day and very pleasant taxiing out onto the bay. The water was smooth, and it felt like being in a motor boat. Finally, Trubee turned her into the wind and opened the throttle. The roar of that engine made my heart beat wildly. You could feel the thrust as the boat raced faster and faster on the water. Then it got up on the step and was just clipping along.

You could feel the waves going chop, chop, chop, and finally we hit one and bounced. After that, it was smooth again. I thought, My God, we're flying! The water was going by us at a terrific rate, but as we rose into the air, it appeared to slow down. When we got up four hundred feet, it was moving very slowly. You could see for miles around. The wind was tearing across our windshield. We looked out, and I thought, Oh boy, this is the life. I'm riding Pegasus now!

You could see all the way down to the eastern end of Long Island Sound. A lot of sailboats were out, even though it was cold. It had been a mild winter, and there was no ice in the harbors.

We headed east, flying over the beautiful estates of Long Island with their lovely manicured lawns. Some of them had boat houses, and I saw a polo field or two. It was just lovely country, covered here and there with light patches of snow.

We flew down the Sound for a ways, and then Trubee did a wonderful thing. He let me take the controls while he gently followed me through. We flew level for a minute so that I could get the feel of the plane. Then at his signal, I made a very gentle turn to the left. The world was just beautiful. As we were turning, we saw that the rim of the horizon was cutting diagonally across the nose of the machine. We came clear around a hundred eighty degrees and headed back down the Sound on a westerly course.

'Now let's go the other way!' he shouted.

So we made a turn to the right. He followed through, and after we came around, he took his hands and feet off the controls. He was going to let me do it alone. Well, for a minute there, I held the controls, and the boat seemed to be going up. I pushed the wheel—but too fast.

He laughed and grabbed the controls for a minute. 'Not so much, just a little pressure.'

Pretty soon I got the idea of flying level, but then a wing would dip down a little bit, and he'd motion me to get it back up again. In a few minutes, I could keep flying straight and level.

Of course, when I started to make the turn, I used the rudder and ailerons. I pushed the left rudder and turned the wheel to the left, but I kept on holding the rudder. To my shock, the nose started down, and the machine started to speed up. Davidson pulled it up and shook his head.

He showed me that once I got in a turn, I had to equalize the rudder again. Otherwise the machine would turn and dive. With the plane on its side in a steep bank, the rudder took the place of the elevator. If you maintained constant pressure, you would dive into the drink.

We flew around for about another forty-five minutes. I was in absolute heaven, laughing and singing and having a marvelous time. We flew past the hangars and the slips, waving to the people on shore, and passed over the Davidsons' house. Finally, Trubee brought us in, settling the plane down on the water. It was just as gentle as it could be. All of a sudden, we weren't an airplane but a speedboat again.

In a way, it was sort of sad. With the throttle closed, we sank down in the water very rapidly. Then there was nothing but the sound of the beating waves, the idling motor, and my pounding heart.

We taxied over to the slip, slid up to the hangar door, and shut off the engine. Trubee shoved his goggles back on his helmet, and we grinned at each other. I don't know, but somehow we were almost like blood brothers. I thought that Trubee was the best guy I'd ever known, and I hoped that he thought the same of me. I knew that if there was ever anything I could do for him, I would damn well do it.

Before he left for Georgia after Christmas, Trubee said he had talked with his father and his brother, and they wanted me in the unit.

'You'll have to go through the same preparatory work the rest of us did,' he said. 'There's a tough physical examination given by a doctor here in Glen Cove. Then you'll have to pass some aptitude tests, which you will probably fail,' he said with a grin.

'I'm ready, fit, willing, and able, right now!'

Trubee said he thought I'd make a hell of a good pilot. 'You've got coordination, and God knows, you've got plenty of guts. I just don't know about your brains,' he said, laughing.

I grinned back. Guys don't kid other guys they don't like.

'Trubee, I'll do my best to be the very damn best pilot I can.'

'I know you will. You're that kind of guy. As you know, Dad and I are going south for a few days. By the time we get back, you may have passed most of this stuff. I'll get McCulloch to give you some flying time.'

'You mean the instructor?'

'Yes, I let you get a feel of the airplane, but I'm not really qualified as an instructor. He is, and he's damn good. He can make that *Mary Ann* talk. He's just the kind of guy you need. You'll enjoy working with him. The only problem is, you've got to get the son-of-a-gun out of bed in the morning. He's never been known as an early bird.'

It all went just as Trubee said it would. While he was down south, I stayed on in Long Island and took all the physical and aptitude tests. I had no trouble with any of them.

I did a lot of flying under the watchful eyes of McCulloch in the next few days, and I soloed before the first of the year.

The rest of the guys couldn't believe it. When that great event occurred, my total flight time was only four hours and fifteen minutes. McCulloch told the guys, 'Jeez, this Cartwright takes to flying like a cowboy to a horse. He's just born to fly.'

That made me feel very good. I felt that I could do anything with a plane, but of course, overconfidence was something every young aviator had to watch out for. Otherwise, you could break your neck!"

"What an experience," Becky said, interrupting Steven's narrative. "I can just see you as a young man, eager as you could be. How you must have gone after that thing!"

"Thank you for that, Becky. You seem to understand exactly the way I felt about it. I was just so proud to be with those guys. We were so young and idealistic.

That period after the solo was one of the happiest in my life. I loved flying! I was absolutely spoiled for anything else. When you eased back on the wheel and broke loose from the water, then started climbing into the sky, the whole world dropped away from you. I'll tell you, it was just incredible. I was in a wonder world all by myself—the world of the airman.

Don't get me wrong! I studied hard in ground school and practiced in the air. I knew I was doing well because McCulloch was constantly making remarks like, 'Well, I'll be damned,' or 'That's beautiful. That's the way to handle it. Everything's just fine. I'm very pleased.'

I don't think there was much doubt among the fellows that I was getting to be one of the best pilots in the group, and I knew that Trubee appreciated my achievements."

Becky gazed at Steven's rugged features, accented now by the firelight. "You must have felt free as an eagle," she said. "I wonder if that is how the Indians felt when they first took to riding the painted horses."

"I don't know, but I rather suspect so. In any case, I certainly felt that way. I decided that my life was in the sky and that I had to stay there. It was so crisp and clean and decent. I got away from the roar of the traffic, any competition with others, worries about school. Riding around in the skies for a while just did something magical for my soul.

By this time, it seemed as if war were only a short way off. The university had stated that if any of the boys had to leave their classes to pick up the 'khaki and the gun instead of the cap and gown,' they would be able to reenter their class when they came back.

On April 14, 1917, two days after Woodrow Wilson addressed the joint session of Congress asking for a declaration of war against Germany, we were officially at war.

Colonel Thompson, Mr. Davidson's friend, had come aboard to manage the unit while the rest of us concentrated on flying and maintaining the aircraft. Thompson was a great big jovial fellow, very sincere about his work. We all liked him and appreciated the load he was carrying.

The first thing he did was locate a place in Huntington, Long Island, about thirty miles down the coast, for a new enlarged facility. We knew nothing about the details, but Thompson got the backing of J. P. Morgan and other mutual friends. In total, they put almost a quarter of a million dollars into that facility.

One afternoon, Trubee, who was by now my fast friend, confided that he had to take a damn flight test that day but that he wasn't feeling very well. In fact, he'd had a slight fainting spell that morning. I suggested that he put off the test, but being the kind of guy he was, he said no, he was going to go through with it, and that was all there was to it.

In any case, he took off, climbed out, and came back over a yacht at six thousand feet and into position headed upwind. The task was to cut your gun and then, with the engine idling, make two 360-degree turns and land in a space set off by four buoys. He wasn't permitted to touch the throttle during the descent except to clear out the engine once at the three-thousand-foot level. At that point, he closed the throttle to start his long spiral down and his final 360-degree test turn. He had to make the bank just right, and the rate of descent had to be exact or he was going to miss the area. As he got down to a very slow airspeed, I heard the whistling of the wires, and it sounded as though he were struggling. I don't know whether he did not respond as quickly as he normally did, or just what happened. But I do remember seeing him make his final turn and thinking he'd slowed his air speed too much. By flattening his glide and steepening on his bank, he was getting close to the stall point.

That's just what happened. He passed over the yacht, but suddenly the whole machine snapped off in a spin, made half a rotation, and dove into the water with a huge splash.

There was the horrifying sound of the boat hull smashing, of fabric ripping, spars snapping. Then came the sudden silence of the engine. It didn't seem that anyone could have survived the crash.

A speedboat shot out from the yacht and roared to the location of the crash. A diver jumped into the water to try to hold the aircraft up and keep it from sinking until they could get Trubee out. He was about half submerged, but he was in such a position that he was able to breathe. He was still alive, but in great pain. I dove into the water and swam over to him.

The job of getting him out of the airplane was very diffi-cult. Several other boats had come very quickly, and ropes were put around the flying boat so that there would be no chance of its sinking to the bottom. Axes, crowbars, and anything they could get their hands on were used to cut the shattered debris loose.

In the most excruciating agony, Trubee was removed from the wreckage and laid on the floor of the speedboat. I was right there with him, holding his hand, wishing there was some way to ease his pain. We were quickly transferred to the 'shuttle,' a commuter boat that was used as a backup for the water support system in the landing area. We went to Peacock Point to pick up Mr. and Mrs. Davidson, then sped directly to the New York Yacht Club landing and to St. Luke's Hospital.

None of us knew what the real trouble was, but it was obvious that Trubee had suffered a major injury, because he couldn't move his arms or legs and was in terrific pain. I held his

hand while he kept saying, 'We're doing okay, aren't we, Cowboy?'

'You bet we are Trubee, ole buddy.'

He whispered with a tight smile, 'We just can't get the
West out of you, can we, Cowboy?'

Later after the surgeon examined him, we learned that his
back was broken.

THE FLYIN' MEN

The time the unit spent at the Huntington facility was very productive. We had a lot of air-planes by then, and Colonel Thompson handled things so that we were making maximum use of the equipment and putting in a lot of flying hours.

We were no longer an independent civil flying club. Ever since our induction into the service, right after the declaration of war, we were officers in the United States Navy.

Before his crash, Trubee had been made a lieutenant junior grade because he had been the leader of the unit. The rest of us became ensigns. As far as I was concerned, it was a pretty good deal to get the commission. At least during the war, I had the same status as an ensign who had gone all the way through the Naval Academy at Annapolis.

I was only a freshman at Yale, and to be commissioned with

the same rank as a graduate of the four-year naval course was certainly a big boost. Of course, our commissions were temporary, while Annapolis commissions were permanent.

We no longer thought of ourselves as the unit. We were now naval aviators.

The first two fellows to be pulled out were Di Gates and Bob Lovett. They went overseas in the middle of August, while the rest of us continued with our training.

I was in the next bunch to go. There were seven of us— MacIlwaine, Leudon, Smith, Walker, Beach, Ingalls, and me. On September 17, 1917, we took the SS *St. Paul*, part of a convoy of twelve ships, from New York. The voyage to Liverpool took ten days.

Crossing the ocean after the declaration of war was an interesting sort of operation. The submarine campaign to starve out Great Britain was being waged vigorously by the Germans. The only thing in our favor was the fact that they didn't have enough submarines to cover the whole Atlantic Ocean. But there was always a chance that a stray sub might be close enough to put a torpedo into us."

"That must have been pretty scary," Becky said.

"Well, to a landlubber from Colorado, it was certainly a bit twitchy. I'd go to the stern of the ship and see that tremendous wake, stretching away to the horizon, and then I'd think about the ocean being ice-cold water for ten thousand feet down. The thought filled me with terrible awe. Every square inch of that ship was packed with troops, as well as a contingent of Red Cross nurses. It was quite obvious that there weren't enough lifeboats to take care of all of us, and that a good many souls would be lost if we ever got hit.

Matters became much more intense when we got into what

was called the danger zone. This was an imaginary line about two hundred fifty miles west of Ireland.

At that point, of course, we ran with lights completely off at night. Not even a cigarette was permitted on deck. The tension was too great to really get much sleep. We stayed up on deck most of the time since you didn't want to be down in the hold of the ship when it was torpedoed.

I must say that our first day in the danger zone, I had the scare of my life. We were up toward the bow of the ship looking for other ships or a periscope when I suddenly saw a torpedo coming straight for us off our starboard bow. I could see it making foam and just coming on like the dickens.

I yelled to Ingalls, who was beside me, 'My God! There's a torpedo! We're going to take a hell of a hit in a minute!'

Well, I was the laughingstock of the crew by the time the episode was over, for what I had seen was not a torpedo but a dolphin. It was racing toward the ship and had entered into the bow wave, as dolphins always do. It ran along with us, accompanying us in the friendliest manner. A friendly dolphin is far, far better than an enemy torpedo. They could kid all they wanted about Cowboy Cartwright and his dolphins.

When we were a little farther into the so-called danger zone, a cheer went up from the bow of the ship.

Looking out over the water, we saw a fleet of fast destroyers coming to give us an escort. Those little ships were traveling very fast—some said forty to fifty miles an hour. They all carried depth charges and could handle submarines. They came up and circled around on both sides of the convoy. It was a marvelous sight and, of course, a great comfort.

In another twenty-four hours, we sighted land. In the

morning, we docked at Liverpool. It was a wonderful sensation to be on solid land again.

That afternoon we took the train to London. The countryside was the greenest that one could imagine. There were neat farms on either side of the tracks, and not one square yard of the land was wasted. Every tract had been put into food production.

We all knew the sad story. The British Isles couldn't support themselves without imported foods. Their population was too great and their agricultural production too small. This was the whole key to the German blockade. It was a serious matter.

We arrived in London in the evening and were very discouraged by the dark mood of the city. It was representative of the country as a whole. Everyone was tired of the war. They had had three terrible years, and England had been bled white by the Somme offensive the year before. Trench warfare and the machine gun had changed the entire nature of war. It had become a hideous hell.

The machine gun was strictly a defensive weapon. It made the advance of infantry extremely difficult. The trenches were built not only to protect the soldiers from rifle fire and shelling but to provide substantial defense. Both the Allies and the Germans had placed barbed-wire entanglements in front of the trenches. The barbed wire was laid in a zigzag pattern and seemed to guarantee the deadliness of the machine gun. The wire held the troops in the line of fire while one machine gun fired from the 'zig' and another from the 'zag.' Where the wires crossed, the fire crossed.

The efficacy of the design was confirmed by the fact that the whole western front had not moved more than thirty miles back and forth for three years. Millions of men had obeyed that dreaded command to 'go over the top' and been slaughtered in the attempt to break the enemy lines on the other side.

As soon as we arrived in London, we reported to the U.S. Naval Air Office. Each of us was assigned to a different location, seemingly without regard to an overall plan. Some were lucky, and some were not.

I was one of the lucky ones. I was sent to Gosport, in the south of England, across the bay from Portsmouth, where the British had established one of the best aviation schools. At Gosport, they had several different types of airplanes, and the training was conducted by very competent English instructors, many of whom had been on the western front in actual aerial combat. They really knew their business. The planes were all land aircraft with wheels. There were no flying boats.

We were started off in Avro 540's. It was a nice two-seater biplane with double bay struts on the wings and an eighty horsepower rotary Le Rhone engine. It was light and very easy to fly. The beautiful graceful wings and fuselage were covered with Irish linen. When I first saw the wings of the Avro and touched its drumlike surfaces, I was reminded of the *Mary Ann*.

At Gosport, I was introduced to another very interesting device: the speaking tube, which operated between the student and the instructor. The student, sitting in the rear cockpit, watched the helmeted head of his instructor in front of him. The instructor's hand signals indicated turns to right and left, as well as nose up or down. But the instructor could also talk through the 'gosport' or tube to the student, who was equipped with earphones. The gosport helmet was used in open cockpit airplanes for many years.

In any case, we had about eight or ten hours in the Avros, and I must admit, it was quite nice to be flying a craft that ran along the meadow grasses and then took off into the air very lightly. It was very different from the heavy hulls of the flying boats.

For the first time, we received acrobatic training. Great precision was required of us in maneuvering turns, figure eights, lazy eights, chandelles, slow rolls, and snap rolls. It was a whole new world and gave us a good idea of the aerial combat skills we would need to stay alive. There was no question that these English instructors were top rank. The training was excellent, and there was never any delay in getting flight time, as there were plenty of airplanes.

Very soon, I managed to solo in the Avro with the help of an instructor who, whenever I would do some kind of maneuver correctly, would say in his broad British accent, 'Oh, I say, that's quite all right.' The instructors had no inclination to dominate or bully the students. England had suffered in the war too long for that. These people were involved in the dangerous game of flying, and they didn't play games. Actually, one out of every three pilots in the Flying Corps was killed. There was simply no room for monkey business.

I was also impressed by the very high standard of maintenance at which these machines were kept. I don't recall a single engine failure at any time while flying at Gosport. People at other bases didn't fare as well. Engine failure occurred frequently, and if it took place immediately after takeoff, it was almost always fatal.

While we were there, we were urged to fly as much as possible, at any time and anywhere within the local area, and to practice any maneuvers that we thought needed work. All sorts of aerobatics were encouraged, as well as mock dogfights. Some very good pilots were developed as a result. Some of them could land a Sopwith Camel from a full roll. I did it a few times, and believe me, you were busy every bit of the way.

After this thoroughly delightful experience at Gosport, which lasted about three weeks, we were shipped to Ayr in Scotland for the aerial gunnery school.

Of course, with the practice that I'd had on the ranch with a rifle and the great instruction I'd had from Brules in handling guns, I was totally familiar with the trajectory of firearms.

It turned out that lots of the fellows thought the machine gun, when aimed, would fire at the same level at three hundred yards as it would at one hundred. They failed to take into consideration the drop that's a factor in every gun barrel. Whether it's a mounted machine gun or one held to the shoulder, the bullet follows a parabola, which becomes very pronounced at three hundred yards. If you don't compensate for this, you can keep right on firing and missing. Add another 150 yards to the range, and a thirty-caliber bullet will drop about six feet.

In our practice sessions, tracer bullets went out about every ten rounds, and they gave you a pretty good idea of where the bullets were going. You needed all the help you could get in aerial combat. There were too many angles, too many things going on, and somebody might well be shooting at you while you were concentrating on some other guy.

Ayr was a rather strange place for aviation activity. It was on the west coast of Scotland, where it was frequently raining or fog-bound. But we did receive very fine training, which everyone seemed to think effective.

When we were through at Ayr, we came back to London and were told we would be going to the front in a few days. Actually, there was a long delay. Among other things, they'd decided that the pressure of the submarine warfare was so great that every effort should be directed to breaking that strangle-hold.

In looking over my logbooks, they discovered that I had experience as a flying boat pilot. They asked me how I felt about it. I loved the fighters—and it was a lot more fun in an SE-5 or a Sopwith Camel than in an H-6 or H-12 flying boat. The maneuverability was so much greater, the speed was faster, and you got a much stronger sense of freedom.

But in thinking it over, I realized I could probably do more for the war effort in the flying boat than in the fighter plane. There were hundreds and hundreds of fighter pilots, but there weren't very many aviators who knew much about flying boats.

Spotting and destroying the German submarines that were squeezing the life out of the British Isles was extremely important. Also, because I had loved flying over Long Island Sound so much, flying the English Channel appealed to me greatly. Therefore, without much further ado, I was sent to Dunkirk as a flying boat pilot.

Dunkirk was at the western end of the front that stretched to the Swiss border. It had been pretty badly pounded by German bombers—the big Gothas and Zeppelins—which had also struck endless raids on London. As a matter of fact, I have a picture of a building just two doors away from the Naval Aviation Headquarters—it was completely destroyed by aerial bombardment. It wasn't by any means the only building that had suffered.

When I first went to Dunkirk, there weren't enough flying boats to keep the pilots busy, but they were getting new machines every day, and I was assured that it wouldn't be long before I was flying. When the day finally came for me to go down to the slips for a flying boat, I went with a hardened veteran, an English chap who had been flying there for some months.

We taxied slowly out into the harbor until the engines warmed up. I opened the throttle and got a good run, then eased up on the step, broke loose, and climbed up for an aerial view of the English Channel.

I had the same sensation as when I was flying over Long Island Sound, except the Channel was a far grimmer place. Destroyers and escort ships plied the waters following the convoys, and there were many airplanes milling around.

One thing the flying boats had to be careful of was fighter planes coming from the German side. Any fighter could outmaneuver a flying boat very easily. A flying boat was really quite clumsy, and a fast fighter could make mincemeat out of one if it got the chance.

You had to keep on the lookout all the time and watch what you were doing because a flying boat was really a sitting duck. The best way to get rid of a fighter was to go into a fog bank, if you could find one. If you could see a fighter coming in the distance, you tried to move over to the English coast as fast as possible. Not many German fighters came over the English coast because they feared the anti-aircraft fire and the heavy fighter patrols.

The maintenance was not nearly as good at Dunkirk as it had been at Gosport. When you experienced difficulty—say, a dead engine—you had no means of feathering a prop and reducing the drag. The best you could do was shut the engine down completely, and even then it would keep windmilling, which would produce a great drag on one side. You would then rapidly lose altitude and would have to find someplace to come down fast. Landing in the middle of the English Channel, with fifteen-foot waves, was almost sure death.

It was a sporty time in Dunkirk, especially the bomb raids at night. I'll never forget the sound of the Gotha bombers. It was as if their engines weren't synchronized—they had a *wroom, wroom* sound back and forth, like a beat. Whereas the motors of the English Handley Page bombers ran rather evenly and gave out a steady hum. You learned about things like that as time went on.

I must say that a bomb raid was no fun when you were on the receiving side of it. You would hear the bombs crashing all around and wonder whether the next one was going to come down right on your head.

Dunkirk didn't really have any bomb shelters or anything like the subways in London. Sometimes you'd go into the cellar of a house, but it never seemed like a good idea because if the house got a straight hit, you'd be buried in it. A better alternative was to go to the railroad yards and crawl in under one of the freight cars parked on the sidings. If they were loaded with cargo, they provided pretty fair cover—at least ten or twelve feet of something that was reasonably solid.

One night I crawled under a freight car with a couple of friends of mine. We'd been at Naval Aviation Headquarters together and were walking back toward our billet when the Gothas came over. At that moment, we were crossing a railroad track and saw the shadows of several freight cars just in front of us.

We crawled underneath in a hurry and, to our amusement, found several other fellows in the same place having a little fun. They had been at some sort of party and were reasonably inebriated. Although we hadn't had anything to drink at that point, we didn't dismiss the idea of straightening out that situation in the very near future if we could survive the bomb raid. The sirens were screaming, the anti-aircraft was thundering, and the long shafts of powerful searchlights were scanning the night in search of the big Gothas.

It was great fun talking to these guys. They were Americans with the British Flying Corps, and most of them seemed to be college fellows.

I remember one of the fellows saying, 'Charlie, if we live through this and get out of this damn mess, what the hell do we want to go back to work in New York or someplace like that for? Why don't we go down to the South Seas, have a hell of a good time, and live out our lives making love to beautiful Polynesian girls in grass skirts?'

'You've got something, Jim,' the other guy said. 'We'll be lucky as hell if we get through, but if we do, we ought to live it up. We ought to have a hell of a time.'

Later, I learned that their names were James Norman Hall and Charles Nordhoff. After the war, those two did indeed go to the South Seas together, and while wandering about that part of the South Pacific, they discovered some old stories and legends and began to write books. They turned into great authors and wrote best sellers like *Mutiny on the Bounty*, *Men Against the Sea*, *Pitcairn Island*, *Hurricane*, and many other very famous books."

"Life is strange that way," said Becky. "To think that you could sit under a boxcar and end up ducking German bombs with world-renowned authors."

"It certainly is."

"Steven, did you ever fly fighters in combat?"

"Well, as you know, I was trained on almost everything while I was in England, but I went straight to the flying boats."

"Which was the best plane you flew?" asked Becky.

"I thought the SE-5, a British fighter, was the best plane at that time. It was absolutely beautiful. It had gentle dihedral, which meant the wings were sloped upward from the center of the airplane on each side, very much like the curve of a hawk's wing.

I know one thing. The SE-5 would fly hands-off if you had it trimmed up right. You could take your hands and feet off the controls, which you sure could not do with the Sopwith Camel. In addition, it did about 130 miles per hour flat-out. At least the factory said it did. I thought it was the best airplane of all, the Rolls-Royce of the whole works.

Later on in France, I flew the French SPAD. You could dive that airplane at 250 miles per hour before pieces came off. You couldn't do that in an SE-5 or a Camel. But give me the SE-5—it was a thing of beauty to men who loved to fly.

That winter of 1917–1918 was particularly rainy and foggy on the English Channel. There would be periods, sometimes as long as seven or eight days, when it would be impossible for us to fly. When occasionally we got some passable flying weather, we would try to make the most of it. Every flying boat on the base would be out, all going in different directions looking for any trace of the enemy.

In spring, because England is so far north, daylight was long, and when the weather was good, flying conditions were glorious. We flew an incredible number of hours. Mostly, it was just skirting the coast of Britain, traveling as far north as Scotland and along the south shore of England as far as Plymouth and even Cornwall.

THE LEGEND OF THE PAINTED HORSE

We did have some success as far as submarines were concerned. Several of the boys spotted submarines either surfacing or just under the surface of the water. They might drop a depth charge, but not with any great accuracy. So they radioed the position of the submarine, and the destroyers would be there in a hurry.

One glorious evening we were invited to the Royal Flying Corps officers' club at a squadron located ten miles down the coast toward Calais. Those British fighter pilots were great fellows. Despite their long service and despite the tragic episodes they had inevitably witnessed, they still had spirit and a very keen taste for barleycorn.

If you ever got to an officers' mess, you soon found that everyone crowded around the bar. There was lots of drinking, and if a fellow could play the piano, that made it all the merrier. The gang would stand around and drink themselves into a real riot and sing. The songs that were sung at British Flying Corps messes were outrageously shocking and vulgar, but they were also exceedingly clever and funny.

An officer would stand up and sing a verse, filthy beyond belief but with a splendid rhyming end. A cheer would go up, with lots of laughter, then another guy would stand up and sing the next verse. It was great fun and really put sedate practices to shame.

As a matter of fact, during the Second World War, the naval flight squadrons used *The Fleet Air Arm Songbook*, which was a collection of the dirtiest songs you've ever heard in your life. When sung in the proper spirit, they produced roars of laughter. I was presented with one of these books in 1943.

This camaraderie and riotous singing at the officers' mess of the British squadrons was one of the few things that made the war bearable.

We flew on, all through July, at Dunkirk. Then to my great joy, I was ordered back to Gosport as a flight instructor, a flight instructor on fighters.

WAR IS HELL?

When I arrived back in Gosport, I found I actually had very mixed feelings about being assigned as an instructor. A lot of my buddies were out there flying at the front, getting shot up and taking terrible chances. Here I was back in a cushy job. I felt a little guilty about it.

I had never been in a real dogfight, though I always felt confident that if I were in one, I could do a pretty good job. But now I rationalized that I shouldn't push my luck. The war was going to last probably another two or three years, and there would be plenty of other chances to get to the front and get killed. Besides, I'd got a promotion to lieutenant junior grade, so I decided to leave well enough alone for a while at least.

For the next month while I was at Gosport, I frequently went up to London to see my friends. I took up with a very attractive English girl, and we had some jolly times together.

Everybody that I knew—Naval Air Arm and Royal Flying Corps—used to gather at the Savoy Hotel. The bar at the Savoy did a flourishing business. Sometimes fellows would bring girls, and sometimes the girls would just come and sit around in the lobby. If you were gentlemanly about it, you might go up to a lady, bow, introduce yourself, and ask her if she'd care to have a drink or to dance. There was always a dance band there, which made matters much easier.

Of course, girls of questionable reputation sometimes showed up, but the hotel management was pretty strict about them. In most cases, they were easily spotted and were very politely ushered out the front door.

A few of the fellows had relatives in London, and when they paid a visit to their homes, they were sometimes introduced to girls. There were also nice old ladies in London who made a specialty of seeing that the American and English boys had a chance to meet 'nice girls.'

The lights in the Savoy were kept on well into the night, but of course, they were completely blacked out from the outside, and it wasn't until you entered the hotel that you realized there was a party going on.

It was at the Savoy bar that I ran into a great guy. His name was Elliott Scott, and he was from Princeton.

The first time I met him, he had two other friends with him. One was a guy by the name of Callahan, who I later found out was one hell of a piano player. In fact, he was just about the best jazz player I'd ever heard. The other fellow was named McCormick. Those three guys seemed like real good buddies and were at the center of whatever was going on. All three of them had made the acquaintance of quite a few 'nice girls,' and they were never without female company, as far as I could see.

They had rented a nicely furnished house in the Mayfair district. How the hell they got a hold of it, I don't know, but apparently Scott's folks had a lot of money. They owned a big cotton plantation and mill in South Carolina. I think his dad sent him something like a thousand dollars to go and have a nice time before he went over to the front. That was a lot of money back then. These fellows just seemed to be having a great time and were, sort of, the leaders of the gang.

Scott went on to become a famous American ace. I forget how many victories he had. But Callahan was, I guess, the best natural flyer I ever knew. I heard he was the first guy to land a Sopwith Camel from a roll. He'd done that at Gosport the month before I was in there. Remember, I told you I learned to do that too at Gosport? That took real airmanship!

Anyway, when Scott and I first struck up a conversation, I told him I'd gone to Yale.

'That's a great shame!' he said. 'Otherwise you look like a nice fellow. Where do you come from?'

'Colorado.'

With that he perked up. 'What does your dad do?'

'He owns a big ranch in the southwestern corner of the state in the wild country called the Four Corners.'

'I've heard about that country,' he said. 'Cliff dwellings or something like that.'

'That's right,' I replied. 'Pretty remote—everything is a hundred miles from everything else down there.'

He laughed. 'Isn't that interesting. I've always wanted to go out west. I suppose you ride broncos and rope and brand and do all those things that cowboys are supposed to do.'

'I had to do it. My dad wouldn't stand for me being around and not pulling my weight.'

Later that same evening, Scott invited me out to their house in Mayfair. I had another fellow with me from Naval Air Arm, and Scott invited him as well. We both went along eagerly, very pleased to be included.

'Tell me, so I don't break any rules around here—when do the lights go out?' I asked.

'Only with the light of day,' he replied.

'Okay, that gives me a pretty good idea.'

Old Callahan got going on that piano, and the girls helped pull back the rugs so we could dance. The guys told jokes, we sang, and everyone had a hell of a good time.

Scott was the guy who introduced the famous southern mint julep to the Air Corps. I mean not only the U.S. Army and Navy, but the British Flying Corps too—in fact, all the Allied services.

He really knew how to make a mint julep! He had learned how from his old man. He would take that old Kentucky bourbon and mix it with enough sugar and mint leaves. He seemed to get all kinds of things from home, including the mint leaves. It was amazing to me how that drink could possibly turn out that good. And of course, it had the kick of a mule.

I want to make it clear that those parties in Mayfair weren't anything like those in an officers' mess. They sang all kinds of songs, but I don't remember hearing a risqué word in any of them. Those guys were pretty damn straight about things when ladies were present.

One time, a couple of fellows, officers in the U.S. Army Air Corps who knew Scott, came to the door. They had a couple of girls with them who seemed to have, shall we say, a slight professional background.

Scott was very polite but said, 'You fellows are welcome

here anytime, but I'm sorry, we won't have those kind of girls in this place.'

The girls were mad as hell, of course, and the fellows got a little uppity. They said, well, they didn't think Scott's reputation was so very good either.

'If it isn't any good now,' Scott said, 'we're trying to improve it. Thank you very much, and we'll see you sometime when you're in better company.'

Later Scott said to me, 'As far as I know, as long as we've had this place, we have kept it clean upstairs and down.'

As I said, Scott became an ace, and after the war he wrote a number of books about flying in the early days.

It was while I was instructing at Gosport that I had the chance to ferry an SE-5A to an English squadron at the front near Armentières in France. I was well received when I landed there and was told there was no sense in trying to get back to England by surface travel without several days' preparation. Channel passage was bad, but perhaps there would be some flights going back soon. They suggested that I hang around for a while, and I was pleased to do so because I knew a lot of the guys.

On the same aerodrome, there was an American squadron called the Hat in the Ring. It was commanded by Eddie Rickenbacker, the foremost American ace. He ended the war with twenty-six victories. Considering the short time that the Americans were involved, that was a very good score. Of course, it didn't compare with some of the British aces, like Billy Bishop, who had, I think, seventy-six kills overall. Richthofen, the great German ace, was up to eighty, I think.

Still, Rickenbacker was recognized as a great flyer. There had been some other fine flyers in that squadron like Raoul

Lufbery, but by the time I got there, they had been killed. The unit had been taken from the Lafayette Escadrille and eventually moved into the Hat in the Ring Squadron.

I must say, I was very happy to meet a lot of the fellows there, but particularly Frank Luke from Phoenix, who was a cowboy and also a hell of a pilot. He was the sort of fellow who kept pretty much to himself. That made a difference in the way a lot of people thought about him, but as far as I was concerned, he was A-one. During the war, he earned a reputation as a balloon buster. I think they later dedicated an airport to him in Arizona called Luke Field.

Anyway, I had a jolly time with that squadron. I asked them about flying a SPAD, but they couldn't spare one at the time because they were flying heavy patrols. Of course, none of them knew if I was a good pilot or not. Maybe they thought I would pile up one of their machines.

When I told the operations officer I had about four hundred hours in Camels and SE-5s, he came up with an even better idea.

'Oh, God,' he said, 'if you can fly a Sopwith Camel, you can fly a SPAD easily. We've got two or three new machines down at the factory in Toulon and haven't been able to spare any ferry pilots to bring them up here to the front. How about you going down to get one?'

Of course, I jumped at the chance. They put me in an old DH9 with a 280-horse Rolls engine in it. It was a two-seater and a hell of a nice plane with lots of room. It sort of reminded me of the old Avro. Of course, it had a lot more get-up-and-go— 280 horse against eighty in the Avro. The pilot took me down to Toulon and gave me a ground check on the SPAD. I took off, flew it around a little bit, put it through loops, rolls, and spins, and then set it back down nicely. The instructor director was sure that I could take it back to the front the next day.

While I was standing there with him, I saw a guy taking off in a SPAD. Those 180-model E Hispano-Suiza engines were good engines, but like everything else during the war, they were being built so fast that things could go wrong. You never knew if a fuel line would break loose or something. The plane roared down the field, took off, and hadn't any more than broken ground when it lost power completely. It probably wasn't any more than eight or ten feet in the air. The airplane had just barely reached flying speed when the motor quit. It simply went back down on the ground hard, busted its undercarriage, went up on its nose for a minute, then flopped back down on its tail.

It was the funniest-looking thing I ever saw. I started to laugh.

The French officer standing with me turned on me fiercely and said, 'Non, non. Il est mort! He is dead!'

I found out right then that that kind of a crash landing in a SPAD was going to kill the pilot. Your head was so close to the gun butts and the rest of the instrument panel that if you hit something solid and hard with a terrific wallop, your neck would be broken.

That's exactly what happened. They pulled this poor fellow out, and he was gone. I felt like hell and apologized, but they waved me off. I obviously didn't know what a dead engine that close to the ground could do to a SPAD and the man flying it. They forgave me, but I must say that I felt quite ashamed for a long time."

"Oh, Steven, how awful!" Becky cried.

"It was, but war is full of tragedy, and when you are young

and filled with a sense of fighting for something grand and glorious, you can handle it better."

"What did you do then? Did you fly the SPAD back to the front the next day?"

"Yes. I took off and was merrily cruising along at five thousand feet over the Loire Valley when all of a sudden that Hisso began burping and popping. It would run for a minute, and then stop and begin backfiring. I thought it was either the ignition or a clogged fuel line. But it was cutting off somewhere. I couldn't figure out what the hell was the matter. I had to find a place to put that SPAD down quickly, which meant some kind of field. But it was springtime and the crops were high in all the farming fields.

I had plenty of time because I was at five thousand feet, but a SPAD is heavy and will descend very rapidly with a dead engine. I knew it landed at seventy miles an hour with no brakes, just the tail skid, and that I had to set her down on three points and keep that stick back in my lap to make the tail skid dig in and brake the roll. I saw a château with a great broad lawn in front of it. It looked like the best flying field around. From a smokestack in a nearby village, I could tell which way the wind was blowing. I brought the SPAD in on a nice curve and set her down just as daintily as I knew how. When she rolled to a stop, I climbed out of the cockpit.

People came running from all over. Even the marquis came striding down from the château. He was a most gracious, handsome, dignified gentleman and was very glad to see an American aviator flying a French airplane. He spoke to me in his language, and I stumbled around in my schoolbook French, trying to explain what had happened, but it really wasn't necessary. It was easy to see that the airplane had gone "kaput," as he said, and that was all there was to it.

I asked for a telephone to call headquarters, and he took me into the château, which was a stunningly beautiful house. He had one of those old telephones that you crank and ring and ring and then call out in French. I had great difficulty, but the marquis helped, and I finally got through to the squadron operations officer.

He said, 'Stay right where you are, Cartwright—don't move. We'll send a crew over there. Put that Frenchman back on the phone, and tell him to give me directions on how to get there.'

The marquis spoke only French, but somehow the other seemed to understand, for the marquis finally hung up and said, 'Voilà!'

The old marquis had two of the most beautiful daughters you could ever lay eyes on. One was about sixteen, and the other about eighteen. By that time, I was quite an elderly fellow of almost twenty. The marquis insisted that I wait at the château, and I was happy to accept. There was a tennis court where we played mixed doubles all afternoon."

"It all sounds wonderful and certainly far removed from the war," said Becky. "Had they seen many planes or pilots before?"

"No, they hadn't," replied Steven. "Of course, they had seen airplanes, but they had never seen an aviator up close. Now here was a guy coming down out of the sky rigged up in goggles, helmet, and flying suit. I'm sure the romance of the uniform greatly added to my image.

Dinner was served in elegant fashion, and afterward we sipped on a fine old cognac while the oldest daughter played the piano. I tried to tell them about my life in the United States, but I'm not sure how much they understood since my French was so bad.

The mechanics showed up the next morning, and we played tennis again while they worked on the airplane. It was late afternoon when they finished, and the crew chief broke up our tennis game by asking me to run up the engine and check everything out. I climbed into my flying suit and got ready to go. But then there were other adjustments I felt had to be made, and more fuel that had to be poured into the tank, and so forth."

"Steven, did you deliberately find fault with the condition of the plane?"

"Becky, I'm not sure that I didn't purposely delay matters because I thought another evening at the château might hold lots of promise. Obviously, we couldn't fly after dark in a fighter plane on the Western Front. That would have been crazy.

Anyway, I remember sitting in the cockpit, pulling my goggles down over my eyes, and trying my best to look like the hero of the Western Front. The chief mechanic gave the call to 'switch off' and turned the prop over two or three times very dexterously. When he got the blade level, he said, 'Contact,' and I threw the switch on. The Hisso had twin magnetos, which meant it had two sources of electrical power, instead of just one. So with the switch in both mag positions, the mechanic took hold of the prop. He got just the tip of his fingers over it and stood on his left leg and swung his right leg forward and then back to keep it away from the arc of the prop. Then he jerked the prop through the arc against that heavy compression, which sort of carried him away in the process.

Twisting props was dangerous business, and some fellows were killed doing it. When you were around an airplane with the engine running, you had to be very, very careful. Stepping on tires to get a look at the engine was a dangerous thing to do. There was a lot of rain in England, and the tires would get wet and slick. A fellow could fall right into the prop, and that would be the end of it.

Well, the chief mechanic was very expert and swung the prop through, and the Hisso bellowed out with a roar. I had no brakes or anything to run the engine up. I wanted to run it up to maximum RPM and check the mags. We had chocks on both wheels, and as an extra precaution, a mechanic got on either wing and strained to hold it down. I opened the throttle wide, and the engine roared like a demon.

I had a little strip of leather at the back of my helmet where the helmet had been pulled together and tied up. It streamed out maybe ten inches or a foot straight out behind me with the wind from the whirling propeller. The airplane was roaring and the tail was up. Oh boy, I was such a sight. The girls were jumping up and down, screaming and dancing.

I finally shut the engine off and said, 'She's okay, but it's too late to get to the squadron tonight.' "

"Oh, Steven!"

"So once again and with great enthusiasm, the marquis invited me back to the château. He had an old gramophone, which we played, and I danced with the girls. The old gentleman was just as happy as he could be. Apparently his wife had passed away sometime before, and he was raising these daughters alone. He thought they were having a wonderful time with this American aviator and wanted it to last as long as possible.

A little before midnight we reluctantly went to bed because I had to leave at dawn. It was a very, very interesting experience, because those two young girls didn't just leave it at that.

After the lights were out, the eldest knocked on my door. She stayed for several hours. I had just fallen back to sleep when the youngest entered my room. My guess was they just wanted to sleep with an aviator. And I had done nothing to discourage it.

When I got out to the SPAD early in the morning, the mechanics were waiting for me. A crowd of farmers had also gathered to watch the plane take off. I climbed into the cockpit and went through the business of turning the prop over with the ignition switch shut off. When the mechanic got the prop just right, he yelled, 'Contact!' I switched to double mags, and he reached up with that glorious twisting kick of his and pulled the prop through. That Hisso broke into a thunderous roar.

There was a long stream of airslip behind, kicking up the dust and throwing the plants over. I played the hero as long as I could. Finally, I taxied out to the far end of the field, turned into the wind, and firmly pushed the gun to that SPAD. She raised her tail and started to roll. Part of the field was a little rough. I felt her getting lighter and lighter and eased back on the stick. She was airborne.

That Hisso had plenty of power, and I moved right up from sixty or seventy miles an hour to a hundred and ten. I climbed out a ways. I didn't intend to go too far. I got a little altitude, maybe fifteen hundred feet, then turned around and got lined up to come in downwind with all the speed I could get. I put the nose down, and boy, she began to move.

I watched that airspeed come up to 130, 150, to 175. The airplane wouldn't have done that in level flight, but she sure as hell would do it on a downhill run with the wind behind it. Knowing a SPAD was built like a brick outhouse, I had no trepidation about taking it to these speeds. Of course, I wouldn't have done it in a Nieuport because the wings wouldn't have stayed on, but a SPAD could take it.

I flew past the crowd assembled on the château lawn, and I couldn't have been more than ten feet off the ground and going like hell. I shot along for about seventy-five or a hundred yards, then I pulled that thing up and did two rolls. As I circled and passed over the crowd, I waggled my wings."

"I can imagine the sight," said Becky. "The old marquis waving his hat with enthusiasm, and the girls jumping up and down and screaming. It sounds as though you had a great time. Where did you go then?"

"I headed back to the front and brought the machine into the Hat in the Ring Squadron before noon.

The next week I made my way by various means back to Gosport. When I saw my friends there, I related my heroics without being at all modest. If anything needed embellishment, I was careful to add it as a pièce de résistance."

Becky laughed. "Steven, it must have been the boy in you, the real bad boy!"

"Yeah"—he grinned—"must have been.

My days at Gosport came to an end when I was ordered to the Admiralty, the naval office in London. They asked what flying boats I had piloted.

I told them I had flown the little boats as well as the Big America, which was the H-12. It was a Curtiss flying boat with two Rolls-Royce Eagle 250-horsepower engines. It had cruised very nicely, broke from the surface of the water as though it really wanted to fly, and had a very substantial range of about two hundred miles. The H-12 was much larger than the H-6's we had been using before, which were known as Little Americas. The Big America could carry four people: a pilot, copilot, navigator, and gunner, with three machine guns. It was such a successful boat that the British ordered almost two hundred of them.

Now I was informed that the Big America was no longer the big boy. The airplane that we had all been waiting for was the H-16, a Curtiss flying boat powered by two American Liberty 400-horsepower engines. The roar from that machine was like an unleashed war dog, thundering and snarling as it raced toward his prey. It was a truly incredible sound! The H-16 was a hell of an airplane, and I was eager to fly it.

It could carry five people and had a range of about four hundred miles. What Curtiss had been trying to do, with the assistance of an English aerodynamist, was to build a flying boat that would be capable of carrying passengers across the ocean. Except for the range, he wasn't too far off with the H-16.

In fact it was only about eighteen years later that Pan Am began sending its flying boats, the Clipper Ships, over both the Caribbean and the Pacific.

The British were putting the H-16's into Portsmouth Naval Base, and I was being assigned to fly them. That was just great. With a four-hundred-mile range, you can do a lot of things. From Portsmouth you could fly clear down to Land's End without any problem, and you could go damn near as far as Scapa Flow to the north.

When they asked me if I would be interested, I could hardly contain myself. 'You bet!' The English officer laughed at my undignified response."

"I can just see you," said Becky "in all your glory as captain of a big new plane."

"It was really exciting," said Steven. "One time I flew the H-16 from Portsmouth down to Land's End at the southern tip

of England and back to the harbor at Plymouth. From a reasonable altitude, it was possible to see quite far down beneath the
sea if the water was clear. I circled the harbor in preparation for
landing when I saw a large object lying on the bottom. At first, I
thought it was an old ship or maybe even a whale. That seemed
highly unlikely, and I took another look and screamed above
the roar of the Liberty engines, 'Jesus Christ, that's a German
submarine.' "

Becky jumped and threw both hands up to her mouth, "My
God, what did you do?"

"I cut the gun on both engines, scaring the crew to death,
put the nose down, and landed that big boat in a matter of
seconds. I set her down fast, but she soon started settling off the
step. I didn't allow her to slow down too much but slammed the
gun to those Libertys, and we roared across the harbor and shot
up the slope of the slips of the RNA seaplane base, scaring the
daylights out of the scrambling dock crew.

I killed the engines and stood up in the cockpit, shoved my
goggles back, and yelled like hell for the duty officer. He came
running out of the dock office boiling with rage that some stupid
naval aviator would handle one of his majestic giant flying boats
in such a flagrantly and senselessly dangerous fashion, terrifying
the dock crews and endangering life and equipment.

I saw he was a commodore, so I quickly saluted. He started
giving me hell but eased up when he saw the American insignia
on my flying suit and the American flag painted on the bow of
the H-16. Still he was hard to please, but when I told him a
German submarine was lying in the bottom of the harbor, he
changed gears.

It took him a minute or two to gather his wits, and he kept

urging me to point out the spot, but on the level of the sea this was impossible.

'Let's have a look at the harbor chart,' he said.

We ran to his office to look at the chart on the wall, and after a minute I got the coordinates and pointed to the spot.

He furiously cranked on an old telephone, then bellowed out orders and things began to happen. Five Sopwith Camels took off, buzzed about continuously, diving down to within ten feet of the water, indicating the invader's position. Sirens wailed, and seamen ran for their ships. Within minutes the harbor was churning as four destroyers darted out from their moorings.

They made for the designated point and passed over the submarine in a staggered formation, laying their depth charges as they passed. Even when you are on shipboard with the roar of the sea, depth charges make a hell of an explosion, but when you are on shore standing in relative quiet, they sound catastrophic.

The destroyers whirled about and passed over the designated spot and hurled four more canisters into the tortured waters. A few minutes later, a heavy oil slick appeared on the surface, and it was obvious the U-boat had been sent to Davy Jones's locker.

Later when all the excitement was over, I took advantage of the daylight and flew back to Portsmouth.

Several days later there was a board of inquiry into the whole matter, but nothing was said about my reckless handling of the H-16. I didn't get a medal, but neither did I get a reprimand. Finally, as if reluctantly, I got a citation commending me for exceptional perception in observing dangerous enemy activity. Not long after this episode, I was promoted to lieutenant."

"Wow," said Becky, "that must have been something. Did you have any other really exciting trips from Portsmouth?"

"Yes, on one trip I found a connecting link in the trail of the painted horse."

"What was that?" Becky asked.

"On one mission we flew an H-16 up the east coast of England, the Channel side, and refueled at Dundee. We really didn't need to do that, but I wasn't taking any chances as far as the range of the aircraft was concerned. I went out of Dundee with full tanks and flew to Scapa Flow, up in the northernmost tip of Scotland. It was a distance of only about 160 miles, but I didn't want to get caught short of fuel and have to land in the North Sea with those tremendous waves. There would have been nothing left of that flying boat if that had happened."

"Not to mention you and the rest of the crew," she said.

He grinned and went on. "When I arrived in Scapa Flow, I saw what was left of the great British fleet. It was only partially restored after its bloody conflict with the German fleet in 1916, the world's last big battleship contest for the supremacy of the sea. In the summer of 1916, the German fleet had come puffing out of Kiel to challenge the 350-year-old adage 'Britannia rules the waves.' The British fleet responded by steaming out of Scapa Flow to meet the foe.

The Battle of Jutland proved two things. One, that equally heavily armed battleships with eighteen-inch guns could pound their adversaries to pieces if they could get off the first shots accurately. Two, that it was the end of the battleship era.

With the advent of the airplane, the striking distance of opponents could be expanded a hundred times. The eighteen-inch guns had seen their end. Both sides limped back to their respective naval bases and nursed their wounds, and there was no more of that foolishness for the rest of World War I.

While at Scapa Flow, I was ordered to fly to the British naval harbor in the Shetland Islands. There were no seaplane slips there for me to power up on, but there was a floating dock to refuel flying boats. I pulled over to the support, shut off my engines just a few yards from the barge, and was drawn in by the sea crews, who were really excited to see the new H-16.

I climbed out of the cockpit and stood on the floating dock. Unfortunately, there wasn't enough time to go ashore. We were only there a few hours. I had the powerful field glasses that I always carried after Brules told me how much good his pair had done for him over the years.

I scanned the town with its fort and old cathedral and then extended my gaze to the outlying fields and pastures. In the distance, I saw what looked like a bunch of white horses, but on bringing them in closer, I saw that they were not whites but paints. The horses seemed very small, and at first I thought it was because they were very far away. But then I realized that they were small because they were just ponies. They were Shetland ponies, painted Shetland ponies.

My mind began to whirl. I thought back to the beautiful painted horses that Wild Rose had presented to Brules as sort of a dowry. I remembered how beautiful they looked up on the side of the hills at home, and for a few moments, if I forgot about their size, I could almost believe I was back at the ranch.

Then my mind began to fly through the clouds. As if in a vision, I suddenly realized that these little painted ponies were one of the links in the great chain of painted horses that had come from the Kinghan Mountains of northern China, across Siberia to Persia, and the Scandinavian highlands to this place, the Shetland Islands. But how, I asked myself, did they get across the Atlantic to the basin of the Columbia River, a distance of some six thousand miles?

I began to wonder why these animals were so small. Maybe these little ponies weren't related to the full-sized painted horses. Were they a smaller breed? Suddenly the whole chain of events became very clear to me.

They couldn't have swum here. They must have been brought here by men. They had to have been transported from Scandinavia on Viking ships a thousand years ago.

The reason they were so undersized was the same reason that the Scottish stag was so small. Like the stag, they had been left to graze in a small area for a thousand years. Their food supply was limited by the confines of the land, and as the generations went on, they became smaller and smaller.

The reverse of this process was demonstrated when the Duke of Argyle moved three stags and seven hinds to the broad ranges of New Zealand about 1895. The stag had no natural enemy there, nor were there severe winters. Over a period of time, the New Zealand stag grew to almost double the proportions of the English stag. It had ample food, no predator kill, and no winter kill.

When I saw all this, I got so excited I could hardly speak. I didn't discuss my theory with anyone. My ideas were still in the formative stages, and besides, they would have been of very little interest to anyone else. But for me, it was a moment of insight I'll never forget."

"Oh, Steven, how exciting. But did you have time to keep on with your research into the painted horse?"

"No, I would have liked to, but I had to get back to the business of the war."

III

"How much longer were you in England?"

"Actually, shortly thereafter, on the eleventh of November, we got the news that the armistice had been signed.

London went wild. You cannot imagine what it meant to people that this dreadful war, with all its devastation and suffering, had ended.

It was to be the war to end all wars, but unfortunately war is a natural way of life for mankind."

"Steven, you are so right," Becky said. "I don't believe that there will ever be a last war for the human race. Did you come straight home then?"

"After the armistice was signed, we thought we'd be going home right away, but it didn't happen that easily. There were almost two million men in Europe and a shortage of ocean-going vessels to take us back to the United States. As they should have, the boys who had been in the trenches, the wounded, the sick at heart—they went first.

It wasn't until the end of March 1919 that I finally left Southampton for home on the SS *Farragut*.

As soon as I got back to the States, I contacted Yale. The registrar's office assured me that I would not be penalized for lost class time. I would go back as a sophomore in the fall of 1919 and graduate in the spring of 1922. That was fine with me.

But first I thought the best thing in the world would be to go back to the ranch and get my feet on the ground. I longed to see my mother and father, and of course, I hoped to visit old Brules again. I didn't even know if he was still alive. Knowing how my mother felt about him, I had never mentioned his name in my letters to her or suggested that she try to find out how he was doing.

HOME AT LAST

When I was discharged in April 1919, I hightailed it back to the ranch as fast as I could. I took the long train ride across the country to Denver, on to Alamosa, then rode the narrow gauge across the San Juans to Durango, and on to Rico, which was the railroad station nearest the ranch. It was a joyous return, I can tell you that.

Dad and Mom met me with the buckboard, some horses, and a few of the cowhands. Even though the war had been over for a good six months, the buckboard was decorated with American flags, and the cowboys were carrying flags on long poles stuck in stirrup sockets as though they were cavalry riders. I was hoping that Brules wouldn't see them because, God knows, they didn't look anything like cavalry. But they were giving me a hero's welcome and had brought along my favorite horse. I was delighted not to have to ride in the buckboard, and we all went home in a kind of triumphant procession.

Even though I was itching to get up the mountain, I spent lots of time after I first got there with Mother and Dad. Mother had been in tears most of the time I was on the front, fearing that I might never come back. Although I had written home often, she told me that there were long periods when she didn't hear from me. Transatlantic mail was very slow, and she was worried almost to death.

After I'd been home a week or so and my parents were reassured of my well-being, I could give in to my urge to go up old Lone Cone.

So one afternoon I got my horse, tied a bedroll and some essentials on the back of the saddle, and hit out for the high country.

I kept turning back to see the valley as we climbed. I was thinking about things, the way one does when one gets into the forest and looks out over the plains. I surveyed the grandeur of the La Sals and turned toward the Blues. I was still on the northern side of the mountain and couldn't yet see south to Sleeping Ute, but I knew it would be within my range of vision when I got to the shelf at the eight-thousand-foot level. There was something very healing about the beauty and majesty of the ranch.

The frightening thought that something could have happened to Brules suddenly struck me. After all, he was an old man. Was there a chance that he hadn't made it through the winter? He used to say, 'I'll see you next year if I don't winter kill.' I tried not to think about it, but I still felt uneasy.

There was more truth than humor in his statement. At an altitude of eight thousand feet in Colorado, the winter weather can be pretty hard. If the fire should go out and an old man had something go wrong with him, it could be a very dangerous situation.

No, I thought, Brules is as tough as a pine knot. He'll be there.

When I burst out onto the shelf and came up to the old branding camp in the meadow, I worked my way around to the southwest where old Brules lived. I must say that my heart pounded with delight when I saw smoke coming out of the chimney of his cabin.

He wasn't there, even though the door was open. It appeared that he had gone out somewhere, maybe to the spring with his water bucket. But he would be back in a few minutes, I was sure. So I just stayed at the edge of the clearing and waited.

I was quiet, not wanting to startle him in any way. In a few minutes, he came back, and sure enough, he was lugging a water bucket from the creek. I pushed my horse out a few steps into the clearing and called to him.

He turned in surprise and kept looking and looking. He couldn't quite make out who it was. So I slid off the saddle and called, 'It's Steven!'

He stared at me a minute, then he gave a war whoop, threw his old hat way up in the air, and came trundling toward me with his arms wide open. I rushed toward him, and we both threw our arms around each other in a *gran abrazo*. There were tears in both our eyes. He kept pounding me on the back, hugging me, then standing back, holding me by the elbows, and crying, 'By God, a flyin' man, a flyin' man!'

I have no idea how he learned I was an aviator, or 'flyin' man,' but I presume it must have been from one of the cowboys.

His greeting was so genuine. There was a bond of some kind between us, a feeling of kinship that could not be denied.

This time, he invited me into his cabin. It seems that I wasn't going to be relegated to a bedroll outside, as I had been on other occasions. I put my horse in the corral and gave him a little grain. It was getting on toward dark.

'You come on in here,' Brules said. 'Let's stoke up the fire. I want to hear all about everythin'.'

He had an old kerosene lantern which gave just enough light to make out the furnishings of the room. I was delighted to see my old Navajo blanket gracing his bed.

He saw me looking at it and said, 'Son, I ain't never forget-tin' when you left that Navajo blanket. That was when you pulled out and was headed off to college. Little did I think that you was goin' to get in that terrible war over there. I've looked at that blanket for the last three years now and just wondered when in hell I was ever goin' to see my boy again. By Jove, I tell you, I've had no word from you, and I didn't know what to do.'

Well, when ole Brules said 'I've had no word from you,' it was like driving a knife through my heart.

You dumb dodo, I thought. Why didn't you write him? You could've sent him a picture or a postcard. Anything that would have let him know you hadn't forgotten him.

But then how would it have gotten up the mountain to him?

Of course, I'd been busy trying to stay alive all that time. Sometimes I didn't give as much thought to the folks at home. The idea of trying to get a letter off to old Brules had never entered my head. And even if I'd written one, how would he have read it? He couldn't read.

But here we were sitting in his cabin, eight thousand feet

up in the Rockies, with the bear skin on the floor and the big elk-horn gun rack that held his 1873 Winchester with the worn stock and tightly bound pistol grip. It seemed like a hundred years ago that he had bound it to keep the crack from spreading. Then there was the Buffalo Sharps that old General Crook had given him after the Geronimo wars. I'll tell you Brules would rather have had that Sharps from General Crook than the Congressional Medal of Honor.

The Sharps always interested me. Gosh, it had a shell that was about seven inches long. It was designed to kill buffalo at a far distance at the time when they were getting scarce and awfully spooky about hunters. And it sure did work.

It's the same kind of gun Billy Dixon is supposed to have used to make his famous shot against Comanche warriors from the Adobe Walls hideout on the Canadian River in the Texas Panhandle.

The whole place had been raided by seven hundred Comanches. About thirty buffalo hunters were quartered up there, and they just shot the hell out of those Comanches. As a matter of fact, they only lost three men. Two guys who were sleeping in a covered wagon were murdered as soon as the charge came close to the house. The other one was old Hanrahan, who was accidentally shot when his wife passed him a loaded gun. It went off, sending a bullet up through his chin and right out the top of his head.

Otherwise, it was a pretty sporty fight. Brules told me how he later saved a guy named Shellabarger, who had gotten lost out on the prairie and was out of water. He'd been in the fight and told Brules all about it.

Old Billy Dixon was one of the great frontiersmen, and that shot of his knocked a Comanche off his horse from a long ways away. When General Miles rescued the hunters and drove off the Comanches, he had a surveyor with him who measured the distance. Now some of these Texas tales could be a little exaggerated, but the surveyor said, and those guys are inclined to be accurate, that the shot measured 1,538 yards.

I know, if Brules had been shooting, I would have believed it.

Brules and I sat around the stove that night and got to telling stories back and forth. He wasn't calling me 'boy' anymore, he was calling me 'son,' and I realized I had been promoted. His genuine affection for me was very touching.

He couldn't get enough of the idea that I had been 'a flyin' man.'

Of course, he had never seen an airplane. There had never been any airplanes over the southwestern part of Colorado at that early date. Airplanes that flew to the coast would either go north through Salt Lake to San Francisco or, if they were going to L.A., down through Albuquerque. No one thought of coming straight across the rock pile. A lot of this country was, to most people, almost unknown. It wasn't until they got aeronautical maps, about thirty years later, that they could really tell about this country.

I told Brules about the night flying I had done and how it scared the hell out of me. I told him about flying those big boats and what they were like, especially the H-16 with the two four-hundred-horse Libertys in it. 'Flying an H-16,' I said, 'must be like riding the marvelous mystical flying horse the Greeks called Pegasus, fast and with lots of power.'

Brules turned to me, paused for a minute, and then said, 'You don't suppose that there Pegasus was a piebald, do you?'

We both burst out laughing. Old Brules had never forgotten his favorite horse, Piebald, that the Comanches had taken from him when they captured him and that dance-hall girl.

Finally I said, 'You know, we ought to go hunting one of these days.'

'Boy, I'd sure love to do that,' Brules replied. 'But we shouldn't go until them bulls have good racks on 'em. And that's goin' to be sometime in August at the earliest.'

I agreed and told him that when the time came, I knew where there was some crack elk hunting.

'Where's that?' he asked.

'Oh, it's over there up against the Monuments, on the other side of the Uncompahgre. There's that country back up at the head of the three forks of the Cimarron. That's still wild.'

'When do we pack up?' Brules asked.

'I'll try to come up here and spend some time with you about the end of August. I'm not going to leave this country until I have to go back to school in September.'

'My God,' Brules said, 'you have to go back to school again?'

'Yeah, I do. I only finished my first year. I've missed two years.'

'How do you feel about going back to college with a bunch of kids two years younger than you are? You having been through a war and bein' a flyin' man and all that?'

'It's going to be an adjustment,' I replied. I was amazed at the sharpness of the old man and how he picked up something like that. 'Now while I fix supper, you tell me whatever happened to your Indian friend, Wesha. I guess you were very fond of him, weren't you?'

'Oh, yes,' he said. 'He was the greatest warrior who ever lived. We were "blood brothers," and I loved him.'

'When did you last see him?'

'I ain't seen him in years,' he said. 'I heard about him a couple of times. He'd gone up to the Yukon Territory when he was a middle-aged man to do some big game guidin'.'

'You went with Wesha on the Sioux campaign of 'seventy-six. Rode out with eighty warriors and went to Cloud Peak camp and joined Crook's command, didn't you?'

'Yep, that's right.'

'Mr. Brules, can I ask something of you, really?'

'Sure, son.'

'Well, sir, I would really like to hear the story of your scouting with General Crook. Weren't you in the Battle of the Little Bighorn?'

'Yep, yep, I sure was.'

'And you were in the Battle of the Rosebud too, weren't you?'

'Yep, I guess you'd call it a battle the way them damn fool pony soldiers was a actin'.'

'Mr. Brules, I know the story of your life up until you came up here with Wild Rose and you had the baby and all that. You told me all about taking Morning Star to Wyoming and about your starting out on your ride with Wesha to join up with General Crook. But from there on, I don't know anything. And I wish you'd tell me, sir.'

'Well, son, it's a long time ago, and there's a lot of good and bad memories. I never wanted to tell anybody. But you being my favorite young man—if you're willin' to listen, I'll be tellin' you. Now come on, let's be havin' somethin' to eat now. After supper, when we get cleaned up here, we'll get the stove stoked again, and we'll sit here and talk about it.'

That was how I heard the story of Brules's adventures when

he accompanied Wesha and the eighty Shoshone warriors to Cloud Peak, General Crook's camp. That's the spot where Crook was waiting with twelve hundred soldiers to advance on the Sioux around the headwaters of the Rosebud. It was eighty miles from the Battle of the Little Bighorn, which took place eight days later.

I listened with fascination and took notes as fast as I could. I learned that Brules had carried an important message from Crook to Custer through country that was crawling with Sioux. Then he became one of Custer's scouts at the time of the Little Bighorn and later patrolled the Yellowstone. I heard how he became involved with Miles in his campaign against the Nez Percé and about Chief Joseph, of whom he thought so highly. And later how he journeyed back to Lone Cone and hunted for grizzlies in the south. He told me how after three years of going without a woman, he took up with a beautiful Mormon girl from a ranch near Moab.

I thought his story, just as he told it, was really an account of the Old West. When he was telling it to me, I felt as if I were right there all the time. I thought that eventually I should write it down so that there would be a record of Brules's life. I wanted people to know the real story of that old mountain man who lived way up on Lone Cone, the one everybody regarded as an outlaw, a misfit, and a person of no consequence. I wanted them to know what a magnificent man he really was. Eventually I did write the book, and I called it *The Scout*.

Long after midnight, Brules finished his story. It ended with that sacrifice that Brules made for the young woman who had made her way to his heart. They had married, and she had followed him for years.

'Mr. Brules, I didn't know you'd married again. What happened to her?' I asked.

'Well, son, Melisande was a beauty and full of spunk. She could ride, and I taught her how to shoot. General Crook thought she was really somethin' too. Sometimes I got kinda feelin' funny 'bout how much he seemed to like her. We was invited to some pretty fancy shindigs, and I think it was cuz he kinda fancied her. He also let her follow me all over, when I was a scout for him down in Arizona. Boy, we sure had some good times, lovin' each other like we did.'

'Did she come back here to Lone Cone with you after your scouting days?'

'No, I had to go with Crook down into Mexico chasin' after Geronimo and them damn Apaches, and she couldn't go with me. When I got back to Wilcox, I found a telegram waitin' for me sayin' she had gone 'bout plum crazy waitin' and had found work at the Shoo-fly Restaurant in Tucson. I didn't even bother to shave or clean up, though I knowed how she liked me to be clean shaven and all. I guess I must 'ave looked pretty scruffy with a three-months' beard, but I just wanted to get that next train to Tucson to see my wonderful Melisande.

When I got to the restaurant they told me she'd been gone 'bout a month. I 'bout went crazy when they said she'd gone to San Francisco.

She'd sent three or four telegrams, and Mrs. Wallens, the owner of the Shoo-fly, read 'em to me—I dun told her I lost my glasses on the campaign. Anyway, Melisande had met up with this rich railroad gent name of Endicott. Seems he was in Tucson checkin' to see if it would be a good place to build a Harvey House, a pretty fancy restaurant for travelers. Well, guess they spent a bunch a time talkin', and he took a shine to her. He thought she was right smart and asked her if she'd want to manage the new restaurant in Tucson. Tole her she'd have to come to San Francisco for three months of trainin' and that he would pay for it.

I knowed from what she said in the telegrams that she sure 'nuf loved me, but Endicott was showin' her off in San Francisco to all 'em fancy people and stuff, and she was lovin' it.

I was so goddamn mad, I was goin' a kill the son of a bitch. I just knew he was foolin' around with my wife. I went to the telegraph office and had the clerk write out a telegram tellin' Melisande to get her ass back here or I'd be on the next train to take care of Endicott. The clerk wouldn't let me say "ass," so I changed it to "bottom."

I guess that telegram shook 'em both up a mite, cuz I got one right back sayin' she'd be on the next train to Tucson and that he was goin' back to New York.'

'Sounds like you solved that problem, Mr. Brules,' I said. 'Then what happened?'

'Well, she come back all right. Oh, she was a wonderful sight, and I knowed she still felt the same 'bout me. We were lovin' each other all the time. But the way she talked about the big city, I got to worryin' 'bout her really bein' happy married to a scout, me bein' gone on campaigns, an' then someday livin' on a ranch.

She tole me Endicott wanted to marry up with her. It broke my heart, but I finally told her she oughta go back to San Francisco, git hold of Endicott, and go with him.'

'Mr. Brules, how could you, when you loved her so much?'

'Son, I had to. I loved her so much, but I knew she just deserved the kinda life Endicott could give her. So I put her on the train back to San Francisco. She was a sobbin' cuz she loved me, but I knowed it was best for her to go. Oh, I told her that if her life ever soured, she better get hold of me and come back, cuz I was never goin' to stop lovin' her. But I never heard from her again. She sure was beautiful!'

I stayed with Brules that night and part of the next day. In the morning, he showed me where the old pasture had been, and where the painted horses that had been Wild Rose's dowry had been kept. I saw where he had torn down the gates when he had left with Morning Star, knowing that he would not be returning for many years. He had never repaired the gates, but the horses, long since gone wild, sometimes came to the ranch. Even though they were wild, they had not left the area. They were confined not to the five thousand acres of Brules's ranch but roamed the hundreds of thousands of acres that spread throughout that great country west of the San Juans.

He told me he felt their favorite place was the pasture, down below where the trout stream ran through and fell over the falls in the southwestern corner. He often saw them there. He never bothered them because he felt that if he did, they might never come again.

He wouldn't let me leave without a visit to Wild Rose's grave. He had told me there was no marker except for the profusion of wild flowers that grew on it. When he took me there, I saw exactly what he meant. The hillside was covered with rich green upland grass, and there were some pine trees nearby.

The burst of flowers that lay over Wild Rose's grave looked as though it had been cultivated by an expert English gardener. But of course, it had just been natural. It was a patch of the world as beautiful as anything I had ever seen.

Brules also took me down to see the wandering stream that ran through the property. At every bend, you could see trout breaking the surface of the cold clear water for flies, and swimming away when our shadows alarmed them.

In the far distance we could see the Chuska Mountains and old Sleeping Ute. And if we turned around, we could see the towering San Juans, with their spring snow sparkling against the blue sky.

We didn't need to talk. This was paradise. I could picture Brules as he corralled his great stallion for the ride that would save Morning Star. I could see it all just as if I had been there myself.

That afternoon, I went to work cutting firewood for him. When I finished, there seemed to be enough to last the summer and a good part of the winter. I think that he was pleased.

When I arrived back at the ranch, the sun was just setting. As I was unsaddling my horse, my mother came out to the corrals. She hugged me long and hard without saying a word. Evidently, she'd missed me even on my short visit up the mountain.

During that summer, I spent a good deal of time with Father. He had very definite ideas about running the ranch and wanted me to learn the things I needed to know about its management. The ranch, after all, represented the entire basis for the family's wealth.

Dad told me that long ago he had decided to switch from raising Texas longhorn cattle to the Hereford white-face breed. The longhorn was a survivor but didn't have the beef qualities of the white-face. For that reason, he decided in 1896 to make some buying trips back east. Ohio was a good area to buy Herefords.

It was in Granville, Ohio, that he met his future father-in-law, the president of the First National Bank. Of course, I can only imagine how it happened. Here was Father, thirty-five years old, about six foot three, with strong broad shoulders and piercing blue eyes. I'm sure that old Mr. Hamilton took one look at this enterprising young man and thought, Well, at least my Rose should have a chance to take a look.

His daughter, who was back home after graduating from Oberlin College, had shown little interest in college boys her own age. She had majored in music and had turned out to be quite a talented pianist.

Anyway, Mr. Hamilton telephoned his wife and invited my father to dinner.

Later, my grandmother told my mother that she took one look at my father and thought, This is a man of consequence. This is a man who carries a certain sense of destiny and pride.

And Mother once admitted to me that she had great difficulty keeping her eyes off him. She said she was fascinated by the western aura he exuded. Deep in her soul, there was a love for the great open spaces, the vast mountains and distances of the West. And here was a man wearing black western dress boots, who looked as if he were strong enough to live in that wild country.

She told me her heart was racing and that she was afraid she would talk too much. He was very polite and had a charming way about him. And when her father asked him questions about the ranch, he was direct and very purposeful.

He spoke about his first herd of longhorn cattle and how he had bought them at Fort Union, which was just northeast of Albuquerque, and had driven them clear through New Mexico into Colorado. By this time, Mr. Hamilton had sized up my father as one impressive fellow.

Mother told me that Father spoke very positively about the

longhorns, saying they were quite wonderful animals, but that the meat wasn't the best and that their long horns were sometimes dangerous. They killed both horses and men time and again. Those longhorn cattle were wild, not by nature but because they had to scrub around in that tough overgrazed west Texas forage.

As it turned out, Dad did a lot of cattle buying in Ohio after that first trip, and every time he got a chance, he went to see Mother.

I'm sure you know what happened. That next spring of 1897, he proposed to her, and I rather suspect she couldn't accept fast enough.

After their wedding, they went on a trip to Florida. They came across to Colorado on the Southern Pacific to Albuquerque, then up through La Veta Pass to Alamosa and on over Cumbres Pass to Durango. It took almost another day to Rico. I can imagine how the mountains and the canyons thrilled Mother. When she saw southwestern Colorado, I'm sure she knew she'd picked the right man and the right place.

Dad knew the ranching business, and he soon had the best Hereford herd in the state. The white-face were strong, and the ranch quickly became very well known. Dad used to send cattle into the Denver stock show every year and always won a lot of blue ribbons.

It was really a place to be proud of. Easterners who came out here were very impressed with the Broken Bow Ranch. They thought an invitation to the Cartwrights' was something special, and it was. My parents were well respected by everyone.

Although they didn't mix with a lot of the other ranching people, Mom and Dad were always very gracious when those fellows came around to buy cattle. They were well aware that a cup of coffee was the common denominator among the folks in this country. Whenever anybody rode into the ranch, they were always invited in for a cup.

Mother loved to entertain. It made no difference if they were cowboys or presidents or kings, she treated her guests all the same. She did say, though, that it took a little while getting used to a man sitting down at the table for lunch with his hat on. Pretty soon, the word got around that it might be a good idea to leave your hat in the hall if you were going into the Cartwrights' dining room.

Mother loved the western country. She was a damn good horsewoman and could ride like an Indian. She loved packing up in the mountains. She loved the forest. She seemed to understand the land instinctively, and of course, my father was a strong part of it. I guess it's natural that I should be so grounded in this part of the world."

Back to Yale

"So Steven, you went back to Yale in the fall of 1919?" Becky prodded.

"Yes, but in early September, I made what I thought might be my last trip up Lone Cone to say good-bye to Brules. I had promised the old man we would go hunting. We weren't going to have time to go on the big elk hunt we'd talked about, but I had made a promise to my old friend, and I was worried about his having enough meat for the winter.

When I reached the cabin, Brules was as excited as a young kid. I could see that he had made preparations for a hunt. He'd pulled together his 1873 Winchester, ammunition, and the necessary gear and supplies.

'I have to go back to school, Mr. Brules.'

'Ain't we goin' huntin' before you go?' he asked.

'Oh, we sure are. I was hoping we'd have time to go on a

big elk hunt. But with everything I had to do to help out Mom and Dad on the ranch, we're only going to be able to go out for a couple of days.'

'Son, you just give me a few minutes to saddle my horse, load up the packhorse, and we can light right out.'

We crossed over to the San Juans and spent two wonderful days reminiscing and enjoying each other's company. He shot a small four-point bull, which was enough meat to last him most of the winter. When we returned to Lone Cone and unpacked the meat and gear, we both got kind of quiet. We were both dreading the moment of saying good-bye.

Finally Brules asked, 'How long you gonna be away?'

'I've got three more years. But I'll be back every summer.'

'I guess I better let you go then.'

I mounted my horse, leaned over, took Brules's callused hand in mine and held it for a long moment. When I got to the timberline, I turned back and saw him standing there looking at me. He waved, and I waved back and went on down the mountain.

A few days later, I left the ranch and got back to Yale around the middle of September. I had decided to enter the Sheffield Scientific School and to major in civil engineering as opposed to going to the Academic School. As soon as I got settled and my classes arranged, I went to look up Trubee Davidson. He had attended college after recovering from his crash and was now a senior.

Over dinner at his eating club, he said he had heard some very good things about me and wanted to know how it was flying those H-16's.

'Boy,' I said, 'that was really something!'

He wanted to know about the fighters too, and I told him

about all my experiences. We had a great time going back over the two and a half years since we had parted.

'It's been a long tough haul for me,' Trubee said. 'I lost a year of school, of course. There was no sense in my applying to get into the service. They wouldn't accept me in my physical condition. I had to go back into the class behind me. You fellows can't imagine how I felt being left behind while you went off to England and France. I really missed being with you.'

'We missed you too. We thought of you a lot, Trubee, and often spoke of you. But in some ways, you were lucky. You cannot imagine what war does to a man. Being scared stiff a lot of the time sears your soul. And it isn't easy killing another man just because he is wearing a different uniform and flying an airplane that has a black Maltese cross on it. The war wasn't all fun and games. It wasn't the way we pictured it, back when we were flying the *Mary Ann*. It left a lot of us with a shadow on our lives. What was it Tecumseh Sherman said? "War is hell!" '

Trubee was silent for a minute. Then he said, 'Cowboy, I understand, and I'm sure you're right, but every young warrior wants to know the excitement of battle.'

I nodded and left it at that.

'So, tell me, what did you do this summer?' he asked.

'I went back to the ranch.'

'When are you going to have me out there?'

'Any damn time you want to come.'

'I don't think I can ride horseback with my back in this condition,' Trubee said. 'But I certainly want to visit you there sometime.'

'You know, Trubee, you'd be welcome anytime.' I noticed that he had a difficult time sitting upright, and I thought I had seen an occasional flash of pain cross his face.

Then I told him that I had enrolled in the Sheffield Scientific School.

He leaned back in his chair and said, 'Oh, my God, what did you do that for? Why don't you go Ac like the rest of the guys?'

'You mean the Academic School?' I asked. 'Well, I don't know. There are some pretty decent guys going to Sheff.'

'Sure, there are, but those Sheff guys are likely to be a bunch of grinds, keeping their noses in their books all the time. The real action is over here in the Academic School.'

'I can't help it,' I said, laughing. 'The old man wants me to be a civil engineer, and in fact, I kind of think that's the way to go. So I've decided to take the Sheff route.'

'Okay,' he said, 'but that means you're cut out of the senior honor societies like Skull and Bones. You won't be eligible.'

'Yeah,' I said, 'but I'm not going to let some secret society rule my life. What the hell do they do in those damn places anyway?'

'That's where they've got you,' Trubee said. 'You don't know, and if you're not in one, you'll feel kind of left out. But I'll tell you what—there are three or four fraternity houses in Sheff that are pretty good, especially Anthony and Cloister. But that's about as far down as you want to go. It's unfortunate, but that's the way it is at Yale. If you don't get into a good fraternity house in your sophomore year, you might as well go home. It's a hard but true fact. The pledging goes on in the late fall, as you know. You have to make a good fraternity, or you're going to miss out on a hell of a lot of the social life in college. It gives you the opportunity to meet a lot of damn interesting people. And of course, the houses hold good dances, so it's a great way to be introduced to girls.'

I knew that he was talking straight and I'd better pay attention to him. It was damn important to be a part of the right social scene. I understand that they've changed it all now at Yale by instituting the residential college system. Fraternities are not as important as they were, nor are the honor societies. But in those days, they were the social fabric of the college.

'Say,' Trubee said, 'you're going to play football, aren't you?'

'No, I should've been here two weeks ago if I was going to do that.'

'I guess you should have been here getting in condition.'

'Hell, I'm in condition. I've been working on the ranch all summer, remember?'

'I forgot about that. You're probably hard as a rock.'

He sort of punched me in the arm and said, 'Ouch! You're hard, aren't you! You really ought to play.'

'I don't know. I really don't want to play.'

'You ought to,' he said. 'You ought to do something that's noteworthy, that makes you stand out.'

'Well, you know,' I said, 'after all that fighting, I sort of lost interest, Trubee. I really don't know what to do.'

'Listen, Steven,' he said, 'everybody gets that way. You know how I felt with my damn back broken and I couldn't get in the service. I wandered around like a lost soul all during the war. Now that's over, and we've got to take hold of ourselves and do a good job. Don't use the war as an excuse for not making the grade here. We've got other challenges.'

That Trubee was the damnedest guy. He came from such a fine family, and he knew that his job in life was always to strive to do the right thing. That was the way he was going to make everyone happy and do some good in this world. It's just character, that's all. That's the difference between people with character and people who are drifters. He was an inspiration to me, and I thought, Well by God, that's true!

Trubee said, 'Say, why don't you come to Peacock Point this weekend? Everyone is eager to see you.'

'That would be wonderful,' I said. 'I bought a car when I got here, so I can drive down on Saturday afternoon.'

I left New Haven after lunch on Saturday, took the ferry from Bridgeport over to Port Jefferson, and drove down to Peacock Point. It was as if the world that had turned upside down were now right side up again. The estate looked just as it had before the war. I was greeted at the door by Mrs. Davidson, who threw her arms around me and said, 'Oh, Steven, how glad I am to see you alive and well, and out of that terrible war! I've heard some wonderful things about you and all the things you did. Now we can pick up where we left off.'

That's just what I wanted to do too. Trubee was in the living room. He had a little difficulty getting up, but boy, he was enthusiastic about my being there, and so was I. Mr. Davidson was most cordial and said some very nice things about me. It was about four o'clock in the afternoon, and I was in time for a cocktail party. Other guests were expected shortly. They were sure that I would know some of them.

'Now,' Mrs. Davidson said, 'you take your bags up to the green room. That's your room, you know.'

'Thank you.' I smiled. 'I'm very touched. It has such a beautiful view of Long Island Sound, and I can look almost up to Port Washington and our old seaplane base.'

'You've come a long way since then. I understand you're a great flyer now and very experienced.'

'Some of the experience wasn't much fun,' I said.

'Yes, but it's all over now, isn't it?'

'Thankfully, it is. And I'm so happy to be here, ma'am, I can't tell you. Seeing you again is just wonderful.'

She hugged me again, and I went up the stairs to freshen up a bit.

When I came back down, I noticed that things weren't quite as formal as they had been before the war. I guess it was the beginning of the flapper era. With some embarrassment, I realized that the girls' dresses were much shorter than they used to be. Not too bad, I thought to myself.

There were several fellows and girls whom I had met before, and they all said how nice it was to see me back and how healthy and strong I looked. They just knew that I must have spent the summer out at the Colorado ranch.

Sometime later, a middle-aged lady stepped up to me, touched my elbow, and said, "Should I call you Lieutenant Cartwright or just Cowboy?"

'Cowboy, ma'am,' I said with a grin.

Her face looked familiar. Where had I seen her before?

'Perhaps you remember our conversation almost three years ago. You were here with Trubee and very excited about getting into the Yale Naval Aviation Unit. I thought you were one of the most attractive young men I had ever seen, and I knew that you were going to make a crack pilot. I understand that's just what happened.'

'Well, thank you, ma'am. That's very flattering.'

'If you have a few minutes, I wonder if we could sit down over here by the window. I've been waiting to talk to you again.'

Why did she want to talk to me? I wondered.

'Do you remember when you told me that you lived out in southwestern Colorado? You said you were about thirty miles southwest of Telluride, at the foot of Lone Cone Mountain.'

'Oh, my gosh, yes, I do remember now.'

'When we last spoke," she continued, "you mentioned that you knew someone who lived up in that country by the name of Brules.'

'Yes. He's an interesting fellow and a great mountain man.'

'That's exactly right,' she said. 'Tell me, have you seen him recently?'

'As a matter of fact, I saw him a couple of weeks ago.'

'You did? How is he?'

'Oh, he's great. Did you know Brules?'

'Yes, indeed, I knew him. I was married to him for five years.'

'Now I know who you are. You're Melisande!'

'That's right. I go by the name of Sandy now. When I came here from the West, I married Mr. Endicott.'

'Oh, yes, yes, I've heard about him. Wasn't he very influential in the railroad business?'

'He certainly was,' she said.

'You met him down in Santa Fe or Tucson, didn't you?'

'Yes, but how did you know that?'

'Brules told me. You were working as a Harvey girl?'

'Yes,' she said with a twinkle, 'but that was a long time ago.'

'I understand that being a waitress was a very decent profession in those days. But let me say right away, this conversation is entirely between you and me.'

'I'm most grateful to you for saying that.'

'Cat Brules is my dearest friend. In fact, I love him almost like a grandfather.'

'You could be his grandson," she said. "You have a look about you that is quite like him. It's uncanny. I mean that as a compliment. He was the handsomest man I ever saw.'

'He told me you rode with him," I said. "I've heard the wonderful stories about how you went out to join General Crook at Fort McPherson.'

'Did he tell you that? Oh, that was one of the most exciting times of my life. I'd never met anybody important on our ranch, and suddenly I was meeting all these generals, Tecumseh Sherman, chief of staff, Phil Sheridan, the wild cavalry leader, and General Crook, who just took such an interest in Brules.'

'Well, ma'am, I understand he took a substantial interest in you, too. A very gentlemanly one, of course.'

'Yes, as a matter of fact, he and I were good friends. He was always very nice to me and always saw that I sat beside him at dinner parties. He was great. Now tell me about Brules. I loved that man, I really did. Did he tell you how we separated?'

'Yes, ma'am. He told me exactly what happened.'

'I knew it was a terrible sacrifice for him to make,' she said. 'But he didn't want me to be just a scout and a trapper's wife. Of course, I would have loved to have been that for Brules. But I suppose the hardship would have been very great, and there would have been times when I wondered why I hadn't married Endicott.'

'Do you wonder now?' I asked.

'Mr. Endicott was a very fine man. He took good care of me, and I lived a very nice life. I went to Europe many times, just as Brules said I would. I traveled all over the United States and met many famous and interesting people. But in my heart, he was always my dearest love. I never met anybody like Cat Brules.'

My face broke out in a big smile. I said, 'No, ma'am, and you never will. I wish, oh, how I wish, Cat Brules could see you now.'

'Well, to be very honest with you, I wish he were right here in this room.'

'Maybe he wouldn't fit in.'

'If you ever saw him in that dress suit that he had when we went up to Fort McPherson as a guest of General Crook, you'd know that he would fit in anywhere. Oh my,' she continued, 'to think that you just spent time with Brules. I loved him so. I wonder if you could give him a message.'

'Yes, ma'am, absolutely. I'd be delighted.'

'Thank you. Let me give some thought to what it should be.' Then she took my arm, saying, 'Now, shall we join the other guests?'

About a week later, I was in my room in Nathan Hale Hall when the football coach came over with his backfield coach. 'You know, Cartwright,' he said, 'we were a little disappointed that you didn't come out for football this year.'

I told him I hadn't gotten out of the service until the spring of 1919 and that I'd wanted to spend time with my family out west.

He nodded sympathetically. 'Yeah, but if you'd have been here, you might have made the first team. You did very well as a freshman. Now, it's pretty hard—you're probably not in condition.'

'The hell I'm not,' I said. 'I've been working on a ranch all summer!'

'By God, that's right,' he said. 'Hey, stand up here a minute and let me feel your arms.'

'Holy Christ, feel that!' he said to the backfield coach as he felt my arms and punched me in the chest. "You are in pretty good shape.'

'I've been punching cattle and working the trails and doing

some of the planting and plowing. I was trying to get rid of the war fever.'

'Listen,' he said, 'you really ought to come out and give us a shot. You were one of the really promising young freshmen. Now you're a sophomore and eligible for the varsity.'

After talking to him, I was kind of eager to give it a try. He told me to come to the field house next to the Yale Bowl on Monday afternoon so that he could suit me up and see what I could do.

Well, you know, I got out there and got caught up in the excitement of it. Most of the guys I'd never seen before. They'd started college while I was in Europe. A few of the old fellows were still there. They seemed glad to see me, which made me feel pretty good.

Anyway, I went out for practice, and I had a hell of a time because I hadn't studied the plays. I had to have a blackboard session with one of the assistant coaches. He gave me a whole bunch of plays that I wrote down in a notebook so that I could try to learn what the hell I was supposed to be doing.

That afternoon, we fooled around and had a little scrimmage. In those days, you know, there wasn't any of this business of having two teams, one for offense and one for defense. Hell, you played the whole damn game. They never took a man out unless he was hurt because after they put in a substitute, he could never get back in.

The ball was much bigger, and it was harder to get your hand around it, so the passing game wasn't as spectacular as it is today.

I'm not knocking modern football, because I love to see it. But in those days football was pretty much a powerhouse deal. You had to plug your way on the ground three yards, four yards, five yards at a time. Once in a while you threw a forward pass. But generally it was just 'dig in.' Boy, it was rough.

There were no face masks, and the shoulder pads were very primitive. The helmets were made of light leather, not like the big, hard strong helmets they have today.

I enjoyed playing football at Yale immensely. I loved the rock and sock of it. It was big stuff back then. There were no professional football teams, and the Yale Bowl was the biggest stadium ever built up to that time. Yale had good teams in those days. We played all the Ivy League schools—Harvard, Princeton, Brown, Columbia, Dartmouth, Cornell—and sometimes other teams who came from as far away as Georgia. In any case, I played first string right halfback for three years and did my share of scoring. It helped me get over some of the strain of the war and kept me in good condition.

Playing football did something else for me. Athletes got favored treatment when it came to fraternity rushes, and I was very pleased to be invited to join St. Anthony Hall, one of the best fraternities at Sheff, in the fall of my sophomore year.

When you entered a fraternity, it became the center of your social life for the rest of your academic career. In some ways, it was rather confining because it kept you from getting to know students from other houses. But there was a strong esprit in the fraternity, and the bonds formed there have remained very strong throughout my life.

Other guys were taken into St. Anthony's that year who had also been in the service. Some had been in the artillery, some in the infantry, and two had been in the navy. We banded together and called ourselves the 'old men.' Since we were veterans and a couple of years older, the rest of the fellows had a certain amount of respect for us.

I was in the fraternity for three years, and in my senior year, I was honored to be president, as well as president of the Interfraternity Council. I also made the Torch honor society, which was the Sheffield Scientific School's equivalent of a senior honor society like Skull and Bones in the Academic School.

During the university winter breaks, I always stayed back east. Mother had relatives there, and I would visit them rather than going all the way home. One year, I went to Lake Placid where I began to take up the business of skiing. I was just fascinated by it, especially jumping. Then, of course, the Davidsons insisted that I come to Peacock Point for Christmas.

The parties and gay festivities that first Christmas were totally reminiscent of those before the war. At one of the parties, Sandy Endicott approached me.

'I was hoping you would be here,' she said. 'I have something that I would like to send to Brules.'

'What is it?'

'There are three photographs. One of them is of me and my brothers and sisters at my father's ranch. It was taken about a month before Cat Brules came riding in on his beautiful horse, Jupiter. Since we were Mormons, there are a whole bunch of us. My father had a photographer come out from Moab. He had one of those flash things.'

The photograph was an old tintype. Melisande pointed herself out. She was a young woman of about eighteen, the oldest in the group, and absolutely beautiful.

'Oh, God,' I said, 'this is fabulous. What's the next one?'

'He may not remember this,' she said, 'but we had a picture taken together when we were in Santa Fe. He took me for a walk through the plaza to the old governor's palace, and there was a man taking photographs. Brules pulled up a chair and sat down. He took off his coonskin cap and held it in his lap. Then he had me stand at his right side with my hand on his shoulder, just as a wife should. He was very proud.'

'Gee, fantastic,' I said.

'There's one more. It was taken at the great ball at Fort McPherson in North Platte, when we were guests of General Crook. His guests of honor were Tecumseh Sherman, General Sheridan, and General Crook, who was chief of the territory of Nebraska, which extended way out west almost to California.

This is an outfit that he bought for me at Daniels and Fisher in Denver. I also persuaded him to buy something for himself to wear to the ball. My, he was glad when we got to Fort McPherson that we had new clothes.'

'I've never seen Brules in a black outfit like that with a white shirt and tie,' I said.

'What about the hat? Look at the hat.'

'That's the greatest thing I've ever seen. Why, he could be a movie star!'

'He certainly could have been. He was the best looking man I've ever seen in my life.'

'Ma'am, just look at yourself. What a beautiful lady you were! And,' I added quickly, 'still are.'

She beamed. 'I would like it very much if you would see that these photographs get into Cat Brules's hands.'

'Ma'am, are you sure you want to give them up?'

'Only if I can be positive that he will receive them. I want him to remember, because, young man, I can tell you that we were both desperately in love with each other. He was the one who sent me away. He believed it was best for me. I think his sacrifice was great, but I lost too. Would you do me the great kindness of seeing that he receives these?'

'I won't be able to go home until next summer, but I guarantee you that I will get these to him, Mrs. Endicott.'

'Thank you. I know that you will. You are a man of your word. Now, we must go in to dinner,' she said, rising.

Reaching up, she gave me a hug and a kiss on the cheek. I saw her only one or two times after that, and we never mentioned Brules again, but I damn well knew that I would get those pictures to him.

When I went back to the ranch that summer, I went to see Brules right away. 'You can't imagine what I have for you,' I said, holding the photographs behind my back.

'I don't give a damn what it is," Brules said. "I want to see you. You're the best fellow I ever saw.'

'Well, look at these,' I said.

'Who in the hell is that?'

'You don't recognize this little girl over here?'

'Oh, my God,' he said, 'where did you get this?'

'Do you remember this in Santa Fe?'

'Oh, my God, oh, my God,' he kept saying. 'Where the hell did you get these?'

'Do you remember this one?' I asked.

'Hell, yes, that is my wonderful wife, Melisande! It was taken at that great ball when we was guests of General Crook, at Fort McPherson. Oh, my God, where did you get these?' he asked again.

'Melisande gave them to me.'

'You're a damn liar. She's long gone.'

'No, she isn't,' I said. 'She married that fellow.'

'Yeah, well, I figured she did,' he said. 'She was going back to marry that goddamn bastard Endicott.'

'She lived with him until he died about ten years ago. He took good care of her, but she told me that she was never really in love with anybody but you.'

He put his head down a minute. 'Well, she done told you the truth, son. I felt the same way about her. God, how is she?'

'She looks wonderful,' I said.

'Well, I'm figuring it out. She must be between fifty-five and sixty, isn't she?'

'Yeah, but that doesn't mean she isn't a good-looking woman.'

'Why didn't you bring me a picture of the way she looks now?'

'Why don't you just use your imagination, Mr. Brules. Or maybe you want me to take a picture of you and send it to her?'

'Hell no, don't take a picture of me. It would scare her to death.'

'Maybe she feels the same way.'

Old Brules just looked off into the distance and shook his head.

In my senior year, I met a perfectly lovely girl named Ellen Brewster whose family lived in Oyster Bay. We were great dancing partners, and we went everywhere together. You know, I really fell in love with her, and we began to talk seriously about what we would do when I got out of college. I'd be an old man of twenty-four. Maybe we would marry and move out west to our ranch in Colorado. I really think she was very keen on the idea, at least for a while.

But toward the middle of the year, I found that when I called her for a date, she would say, 'Oh, Steven, I wish you had

let me know just a little ahead of time. I've been invited down
to Princeton this weekend.'

Anyway, she was my date for the Yale Senior Prom, and it
was then, as we wandered hand in hand around the New Haven
Lawn Club, that she finally confronted me. 'Steven,' she said,
'there is something I have to tell you. I have dreaded this moment because I love you with all my heart. But I don't think I
can live your kind of life. I don't think I can live on a ranch in
the West, where you are so far from anywhere.'

'Oh, don't worry about that,' I said. "Why don't you come
out this summer, meet Mom and Dad, and let me show you
what it's really like.'

'No, Steven. I have met a wonderful fellow at Princeton.
Actually, he's not one of the undergraduate students. He gradu-
ated three years ago, and he's an associate professor. I really
think the eastern academic life is more suited to me.'

It was a hell of a shock, let me tell you. I thought, Here was
my best gal, and yet—well, of course, I should have been smart
enough to see what was going on. Wake up, wake up, Cartwright, get with the world, you know.

Really, I felt that I couldn't find any other girl who would
appeal to me the way Ellen had. I thought she had broken my
heart, and at that time I was right. But I found out later there
was a lot more to the world.

After graduation, I went back to the ranch in a rather
depressed state. I worked hard, and Dad kept giving me more
and more responsibility, which I enjoyed immensely. We had
guests from time to time, and I met a few young ladies whom I
became interested in temporarily. I did get a letter from Ellen
telling me how happily married she was and how everything was
going well and that she rather liked the life at Princeton.

145

During the next three or four summers, I became more and more inured to the idea of being a bachelor. There really wasn't much chance out on the ranch to meet anyone you would be interested in.

Whenever I could, I would go to Denver, especially to the stock shows, where I would try to meet a few people. From time to time I invited a young woman out to the ranch, but it didn't take me long to find out that they didn't fit in with anything that I had in mind.

So I went through five years as a hard-working cowboy, second in charge of a big ranch. I enjoyed ranch life enormously. The only thing missing, of course, was my better half.

There was another thing that was bothering me. I still had the flying bug. I thought of the thunder of the engines and the spray bursting around the flying boat until all of a sudden we were airborne. I thought how glorious it would be to have that feeling again.

REUNION

About the last of January 1927, I got a letter from our class secretary reminding us that this was our fifth year after graduation and our first reunion back in New Haven.

Boy, I thought, this is one thing I'm going to do. I'm going back to see my old friends, and maybe I'll meet some attractive girls. There must be a really classy gal who would consider marrying a western rancher.

The idea of dude ranching had just gotten started. Right after the war, some eastern fellows had gone to Wyoming and bought ranches. They had done it just for their health and to get over the shock of the war. They had friends come out to visit them, and the friends had such a marvelous time that they thought of going again the next summer and paying their way. Soon some of the ranchers found they were making as much or more money out of the 'dudes' as they were out of the cattle operation. I kept thinking that maybe we could do something like that, but I was afraid that we were just too remote. The transcontinental railroad went through the middle of Wyoming. You could take a train from the east and be in Wyoming in two and a half days. To get to southwestern Colorado, though, you still had another two days to go.

But anyway, I thought I'd go to the reunion and meet a few of my old friends. I told Dad and Mom what I planned to do. By that time, I didn't ask permission. I had a little money. My wages were pretty good as assistant manager, and I didn't have any place to spend it.

I dug out all the fancy stuff I had—tuxedos and the like. Then, I wrote Trubee to tell him that I was coming back for my fifth reunion.

Trubee replied immediately. 'Why don't you come back two or three days ahead of time and come down to Long Island? You can stay with me, and we'll catch up on things. I want to talk to you about some things that are going on in the world of flying. People are starting to think in terms of airlines. I don't know if it will ever amount to anything, but I really would like to visit with you. So please come.'

I took the train back east reading books all the way and bored to death, because I didn't see any passengers who were worth talking to. Trubee came in from Long Island to meet me at Grand Central Station.

God, it was great to see him. We drove out to Peacock Point, and it was just like old times. Mrs. Davidson was as hospitable as ever.

That night, we went to the country club. I was standing in the stag line watching the dancing and waiting to cut in when suddenly my heart turned over. I'd seen a familiar face. It was Ellen. I watched her for a few minutes, then moved to cut in.

'My God, Cowboy, how are you?' she said.

She threw her arms around me right there on the dance floor and gave me a big smack. We danced for a minute or two, and then she said, 'Come on, let's sit down by the bar and have a little visit.'

That was when Ellen told me about her marriage. The Princeton chap was a great guy, she said, very intellectual and all that sort of thing, but he had a drinking problem that got worse and worse. They had no children, and she felt very badly about that, but finally, she said, 'I had to leave him. I just couldn't go on anymore. Everyone understood, including him. So I got a divorce. I didn't ask for anything from him, and he didn't ask anything of me, so it was rather simple. You have no idea, Cowboy, how many times I have thought of you. I'm so delighted to see you!'

She made it very evident that she wanted to take up right where we left off. I was thrilled, of course. She looked even more beautiful as a mature woman than she had as a college girl.

'My goodness, you look wonderful!' she said. 'The life in the West must be great.'

'Why don't you come out and take a look sometime and see what you think?' I said.

'I would love to, I really would.'

'I'll have Mom write you a letter and invite you.'

'Oh, do that,' Ellen said. 'Say, are you going to be here for the reunion?'

'Yes,' I replied.

'How long are you going to be here?'

'A couple of weeks.'

'Oh, good,' she said. 'That gives us time to have some fun!'

We all went up to New Haven together, and I got a big kick out of driving to Port Jefferson and taking the ferry across to Bridgeport. It was just like the old days. We were still young enough that everybody was 'Hail fellow well met.' I saw a lot of guys from St. Anthony and some of the guys I had played with on the football team.

While I was there, we went to a party in the old Quadrangle. I ran into a fellow there that I thought looked familiar. Had he been in the Yale Naval Aviation Unit? Where had I seen him before?

Anyway, I went up and introduced myself. "I know who you are," he said. 'You're Cowboy Cartwright. Everybody around this place knows who the heck you are.'

'Were you at Huntington?' I asked.

'No,' he said, 'I was with the second Yale unit. We went to Lake Erie and did our training there.'

'What's your name?'

'Juan Trippe,' he replied.

'Where did you go from Lake Erie?'

'After we had all been taken into the service, I was at the Naval Aviation Station in England. They put me on H-12's flying the coast. I didn't get there until late in the summer of 1918. Then the armistice came on November eleventh.'

'Do you miss the flying?' I asked.

'I certainly do.'

'I miss it to beat the band!' I said.

'Is that so?' he said. 'Well, you know, I live out on Long Island, and I have a little flying boat that I use all the time to go into New York City. I'm supposed to be doing some work on Wall Street, but I don't like it much. I've had an idea, and I've got some backing from some of the same people who supported the Yale unit—J. P. Morgan and that crowd. They want to start an airline.'

'Do you think it's practical?' I asked.

'Well,' he said, 'it depends. We're a long ways from being able to fly in bad weather. And our radio communications are still very poor. I'm convinced there are not enough airfields around the country to handle big airliners. The air mail is being carried by the DH-4's with the Libertys in them—open cockpit things—and they've got a bunch of lights, rotating beacons, all across the continent to guide pilots at night or in stormy weather. You know those guys get into fearful situations over the Alleghenies and the Rockies. The only way an airline would be practical is if you could fly in the southern part of the hemisphere, where you've got pretty good weather most of the time.'

'You mean around Florida?' I asked.

'Yes,' Juan said, 'around Florida, the Caribbean, and that area. How can we possibly operate an airline across the United States in competition with the railroads? When it's good weather, we can fly those DeHaviland mail planes and make better time than the trains, but as soon as the weather starts closing in, we're all through. We can't do anything, and the trains just keep going on. But if you get someplace where the surface transportation is very poor, where you have to go over large bodies of water or jungles and where the weather is rather good, then the odds are that an airline could be successful.

I've got an idea that we can run an airline from, say, Key West to Havana. You know it would be only an hour's run across there in an H-16. It's a long trip from Miami to Havana in a boat. And it's an uncomfortable trip. How about Miami to Nassau? Those places are hard to get to. It seems to me that is the direction we ought to be taking.

There is a Russian designer named Sikorsky down here in Bridgeport. He built a lot of Russian airplanes—enormous flying machines. You just wouldn't believe it. I don't know how well they flew, but he's a pretty good designer, and he's building a better airplane now. He's going to use a new engine that's just about ready to come out. It is a WASP made by Pratt and Whitney. It's got about 425 horsepower, and it's air-cooled. Sikorsky has designed an amphibian that can land on water or on land. Now that is what we need. There are plenty of these dirt fields that we can get in and out of, but we need something that will land in the harbor too.'

The more he talked, the more excited I got. I told him I'd read in the newspaper about how some guy had bought an airplane, a Ryan Brougham, from the Ryan factory in San Diego. He had the interior all taken out and loaded it with extra gas tanks so it would have a hell of a range. It had a Wright whirlwind motor—a radial, not a rotary.

'Oh, yes,' Juan Trippe said. 'That's exactly what he had put in. But you know that Wright engine has been out for three or four years.'

'I wouldn't know,' I said. 'I've been living on my ranch down in southwestern Colorado. I'm pretty out of touch.'

He laughed. 'It is hard to keep track of these things. It's all changing so fast. We've been fooling with water-cooled motors for years. Those air-cooled rotaries are light, but they have a terrible gyroscopic effect.'

'Why weren't they able to build a radial at that time?' I asked.

'They never got the idea of the master rod," he said. "In

this new engine, instead of the whole engine going around, it stands still. There's a master rod in there, and all the other rods are connected to it. It's this master rod that makes it travel around and not the whole engine. They have been casting these cylinders with fins on them for air-cooling instead of having to machine them, as they did the Le Rhône and the Clerget. The Le Rhone was a good engine, light and powerful for its time, but that gyroscopic effect was hell, and it didn't have any life to it. It was good for just a few hours of flying, and that's no good for an airliner.

You remember flying the SE-5A and the SPAD? They had good engines. You had throttles you could open and close, which is the normal way of operation, instead of having to control the engine by shutting it on and off with an ignition button, like in the Sopwith Camel. The plugs could get all fouled up when you did that. Remember, you always had to keep turning the power on and off. That's why that Camel kept going *Vroom, vroom, vroom* when we would come in to land. That was not a good system.

Of course, the big problem with the water-cooled engine is you're lugging around that big radiator with all that water in it, and it's about fifty percent of the weight of the engine. God only knows what the weight of that four-hundred-horse Liberty engine is. I never flew behind that. All I was flying were the H-12's with the Rolls-Royce Eagle in them.

It's just a whole new world now. This fellow—I've forgotten his name now, it begins with an L—set a record going across the country yesterday. He flew nonstop from San Diego to St. Louis. He has an airmail company there, or was chief pilot for an airmail company. Anyway he's got the backing of some rich

St. Louis people, and he just flew into Roosevelt Field yesterday afternoon. He is going to try to fly nonstop to Europe.

You know Byrd's got that Fokker trimotor, and he's got those Wright whirlwind radial engines. He is going to use three of those engines on his plane when he attempts to fly across the Atlantic. But this guy from St. Louis is going off by himself. We'll never hear of him again.'

'No, I guess not,' I said.

Juan went on trying to bring me up to date on the newest developments in aviation.

'This Pratt and Whitney engine is a hell of a lot better than that whirlwind engine built by Wright down in New Jersey. I saw the engine at the grand opening at the Pratt and Whitney factory in Hartford. They had a dining room table in a hangar and all the parts spread out on a linen cloth. Honestly, you would have thought you were arriving at a feast and that the table was set with silver. Only it wasn't silver, it was hard steel. The crankshaft was there and the connecting rods, the cylinders, all the cable housings, the rocker boxes, the push rod housings, the pistons, and everything else that went with it. It was a beautiful-looking display. That engine developed 425 horsepower. Now that's twenty-five horsepower more than that water-cooled Liberty when it first came out. And this thing is about half the weight of that Liberty. The engine is designed to run about two or three hundred hours without any mainte-nance. That's the kind of engine you need to make a nonstop transatlantic flight. And they'll be doing it one of these days. But for now the Wright engine has to be good enough to do the job.

I think Byrd is going to make it across, but I don't know about this crazy guy from St. Louis, this airmail pilot. I don't know how he's going to stay awake all that time. And God only knows what kind of icing conditions you're going to get in the North Atlantic. That's one of the things that's worrying Byrd. Just because you've got three engines doesn't mean you can't ice up. It's going to be very interesting to see what happens.'

I was fascinated with Tripp's account of the aviation scene.

'You know,' he said, 'we could work the whole Caribbean. Now, you take Venezuela and Colombia and places like that. They don't have airfields, but we could land in the harbors.'

'You can't operate those machines based on a cost per seat mile,' I said.

'Oh, hell, no,' he said. 'We'll have to have an airmail contract. It will be years and years before they will have large enough airplanes to make money on passengers alone.'

That evening, we all went over to Trubee's old eating club on Chapel Street. While we were there, some guy who had a radio in his room came in and said, 'Can you believe it! That Flying Fool took off!'

'What Flying Fool?' we asked.

'That guy Lindbergh! He took off from Roosevelt Field at seven fifty-three this morning.'

'It's a lousy day to fly,' I said. 'It's been raining.'

'Yeah," he said, 'but he's left. I guess he was afraid that Byrd would get off ahead of him and claim the twenty-five-thousand-dollar prize.'

'What prize is that?' I asked.

'The Orteig prize,' he answered.

Of course, $25,000 was a hell of a lot of money in those days. But apparently this guy had been planning on winning and managed to get the backing.

Two other pilots were planning to fly with Byrd in that

Fokker trimotor, and they were using three engines. Even if you had an engine failure in one, you could still make it. And with three guys, they would be able to spell one another. But here was Lindbergh alone on a flight they figure is going to take thirty or forty hours. How was he going to stay awake all that time? And he was a goner if his single engine quit.

Of course, we didn't know then that poor old Lindbergh never even slept the night before he took off. He had been at a show in New York City when they told him that the weather was going to be good over the North Atlantic. He left the city and tried to lie down at a boarding house near Roosevelt Field. But he couldn't sleep and was out at the field by daybreak.

It was the first time that he would take off with a full load of fuel. His tanks hadn't been full when he left San Diego, and he hadn't taken on a full load when he left St. Louis for New York. The distances just didn't require it. I don't know how many gallons he was carrying this time, but the tanks were full and the gravel runway was wet.

Later he said that he ran the engine up until he got the highest RPMs, and the cylinders were good and warm. Then he just let go of the brakes and started to roll down the runway. At first, the plane just staggered along, but finally it got going fast enough to get the tail up. Apparently, it took a long long time to get to flying speed, and there were trees just off the end of the strip. They were coming up fast. He could have cut the gun and closed everything down, but by the time he had to make that decision, he had just about run out of room. He knew if he crashed with all that fuel, he would burn to death. So he stayed with it, and bounced it two or three times on the runway, and finally the plane just barely dragged itself into the air, clearing the telephone lines and the trees by about ten feet.

Of course, there was great excitement. Newspaper headlines screamed, 'The Flying Fool Takes Off!'

He was flying what we call a dead-reckoning course: just take a compass heading and go. All he had was a needle ball and air speed indicator and some damn thing called an earth inductor compass.

Of course, there was no such thing as an automatic pilot in those days, and he was on the controls all the time. He was in and out of the clouds, but he'd had very little instrument training. He was getting most of his instrument training as he started out across the ocean.

We also heard that he had been spotted over Cape Cod about ten-thirty or eleven o'clock in the morning. No one heard another damn thing all afternoon. That was because he had made the first real jump over the water. Instead of following the coastline and playing it safe, he took a compass heading and would see how it worked out. He flew the heading for about four hours, and there he was over Nova Scotia. He had been flying about a hundred miles off the coast all the way. It was risky business, but it was good training.

Of course, this was in May, so it was light well into the evening up north. The next thing we heard was that he had passed over St. John's, Newfoundland. Once he started out over the ocean, of course, we didn't hear anything. He said later that he had a very hard time. He had to climb to stay out of the clouds and the fog, but when he climbed and passed through the clouds, he picked up a lot of ice. So then he had to descend to maybe a hundred or two hundred feet off the water so that the warm air would take the ice off his wings. That was damn tough to do at night.

I ran into Juan Trippe again at one of the fraternity house parties. He was still red hot on this airline deal.

'Juan,' I said, "if anything definite develops, let me know. I'd be very interested."

'Sure,' he said. 'You've had a hell of a lot of hours on boats, haven't you?'

'Yes,' I said. 'I flew the English Channel for about sixteen months. I guess I've got about a thousand hours.'

'Sikorsky's got some plans for a flying boat that will carry about thirty or forty people. It will have four engines and really get out and do something. It's just on paper now, but someday these big flying boats are going to be going everywhere. Until they get decent airports with paved runways, land planes are not going to be able to operate effectively.'

I'll tell you, Becky, between talk of an airline and the 'Flying Fool,' I was getting really stirred up.

The reunion ended that night. The following day, about three in the afternoon our time, ten-thirty P.M. in Paris, Lindbergh landed at Le Bourget.

The whole world went crazy!

That was when I started wondering if living down on the ranch in Colorado was the right thing for me. After all, the old man had his ideas of how it should be run, and I wasn't going to really be in charge until he passed away. I sure didn't want anything to happen to him, but I couldn't help thinking that I might be missing some things in life.

When I left New Haven, I gave Ellen a call. Nothing would do but that I come out to Oyster Bay for a day or two. She wanted to introduce me to her family.

I thought, Well, now is the time. But instead of spending two days, I ended up staying a week. We went into New York for a couple of parties and to the country club where many of the people in that area belonged.

Although I was still a little put off that she had married that Princeton guy when I had been so much in love with her, I couldn't hold it against her in the long run. I told her that we were going to have to do something important here. She said she certainly thought that was in order.

Finally, after lingering as long as I could, I said, 'Let me go back to the ranch and talk to my family. Then maybe you'll come out to the ranch this summer?'

'Oh, I would just love it!' Ellen said.

I thought that was a little funny. She had told me five years before that she would be very lonesome living out on the ranch. That's why she had married the guy from Princeton. But maybe she had had enough of that merry-go-round. In any case, we had a passionate parting.

When I got back home, I reported to the family about everything I had seen and done. Of course, my father was terrifically excited about Lindbergh's flight. I told him that I thought the flying boats would someday be developed into great big monsters that would cross the North Atlantic in maybe twenty hours instead of the five or six days it took by ship. Then I told him about Juan Trippe and his ideas for an airline.

'What's he going to call it?'

'I think because he plans to run between North and South America and across the Caribbean, he wants to call it Pan American.'

'That doesn't sound like a bad notion,' Dad said. 'It wouldn't work here in the United States, with the good rail transportation we've got. But down there, where you have good weather and shipping is your only competition, why, I think he just might have a good idea.'

He didn't ask me whether I was interested in it.

I talked to my mom a little bit about Ellen. Of course, she was convinced that there wasn't anybody who was good enough for me.

'If I keep going on like this,' I said, 'I'll still be a bachelor at the end of my life.'

'Never,' she said. 'But if you really think you love this girl—'

'I don't think, I know I do.'

'Well, then why don't I write her a letter and invite her out here.'

She did just that, and sure enough in August Ellen arrived. She seemed to take a great interest in the ranch. It was something totally new for her. She had never been on a horse in her life. Maybe a pony, but she had never done any real riding. When we showed her those incredible mountains, I think they scared her a little bit. Still, we had a great time together.

When the time came for her to leave, I drove her back over to Rico.

Then I asked her to marry me.

'There is nothing in the world I would rather do,' she said.

We had a very loving parting. 'I'll write to you every day,' she said. 'We must set a date. I'll have to talk to Mother and Father about it. When would be a good time for you?'

'I don't know,' I said. 'You're calling the shots.'

'Well, let's think about it. I don't know if a long engagement is necessary. Spring weddings are always wonderful, but after all, I've been married before.'

'I don't care,' I said. 'Just as long as we get the knot tied before too long.'

'I don't like that expression "get the knot tied." Sounds as though I've got a rope around your neck or something.'

'Well, you kind of do,' I said.

She laughed and boarded the train.

In the early fall, I got a letter from Juan Trippe.

'We've formed a company called Aviation Corporation of America,' he wrote, 'and we are going about establishing an airline.

We're going to use Consolidated Commodores for our first flights, and we're going to run from Miami to Nassau and from Key West to Havana. Even though you haven't been flying for five years, it wouldn't take long for a pilot with your skill to get up to snuff. I just want you to know that I may be sending you a wire someday and asking you to visit me.

We've set up a base at Dinner Key in Florida. Now you remember that was an old naval training setup. The Navy was under tremendous pressure to get trainees out in a hurry, and with the number of flying boats they had, why, they left Dinner Key and moved to Pensacola. And that has been the Naval Training Station ever since.

But the abandoned Dinner Key base is ideal for us. Some of the old hangars are still there, and we can use them. I've got some very fine fellows who want to fly these airplanes. I hope you're going to be one of them.'

He went on to say something about my civil engineering degree and how he thought it might be very useful somewhere down the line. 'Keep us in mind, Cowboy, and let's see where we go from here.'

I was certainly very interested, but I hadn't made up my

mind about leaving the ranch. I must say, though, that when I was out riding up the trail to old Brules's cabin or looking out over that vast landscape, I had an urge to see some of the rest of the world. I didn't want to be standing on the sidelines while the world went by.

I had a lot of confidence in Juan Trippe's ability to set up the airline. He knew that an airline couldn't be profitable if it were supported by passenger ticket sales alone. You had to have a mail contract, and that would take a lot of politicking. Selling the government on the idea of a mail contract to South America was going to be tough. The South Americans weren't going to pay anything for it. But I knew Juan Trippe was very well connected, plenty intelligent, and ambitious. If anybody could pull it together, he could. Years later, the whole world stood witness to the fact that indeed he could and did.

THE BIG HUNT

In the fall, I did what I had been wanting to do for the previous five years. I took old Brules hunting. That year there was a short five-day season for elk.

'What's a season?' Brules asked when I talked to him about it.

'That is the time when you are allowed to shoot elk,' I said.

'What are you talkin' about! Hell, if I want an elk, I just step out of the cabin here, take a little walk, and kill me somethin'.'

'Yeah, I know,' I said. 'And if you're short of grub, Mr. Brules, I don't think anybody is going to say anything about you going out here and knocking down an old dry doe or something like that. God knows, there aren't any game wardens around here anyway. But they've got new rules on all this kind of thing. I don't want you to have a big mess, a big fine. They can even put you in jail. Not only that, you can get a bad name around. They're liable to take your license away for the rest of your life. You wouldn't be allowed to hunt in Colorado at all.'

'Now what the hell is a license?' he asked.

'It's a piece of paper that you buy from the State of Colorado that gives you permission to hunt elk and other game.'

'When did those sons of bitches start doing that?'

'It is hard to believe, but by 1899 the game in Colorado had been almost totally wiped out. It was because of the hunters who shot deer and elk for the military posts during the Indian wars, and also the ranchers and farmers who thought of the game as a supplementary diet and shot an elk or a deer anytime it happened to suit them.

It was just pitiful. All that great game that had been around in your day was just gone. Now, that's not true way over here around Lone Cone. We've always had a lot of game. We're so remote and so far from the railroad that hunters didn't get over into this area very often. We didn't suffer the same terrible depletion as the rest of the state.

To rectify this sad situation, the Game and Fish Department was started in Colorado way back in 1900. For a long time, the season was just closed completely. You weren't allowed to hunt elk or deer at all. The amazing thing was that because the city people no longer came to go hunting, the game began to increase very rapidly.'

'I didn't know anything about that,' said Brules.

After I went into Norwood and bought licenses for both of us, we started to plan our trip.

'Mr. Brules, you know that there are different times and different places where elk come on with big strong heads, big trophy heads, and other times when they slack off a bit. It has to do with genetics. There's a sort of cycle when the big boys come through a herd, then it trims down a little bit. If all the big fellows are killed off, then the herd doesn't turn out the champions.'

'I never thought about it,' he said.

'I told you there's still some good places to hunt. Probably right where we are here there's lots of game.'

'Yeah,' he said, 'but since they've put in that damn Grazing Act in 1912, we've lost a lot of range to the cattle and the diseases. Christ, the bighorns have just gone to hell with the domestic sheep comin' in, and you know, the big elk herds just aren't doin' as well.'

'I told you a long time ago that what we ought to do is get a power wagon and trailer for our horses.'

'Hell,' he said, 'you don't go huntin' elk with a power wagon.'

'No,' I said, 'I don't mean we'd do the hunting that way. But we could cover so much territory. We could start up at Meeker and the White River country and work our way down and hunt the Grand Mesa and maybe go up and hunt the forks of the Cimarron. How about the Monuments and Engineer Mountain and all that area? That's wild country in there.

There's no use going near Telluride or Ouray—those are mining camps. Those guys have wrecked that land for miles around. But we could take the road and go around the San Juans by way of Dallas Pass and Ridgway. We can park at the bottom of Owl Creek Pass, then take the horses up the trail and see what we can find.'

'Well,' he said, 'that sounds pretty good. Yeah, I believe you might have somethin' there, young fella.'

'I'll tell you what,' I said, 'I want to see you use that Buffalo Sharps. I want to see you knock an elk down with that.'

I had another reason for wanting to hunt somewhere else. We had a herd of elk around Lone Cone, but as Brules said, the Taylor Grazing Act had cut down on the numbers, and I thought we would leave that herd alone for a while. Nobody came up to hunt in our country—it was too far from anywhere. Maybe a few ranchers or a few guys from Norwood would get up here, but the rest of the world passed us by.

On the other hand, I knew that there was a lot of country in the Uncompahgre range to the east of us that hadn't been touched, especially at the head of the three forks of the Cimarron. It had to be great hunting country. We just needed to get there. We couldn't ride our horses all the way from the ranch. Hell, it would take a month on horseback.

When the season opened, we hit out for the Cimarron Basin. We took the power wagon and horse trailer as far as we could. Then we off-loaded our horses and packed up Owl Creek Pass just below the north face of Courthouse Rock, crossed over Monument Ridge, and dropped down into the west fork of the Cimarron. We headed south into the headwater basin. From there, we worked our way up narrow game trails until we topped out into the high country. It was great. We could see Engineer Mountain to the west and Uncompahgre Peak to the east.

We saw quite a few elk, but I must say, poor old Brules was really shocked by the way the basin of the Cimarron was so hard grazed.

'Christ, it's all grubbed out,' he said. 'It used to be the grass up there was waist high by late summer. There was lots of game, including bighorns, and you used to have a damn good chance of seeing a grizzly.'

'I think the real devastation of the country came when the miners killed the game up there in the high country to keep their camps supplied.'

'Yeah,' he said, 'they did about half the damage. The other half was done by the Grazing Act.'

'Yes,' I said, 'but the elk seem to be doing all right. I think they are coming back.'

'Yeah, I reckon they're pretty tough, and the deer seem to be coming back too.'

We hunted there for a couple of days without any luck. Then we packed up and worked our way past the middle fork and over toward Uncompahgre Peak, on the east fork of the Cimarron. We set up camp overlooking the big basin below.

We were sitting on the edge of the brim of the basin one lazy afternoon, basking in the warm sunshine under the deep blue sky, when I saw something way down the valley. 'Gee, Mr. Brules, look! For God's sake, look!'

'Yeah,' he said, 'I see 'em. Don't say nothin', son. Just stay out of sight.'

What we had seen was a whole line of elk coming out of the timber down in the valley way below us. They were being led by a big old bull. Boy, he was a dandy. I hadn't seen one like that for a long time. We got to whispering even though we were better than half a mile away, I guess, eight hundred yards at least.

'Do you think that big fifty-caliber of yours would reach him?'

'I wouldn't of brought it along, if I hadn't of thought it would work,' he drawled.

'You going to take a shot?'

'Let me look at that bull again,' he said. 'Hand me them field glasses.'

By Jove, he still had the field glasses that old General Crook had given him when he made the mad dash to Custer's Last Stand. He started lookin' and lookin' and lookin'. The bull stopped walking and grazed a little bit.

'Do you think you can hit him from here?' I whispered.

'I reckon so,' he whispered back.

'Well, what do we do?'

'I got to have a steady rest, for the gun,' he said, 'and the way you are puffin' and blowin', I can't use your shoulder. So let me see, I'll slide over there by that rock.'

He just took his time. 'There's no use gettin' excited. They're not movin' anywhere. They're not gonna run off unless somethin' spooks 'em. I'd kinda like to wait till that bull gets away from the timber and out into the open of that clearing where the sun would shine on him a little bit. I think that would do better.'

I waited breathlessly. I took out my field glasses, which I had in the service. I kept watching the bull, and we kept talking in low whispers.

Finally he said, 'I'll just wait till he gets broadside.'

'That'd be the best, wouldn't it?'

'I'll take him head on if I have to. But I don't really want to try that. I ain't dun much shootin' in two or three years, you know.'

'You can put him down anytime you want. I'm sure you can, Mr. Brules.'

He smiled. 'Yeah, and when you say somethin' like that, that's the time the old man will miss.'

'No, you're not going to miss, Mr. Brules.'

He got over to the rock. He couldn't kneel down very well—he was a little stiff. But he could sit down, and he moved the barrel of the gun so's it was resting on the rock. He began to straighten up, getting everything lined up and sighting down the barrel, getting that bull in line. I could swear that bull was over eight hundred yards away.

That big fifty—my God, the size of those shells. They looked like the fifty-caliber machine gun shells that we were getting at the very end of the war, instead of the thirty-thirty stuff. It's just like a small cannon, you know. It was a lever-action breech block gun. He shoved the handle of the breech loader down with his right hand. The breech block slid back, and the chamber opened. He took one of those fifty-caliber shells and kind of wiped it on his shirt. It was like you'd spit on a baseball before you were going to make a pitch.

He dropped it down in the chamber and saw that it settled in and lay just right. Then he slowly closed the breech block. He settled down, squirmed around a little bit, resighted a couple of times, and got his distance right. He got what he'd thought was the drop at that distance, figured whether the uplift of that calibrated sight was going to take care of it, and pulled back the hammer until she was cocked. He reached down and pulled the first trigger—that was the hair-trigger set—and then, real carefullike, slid his finger in between the two, not touching the hair trigger. Then he squeezed off the shot.

I had never heard a big fifty fired before. I thought it was going to be a hell of a roar, like my .458 African that Winchester made. But it wasn't like that at all. It was almost like a rocket push. Then I remembered that our modern shells are loaded with a variation of dynamite, but this thing is loaded with black powder. It doesn't have the kick, but I guess it has the shove. It's maybe a fraction of a second slower in burning.

When that gun went off, it took maybe an instant or so for the bullet to travel that distance, and then by God, that bull elk just humped up, stood there for a minute, and then fell over. It was unbelievable. At the sound of the shot, the herd, of course, ran off into the timber, leaving the old bull a big pile of hide and horns crumpled in the meadow.

I jumped up and hopped around, shouting, "Jesus, what a shot. What a shot. My God, that's better than half a mile."

Brules didn't say anything. He just opened the breech, and when the shell was ejected, he skillfully caught the empty casing in his right hand. He blew it out and stuck it in his pocket. Then he blew down the barrel. Still, he didn't say anything. He just closed the breech, walked over to his horse, and slid that Buffalo Sharps back into the saddle scabbard.

'Well, she still works,' he said finally.

That was it. But I'll tell you, to me it was a great triumph. It was the longest shot I'd ever seen.

His instinctive action in catching the ejected empty shell case as he opened the breech was the sure mark of an old hunter. A man could take a lead bar and a mold with him, get a good fire started, and mold bullets anywhere. That worked for the old muzzle loaders. But when the modern brass shell case came along, you could make the lead bullet all right, but you couldn't make the case in the field. It had to be machined on a lathe, but out in the mountains, well, there weren't any of those around. If you stood in deep snow or heavy brush and didn't catch your shell, you might not be able to find it. And if you couldn't make a reload, you were out of ammunition.

We broke camp quickly and went down to the bull. We

were moving along as well as we could with the pack train behind us. It was damn steep country, so half the time we were leading the horses and half the time riding. When we got there we saw that he was a dandy! Seven point each side. An imperial head. Oh boy, what an animal. A true monarch.

I knew I would have to dress him out and take off the head and all that, because the old man was pretty stiff by that time.

When we went hunting that fall of 1927, I figured that Brules was about seventy-eight years old. It had been eighteen years that I'd known him, and he was not a young man when I first met him. It was very apparent that he had aged recently, but he still had a twinkle in his eye, and every now and then I would catch him looking at me with a smile on his face. He wouldn't be saying anything, but you could see he was thinking. I never saw him with an unpleasant expression. He always seemed bright and alert. But he wasn't one to talk a great deal or throw a lot of compliments around.

The only time I knew him to do that was when I first came back after a long absence. Mostly, we didn't talk much. We both understood how we felt about each other. We knew what the hell was going on between us, and it didn't require any explanation.

The afternoon of the hunt was glorious, and we made camp right where the elk had been brought down.

'That old bull is going to be pretty tough eating,' I said.

'No, he ain't, if we take those backstraps.'

Old Brules went to work right away cutting out the backstraps. Watching that man with a knife was quite a lesson. He always carried a little whetstone with him. He would spit on it and work the knife back and forth just like an artist. The knife had to be so sharp, he could split a hair with it. Then he went to work and made two slices, made his cuts, and when he was through, he laid the backstraps off to the side.

While he was doing that, I checked out the animal. It was the biggest elk I had ever seen on the range. It had a magnificent rack—it had to be something special. It would be a shame not to mount this rack. And it occurred to me that if I were going to do it, I had better take the whole head and cape.

I immediately started cutting from back of the shoulder and down around the chest and almost to the belly and back up around the other side. When he saw me doing that, he asked, 'What the hell are you doin', boy?'

'Well, Mr. Brules,' I said, 'I think this is a record trophy elk, and I think we ought to take him and have him mounted.'

'What the hell are you talking about—mounted? He's dead. You ain't gonna mount him!'

'I wasn't talking about getting on him, I was talking about getting a taxidermist to fix him up so you could put him up on the wall.'

'Taxidermist? What the hell is that?'

'They are the guys that stuff these animals and fix them up so you can hang them on the wall. They put in glass eyes and all that kind of stuff.'

'Oh, God! I don't want nothin' like that,' he said. 'What the hell do I want something like that for? It would stick way out in the room. Look at my cabin. You couldn't fit it in there.'

'You're right, it won't fit in there. But I was thinking, Mr. Brules, if you would loan me this head—I wouldn't ask you to give it to me, but if you would loan it to me—I would have it mounted, and I would put it in our big ranch house there. The house has a very high steep roof because of the snow loads.'

'Yeah,' he said. 'Now what do you want to do that for?'

'I want to put it up above the fireplace. It's a magnificent head, and it will give the ranch a hell of a lot of class.'

'Well, I never heard of a dumb thing like that,' he said laughing. 'But son, whatever you want to do, you go ahead and do it. Why don't you just cut him off here at the neck?'

'I've got to get him back here at the shoulders, so that it can be put on a kind of shield by the taxidermist.'

He couldn't grasp it all at once, but he seemed to accept it. So I went to work, and I was very careful to take enough of the cape that it wouldn't be pinched up. It would look just the way it ought to.

I got to thinking, Boy, these big racks are scarce. You don't come across them very often anymore, and certainly not as big as this! Look at the spread on this thing, and look at the size of the boss right at the skull.

'You know, Mr. Brules,' I said, 'I think that up in Oak Creek, Colorado, there is a bar there with the world record elk head on the wall. It was killed in about 1910 by some guy up around Hahn's Peak. The number-two world record is in the Elk Lodge in Hotchkiss, Colorado. That's a big son of a gun, and it was killed on top of the Grand Mesa just before I went into the war, about 1915. Jesus, I think this thing is as big as or bigger than either of them.'

'Oh, hell,' he said 'go ahead, do whatever you like. I don't care. It is a very big bull, and I kinda like that. I'm just glad I ain't lost my eye.'

I said, 'You sure as hell haven't! That's an eight-hundred-fifty-yard shot. But of course, that Buffalo Sharps was made with the power to do that.'

'I know,' he said. 'It had to have the power when those buffalo herds was gettin' thin and real spooky. Those hunters couldn't get close to 'em, and they had to have a gun that would reach out.'

'What do you suppose was the longest shot that was ever made with one of these? Do you have any idea? The Buffalo Sharps was one hell of a rifle. God, that cartridge is about seven inches long, isn't it?'

'Somethin' like that, I guess. One thing I do know that Shellabarger done told me about—'

'Who's Shellabarger?' I interrupted.

'Well, don't you remember when you was younger, I was telling you about those Comanche raids? I told you about finding Shellabarger out there on the prairie up around Wagon Mound. He was plumb beat out, dried out, fallin' down, and out of water. I brought him back.'

'Oh, yes, now I remember!' I said. 'He finally recognized you as the Cat Man, didn't he?'

'Yeah,' old Brules said. 'It sure startled him when he looked in my eyes. He'd heard all 'bout those Comanches not wantin' to come in that area on account of the Cat Man. I got them thinkin' I was a spirit. I'd messed up enough of them that they didn't want to come back to that country.'

'Yes, sir, I heard about that, and I wouldn't have blamed them. I'd get the hell out of there too. I wouldn't have wanted you hunting me, Mr. Brules.'

He laughed. 'Well, son, the only thing I would hunt you for is to put my arms around your shoulders and tell you what a hell of a fine young man you are. You done come along something fierce. I can't believe all that stuff you told me about. A flyin' man and all that. That's way out beyond me.'

'Well, Mr. Brules, just like anything else, you get used to it.

You'd probably have made a red-hot pilot if they'd had planes when you were young.'

'No,' he said, 'you'd never git me off the ground.'

'Maybe not, but you were a pioneer of the West, exploring new territories, challenging the unknown, and taming new fron-tiers. I was a pioneer in the sky. We have the same kind of spirit.'

He didn't answer.

'Anyway,' I said, 'I think we ought to take this elk in and see how this old bull measures up. I think he ought to be good for something. I'll bet he'll go in the record book all right.'

'I don't want him in no book.'

'Never mind, sir. You just let me handle it.'

And that's how it ended. The next morning, we quartered out the meat and packed in the panyards on the mules and packed that big rack down to the nearest dirt road, which was at the junction of the three forks of the Cimarron. It was difficult maneuvering through the valley of the east fork. It's beautiful, but rugged country, very much like Yosemite with a lot of rocks standing on end. I left Brules, the elk, and the pack mules there, then went back to where we had left the power wagon and brought that damn thing around.

I rode my horse back up the west fork of the Cimarron and down through the trail in Owl Creek Pass. It was about a twenty-five-mile ride, but I made pretty good time by myself.

When I got to the Dodge power wagon and unsaddled my horse, I ran him into the trailer, buckled everything up, climbed aboard, and went whistling down Owl Creek Pass Road. I came out on the main road and headed toward Montrose. I raced through town and turned off in the direction of Gunnison.

About twenty miles out, I headed south onto the road that led back up to the three forks of the Cimarron.

When I got there, old Brules had his meat hanging right alongside the dirt road where I'd left him. The old boy was sitting beside a fire. I guess he didn't figure I'd be back for a couple of days.

I pulled up, and we loaded in a pretty good hurry and got out. By driving the rest of the night, we got back to the ranch about daybreak.

When we got up close to the ranch, Brules told me to unload him there. He didn't want to go any closer to the ranch house where there was any folks. He was sure funny about that.

'Hell,' I said, 'there's no one there at the moment but my mom and dad. They would be glad as hell to see you.'

'Yeah, well,' he said, 'I've met your dad. He's a real fine man. But I don't know how to talk to a woman, and I don't wanna go in there.'

I was going to push him a little bit, but I could see he was getting uncomfortable. I said, 'Mr. Brules, that's entirely up to you. What do you want to do?'

'Just unpack me right here,' he said. 'I'll take my horse and saddle and them backstraps, and you're welcome to everythin' else. By Jove, I'll head directly up to ole Lone Cone.' He paused, and I knew he was wondering when he would see me again.

'I'll be up to see you in a week or so and bring you some meat,' I said. 'First, I want to get in touch with the Boone and Crockett people to see where this bull measures in the record book.'

'That's the craziest thing I ever heard.'

"Well, sir, I'll see you soon.'

'Okay,' he said. 'We sure had a swell hunt, didn't we?'

'We sure did! Boy, that was great!'

'You know, son, it took me back to the old days. I just loved it up there. That's wild country, and it kind of reminded me of a lot of things. There was one time there where I wasn't feelin' so good.'

'Did you eat something, Mr. Brules?'

'Oh, hell, no,' he said, 'nothing like that. But I couldn't help thinkin' about when I dun took my little Mormon girl up there.'

'You mean Melisande?'

'Yes,' he said. 'She was the most beautiful thing, and I showed her the forks of the Cimarron. She was a farm girl from a little old ranch just outside of Moab, where I picked her up.'

'Yes,' I said. 'I remember. You told me that story.'

He lapsed into a little silence, and he didn't say anymore. It was obvious Brules's love for that woman was very deep and lasting.

He finally came out of his reverie and said, 'Son, come up and see me whenever you get ready. It gets a little bit lonely up there sometimes.'

I stood by the Dodge power wagon for a few minutes and watched as he eased his horse off in a slow walk up the trail that led to the peak. He didn't look back. Once again, I experienced the wonderful closeness I always felt to that man. I thought about the life he had lived in the Old West. The living had been hard, the fighting tough, the loving beautiful. There he was, my old friend, with that fabulous hat of his. That old black hat. Just ambling along.

Back in the power wagon, I drove another fifteen miles to the ranch house with my horse and this big bull. 'How did your hunting go, son?' my dad asked as he came out.

177

'Pretty fair, I think.'

'Where's the old man?'

'He didn't want to come on into the ranch. He wanted to go back up the mountain.'

'Yeah, he's like that,' Dad said. 'There's no use trying to push him.'

'I'll tell you one thing, Dad, he's got a tremendous respect for you. You did a great job for him in proving up his land.'

'Well, son,' he said, 'I hoped I was doing some good for him. But I have to admit I had a selfish motive too. He has no relatives, no one to leave that land to. The deal was that if I financed the proving process, he would hold title while he was alive. And when he died, it would all come to me. He told me there wasn't anybody else he'd rather have it than me. And I couldn't think of anybody I'd rather see have it either.'

I laughed. 'Dad, you made a good trade, all right. But you made the deal like a gentleman, and he thinks a great deal of you.'

'I'm glad to hear that. I know how fond he is of you. Whenever I see him, he just can't stop talking about you. He told me how he met you when you were a little boy, and he's watched you grow up. He said he thinks you are one of the finest fellows he ever knew. I did see him a couple of times while you were away in the service, and I told him you were flying.'

'Oh, so that's how he found out!' I said. 'Dad, you're not prone to spreading family news.'

'No, I'm not. But I thought the old man would really appreciate some information about you. I know how fond he is of you. I hope you approve.'

'It was your call, Dad. Anything you wanted to do was fine. Now, let me show you what we've got here in the truck.'

I opened up the back door of the power wagon and dropped the hatch. Dad took one look inside and let out a long whistle. 'My God, will you look at that thing! How did you get him?'

'Brules brought him down with the longest shot I've ever seen. It was over half a mile.'

'Oh, come on now, son,' he scoffed.

'No, honest, it was a good 850 yards. He was using the old Buffalo Sharps that General Crook gave him.'

'That's the biggest elk I ever saw!' Dad exclaimed, taking a second look.

I agreed and told him about the two records I knew of.

'Yes, I've heard of them,' he said. 'But this is gigantic. What are you going to do with it?'

'I'm going to take it to Jonas Brothers in Denver,' I said. 'We're going to get this thing mounted. It's too big an elk to let it rot away.'

'I agree with you, son. That would be a shame.'

'It also gives me something to remember old Brules by,' I said.

My dad and I measured that thing, and I went in to check the Boone and Crockett book.

'I don't know. It's either the world record or very close to it. Of course, when it dries out, it will shrink a little bit.'

'That's a mighty fine rack. Where are you going to put it?'

'In the house, above the fireplace.'

He said, 'Oh, that's perfect, just perfect. It will give the room a seven-million-dollar look.'

'Yes.'

'There's just one thing, son. We've got to ease Mother into this thing.'

'Yes, sir, I know that. But I'm going to show her.'

'All right, but you're not going to tell her right now what you've got in mind to do with it, are you?' he said, giving me a wink.

'No, sir.'

We got Mother out there, and she looked at it, saying, 'Son, I have never seen anything so magnificent! Isn't that the most beautiful animal! Too bad you had to shoot it.'

'Mother, that elk would have lived only another five years, but if we mount him, he will live at least fifty more.'

She looked at me and smiled. 'You may have something there, but you had better check with me before you hang him up anywhere.'

'Mother, you don't think I would do anything else, do you?' I said.

She gave me a hug and a big kiss and said, 'I'm so glad your hunting turned out so well.'"

PAN AM

"Now I know where that beautiful elk head over the fireplace came from," said Becky. "When I first saw it, I was small, and it was so big. It really frightened me. You know, Steven, when I was little, I was also in awe of you. You were the family hero off flying for Pan Am and having great adventures."

"That must have been my mother talking," Steven replied. "If you had talked to the old man, you would have seen he had entirely different thoughts."

"I know you had your differences," Becky said. "But you both had a high regard for each other, and that is what sustains a relationship in the end."

When Steven didn't comment, she asked, "What are you thinking about?"

"I'm thinking that you are a very intuitive young lady, and that I'm very proud of you."

"That's very flattering, coming from you," she said, blushing. "I thank you."

She leaned down and gave him a kiss on the cheek. He continued to stare into the firelight.

"Now, come on," she said, "I want to hear how you got started with Pan Am."

"I think I told you that I had kept in touch with Trippe after I got back from the Yale class reunion.

He had told me then what he was planning, but it took him a whole year to put it together. In the meantime, I was plugging away here on the ranch. Trippe formed the Aviation Corporation of the Americas and bought two or three rickety airlines. He then combined some of their facilities, personnel, and equipment and was off to build Pan American Airways.

In the spring of 1928, I was out on the range for a few days. When I got back to the ranch house, I learned that one of the cowboys had gone down to Rico and had picked up a five-day-old telegram sent me by Juan Trippe.

'Cowboy, get your spurs,' it read. 'We've got the oats for Pegasus now, and we want you to be one of the riders. Can you manage to come back east as soon as possible for a meeting with me, then plan to head down to our training base at Dinner Key in Florida? We have ordered some Consolidated Commodore boats that will be ready sometime this fall. Although you have had a lot of flying time, you're going to need a little refresher. Now is the time to get going. Please advise right away.'

There were no telephones at the ranch until 1934. If you were in a hurry, you had to send a telegram from the telegraph office in Norwood or the railroad station at Rico. The most common way to communicate was to write a letter, and then you sat there for a couple of weeks until you got an answer. But then,, we were on the outskirts of civilization and couldn't expect anything else.

Since the telegram was five days old, I took the power wagon, beat it down to Rico, and wired him, 'Have been out on the range. Just received your telegram. Leave for New York on the next train. Will advise.'

The morning I left, I rode up the mountain just after daybreak. I reached old Brules's place about eight o'clock. He was overjoyed to see me because it had been two or three weeks since I had visited him. I told him that I was going back east and that I was going to be a flyin' man again. I was going with a company called Pan American Airways, and their base was to be in Florida.

He had heard of Florida all right, but he didn't exactly know where it was. And of course, he knew nothing about the airlines or any of the growth opportunities.

'Well, son, I seen it in your eyes when you come back in 1919. Hell, I knowed that you weren't never going to be happy unless you was flyin'. It was easy to see that you was a flyin' man. You got the eyes of a flyin' man. You got the heart of a flyin' man. What I'm sayin' is that if you'd been born eighty years earlier, by God, you'd a been a scout just like me.'

He gave me a big hug, and I could see tears in the old man's eyes.

'Are you gonna be back next summer?' he asked.

'I will if I can.'

We said good-bye without realizing how many years it would be before we would meet again.

When I arrived in New York, I went right to the Yale Club

and gave Juan Trippe a call at his office. He was delighted to hear from me and said, 'You just stay right where you are, Cowboy. I'm coming over, and we'll have lunch at the club.'

Sure enough he did. I told him I had come in from Chicago that morning. All told, it had taken me five days to get to New York, courtesy of the Denver Rio Grande, Union Pacific, and New York Central railroads.

'My God,' he said, 'where is that ranch? They must pump daylight to you out there.'

We both laughed. 'It is pretty far out,' I said, 'and if you're the kind of guy who gets lonely, you haven't got any business being there.'

'It's wonderful to see you,' he said. 'God, you look tough as hell. Like you could play sixty minutes of football again.'

'I wouldn't want to try that,' I said. Trippe knew what I meant. He had been a Yale football player himself.

'You know,' he said, 'we bought these airlines.' And he proceeded to fill me in on the technical details.

The next thing I did was to telephone Ellen and let her know where I was. I had wired her that I was coming and that I would be in touch with her on my arrival.

'Come right on out to Oyster Bay and stay with us at the house,' she said. 'Mother and Dad want to see you again. I told them that we have plans to get married, and you must come.'

I told her that nothing would please me more. She met me at the station with a big hug and a kiss. Her mother and father greeted me with warmth, and I felt very comfortable about my future, which, of course, included marrying Ellen.

'Steven,' Ellen said, 'you must be very excited about the prospects of going back to flying. I am so proud of you.'

'I certainly am thrilled. And I know you're going to like

living in Florida. Let me go down there and check things out, and then we can make some plans.'

I had another lunch with Trippe before I went to Dinner Key. When I realized the vast scope of what this man was dreaming about and the possibilities of bigger and better flying boats that could travel all over the world, I knew I wanted to be a part of it. Trippe, in his way, was a man of vision, and he accomplished incredible things.

After taking the night train down to Miami, I went out to Dinner Key. A lot had been done by the new Pan American Airways to get things in shape. The old navy hangars had been painted and the slips refurbished. The Commodores had not been delivered yet. But I was delighted to see some familiar flying boats around. There was an H-12 and an H-16, both bought out of navy surplus. There were also a few small boats of the *Mary Ann* category, in which some of the fellows were taking flight checks, getting into shape.

It looked like a project that would require a multimillion-dollar investment before there was any return. There had been no revenue at all until just recently, when Trippe had gotten the mail contracts from Miami to Nassau and Miami to Havana.

Trippe had some other ideas that sort of set the standard that all airlines would follow later. He was the first guy to say that if you were going to run an airline, you had to run it like a railroad. The flight had to go out on time, and there had to be adequate preparation so that flights would not be delayed. That meant the weather had to be well researched before a flight could be okayed. It was better to cancel and go the next day than to find a problem en route that would cause a flight to return to its starting point. All that did was burn fuel and use up time and energy. He was very keen on fiscal responsibility.

It was at this time that Trippe hired an engineer named Priester. Of German background, Priester was a man of great precision. He was responsible for laying out airports and harbors and maintaining flight schedules and pilot training programs. He really supervised the running of the airline from a technical standpoint. He was a valuable asset.

Pan American was run very much like a military operation. It was the first airline to put pilots in uniform—stripes on the sleeves showed the rank. The captain was the senior officer; then the copilot, who was called the first officer; next the navigator; and then after the boats got big enough, the flight engineer and the radio operator. In any case, it was Trippe's idea that the captain boarded the boat first, then the first officer, and so forth, all the way down the scale. Each man knew his place, and their discipline instilled public confidence.

Later on, when the big Clippers were flying, they had inflight stewards and marvelous service. If you wanted a gourmet meal, you took a flying Clipper Ship to Rio. The foundations were laid right there at Dinner Key for a fabulous airline.

When I got down to Miami, I found I already knew some of the fellows. They were old navy pilots, and two or three of them had been in the Yale Naval Aviation Unit. It made for very great esprit. The weather was gorgeous, of course. All down through the Keys, the water was deep blue and the sun shone brightly most of the time. It was a big change from New York, where winter was already setting in.

It was a few days before I flew. But when I did, it was in a little *Mary Ann*-type machine with another pilot. It had been nine years since I had flown, and getting back into it was exciting. When they found out I had almost a thousand hours in the H-series boats, I was immediately considered captain material. I was a little rusty on some of the instrumentation, but on the whole, I caught on quickly.

It wasn't long before I realized that I wanted to do this for the rest of my life. I was thirty years old, and in this company, it felt as if the world were my oyster.

I was exceedingly happy, but I thought it would be even nicer if Ellen were with me. I told her what a beautiful place it was and how much I was enjoying it.

Finally, one day I called her and said, 'What the hell are we waiting for? Why don't you come down here, honey? We'll get married. Either that, or I'll come up there.'

When I suggested that, she said, 'If you come up here, I'll marry you next weekend.' This was on a Friday. The next weekend was nine days away.

'You got a deal,' I said. 'I'll be there.'

'What kind of ceremony do you want?' she asked.

'Whatever will make you happy,' I responded. 'I just want to marry you.'

'Well, I feel the same way. But I would like some of our friends here. Wouldn't you like to have Trubee Davidson?'

'I wouldn't think of doing it without him. I'm going to call him right now and ask him to be my best man.'

She laughed and said, 'I have some friends I'd like to invite. They all think you are the greatest. When they know that I'm finally going to marry Cowboy Cartwright, I'm going to see a lot of envious eyes.'

I called Trubee, and of course, he said, 'Cowboy, I am honored. I wouldn't dream of missing your wedding. I'll be there with bells on. Ellen is a great girl. I was a little disappointed when she quit going around with you and married that stupid professor down at Princeton. He wasn't half the man you are. I'm so glad it's all come around to the way it ought to be.'

The next Friday night, I took the train, which arrived on Saturday morning. We were married in the afternoon and had a party that night. On Sunday night, we returned to Miami and were in Dinner Key by midday the next morning.

When she saw the base and all the excitement of the flying boats coming in and going out, Ellen seemed immensely impressed. I think she was secretly very relieved that she was not going to be stuck out on a ranch in southwestern Colorado.

Ellen loved Florida, and she decorated our cute little house, so that it was a happy place to come to in between trips.

Meanwhile, Trippe was extending lines all over the place. You could hardly keep track of it. With the big Sikorsky S-42's, he started flying from Dinner Key to Havana, instead of out of Key West. He had already been flying from Miami to Nassau, and once he got to Havana, it was a cinch to go down to San Juan, Puerto Rico, and then to Trinidad. From Trinidad, he jumped down to Georgetown, British Guiana, and from there to Paramaribo, Surinam, and Cayenne in French Guiana, and then on to Belém in Brazil near the mouth of the Amazon. Each station was set up with hangars and slips and adequate docks for loading and unloading passengers and for refueling. It was a big job.

The jumps were deliberately kept short in order to keep the fuel loads down and the passenger loads up.

Later on, of course, the boats were much more long-range. Ultimately, Pan Am covered all of South America, Central America, Mexico, and the Caribbean Islands with both flying boats and land planes.

Trippe was a great man for getting mail contracts from the

government. He worked the State Department and U.S. Postal Service to a fare-thee-well. Having Pan Am planes flying in and out of those remote places where the surface transportation was poor was a very good thing for every country. They all wanted the service, including the United States. Pan Am was considered an instrument of state long before it started flying across the Pacific and Atlantic Oceans. In fact, by 1935, it was the largest airline in the world.

Trippe even put in a line from Belém, clear up to Manaus, the great rubber capital of Brazil."

"Manaus, that's a thousand miles up the Amazon, isn't it?" Becky asked.

"Yes, it is. To fly a regular schedule a thousand miles up the Amazon—crocodiles, wild native tribes, and all—was quite a feat.

By the third year, we had Sikorsky S-38's, a great little airplane, equipped with the Pratt and Whitney 425-horsepower WASP engine. That engine would run all day and all night.

Every now and then, Ellen would fly with me when I was on the run to Havana, Vera Cruz, or Cozumel through Mexico City.

The first time we took off from Cozumel and flew across the jungle to Mérida, I pointed out the long line etched straight through the jungle of Yucatán.

'What's that?' Ellen asked. 'Is it a survey line to build a railroad?'

'No, that's the old Mayan road. It was built about the same time the Romans were building their roads and probably in about the same manner. It's paved and runs from the Mayan capital of Cobá down to the seaport of Tulán.'

Later, when we were back in Mérida, I told Ellen we ought to go out and see Chichén Itzá.

'What's Chichén Itzá?' she asked.

'It's the great ruin of the Mayan civilization in Yucatán. About 200 B.C., the Mayans came down from the highlands of Guatemala, where they had been located for at least a thousand or maybe two thousand years. Whether they drove out a lesser tribe or whether it was virgin territory, they don't know. In any case, the Mayans did move to the Yucatán. Around the time of Christ, the ruling family in the area was known as Itzá, and they settled at Chichén because there was a big *chenote* there.'

'What's a *chenote?*' she asked.

'A *chenote* is a well—not an ordinary well. It's very large, about four hundred feet in diameter and maybe eighty feet deep.'

'That is a big well,' she said.

'Yes, a lot of calcium formations underlie the jungle of Yucatán. Apparently this well was full of very good water. It was an advantageous place to build a city, which they called Chichén Itzá, meaning "Mouth of the Wells of Itzá." Itzá was the royal family name.'

'I'd love to see it,' Ellen said enthusiastically.

We made the long, hot, dusty trip on the rough gravel road. But it was well worth it. We saw the Temple of the Warriors, with its big ball court. Nobody knows exactly the rules of the game that was played on it, but the old Spanish Franciscan friars said it involved a leather ball being kicked through a circle. The team that lost was put to death. Seems like a tough sport.

There is another temple at Chichén with a peculiar throne. It looks like a man in the form of a cat, leaning back on his elbows with his knees up and his head turned away gazing out over the city. His belly was the seat, and his knees and head formed the arms. It must have been for a prince or priest to sit on during ceremonies. It was called the Chacmool.

Then there was the pyramid of Kukulcán, which had very narrow, steep steps. You could go up them all right, but coming down was a giddy business. If you slipped, you would roll all the way down.

I don't know if they performed human sacrifices, as the Toltecs and the Aztecs did up in the plateaus of Mexico. Those tribes would lay the victim out on the altar, stab him in the chest with an obsidian knife, cut out his palpitating heart, hold it up to the gods, and then kick the body all the way down the steps of the pyramid. It must have made a bloody stinking mess.

The conquistadores reported on the ferocity of the Aztecs and Toltecs. But the Mayans seem to have been of a gentler nature.

A Mayan tour guide who showed us the well told us that the *chenote* was probably the most authentic edifice in all of Chichén Itzá. Then he gave us a little of its history.

The legend told by the Spanish Franciscans is that during droughts, the priest proclaimed that the gods were disfavoring the nation and holding back the rain. They ominously predicted that crops were going to fail and the whole population was going to starve. It was said that if a human sacrifice was made, the gods would be appeased and the rain would start.

In about 1905, a British archaeologist, Mortimer Wheeler, went to Chichén Itzá with some diving equipment and found evidence to support the old Franciscan friars' stories. The Mayan priest was supposed to sacrifice a virgin decked in gold, who had been tranquilized. He would stand, holding her stiff body high above his head. If, after the chants, a cloud passed over the sun, it meant the sun god claimed the maiden. They would then hurl the living girl into the *chenote* in such a way that when she hit the water, maybe a hundred feet down, her back would be broken. Because she was weighted down with gold, her body would sink to the bottom. Eventually, the archaeologists recovered a number of female skeletons. All of them had broken backs and were wearing gold bracelets on their wrists and ankles.

Ellen was fascinated by the story, but of course, she pooh-poohed the superstitious ideas. 'Can you imagine anyone being foolish enough to think there would be rain after a human sacrifice?' she said.

Ellen walked out on the altar and extended her hands up toward the sky. If the sun is a god, it was certainly shining on her that day. She looked so beautiful.

'Here I am, O Kukulcán. Take me, and let there be rain,' she said, mockingly.

I called her back and said, 'It's all well and good for you to make fun, but you know, some of these people may still believe this. Besides, Chac is the rain god.'

I had been very impressed with the nobility of the Mayan population, not only in Mérida but in the surrounding area of Chichén Itzá.

'It might be considered blasphemy, or at least an insult to their religion, for you to act like that. I'm not sure that it is the thing to do.'

'Oh, you're silly to be worrying about things like that,' she said, laughing.

'Maybe so, but at least I don't want to hurt their feelings.'

'Well, I suppose you're right about that,' she said.

We made that little trip together several times. It was in

the spring of 1935, after visiting the seaport of Progreso, about twenty miles from Mérida, that I got an order to go back to Havana on the next flight because of a crew shortage. We were nicely ensconced in a lovely hotel in Mérida, so I told Ellen that I would go back to Havana and return the following day. As it turned out, instead of being there one day, I was held up for three or four days, flying between Havana and Miami. I couldn't get through to Mérida on the telephone, but I did send Ellen a wire to tell her that I was delayed.

In a return wire, she said, "Dearest love, too bad. I'm going back to Chichén Itzá to study the ruins and the gods."

There was no further word from her when I got home, so I thought I had better get back to Mérida.

I knew the damn flights from Havana only went every other day and that I would have to wait. There were only about eight seats available on an S-38 anyway, but then, passenger traffic in those days was usually not heavy. A lot of people were still afraid to fly on an airplane. Looking back on it, I don't suppose I can blame them.

In any case, I told the station manager, 'Buddy, get me on tomorrow's flight. Really, it's important.'

'I will,' he said.

I was about to leave the house the next morning when the telephone rang. It was the Havana Western Union with a telegram from the assistant Pan Am station manager in Mérida. He was a Spanish fellow and didn't speak English very well, but he was friendly and knew both Ellen and me. He hadn't known where to reach me, so he'd sent a wire to my house.

'Señor,' it read, 'come quick to Mérida. *La señora* in terrible accident. Come quick.'

There wasn't any way to telephone, and I didn't think it

would be worthwhile asking him for details because we would just waste time exchanging wires. The thing for me to do was to try to get on something—anything—going to the Yucatán.

Those Pan Am fellows were all my friends, and when I got out to the Miami terminal, I said to the dispatcher, 'Jesus, I've just had terrible news! You've got to help me!'

'Steven, I'm sorry, that's just awful. But damn it, the thirty-eight is full!'

'God,' I said, 'there must be some way. Maybe I can charter a plane.'

'No, there is nothing around here. Pan American has the only equipment that can make that flight.'

These guys could see that I was really upset. One of them was the chief and a great friend.

'I'm going to make you a crew member,' he said. 'You are now copilot on the manifest.'

'Oh, God, that's great! But what do you do for a copilot from Mérida to Vera Cruz?'

'You just leave it up to me. You want to get there, don't you?'

'Damn right!'

A fellow named Fredericks met me in Mérida. He was some kind of an attaché at the American consulate.

He said, 'I'm very sorry to tell you, Mr. Cartwright, but your wife met with a terrible accident out at Chichén.'

'What the hell happened? How badly off is she?'

'Mr. Cartwright, it was a fatal accident,' he said.

I could have dropped dead right there. My God, my Ellen! 'How did it happen?' I gasped.

'It seems that she took a bad fall off one of the ruins. I don't really know much more than that.'

'God Almighty, where in the hell is she?'

'Her body is down at the morgue.'

'Who brought her in?' I asked.

'The man who is the keeper of the overnight facility at the ruins.'

'What's his name?'

'Pedro Estaban.'

'Where is he? How can I get ahold of him?'

'Let me see if I can arrange it,' he said. 'The telephone service isn't very good. I'll send a messenger to his house and ask him to come out here and talk to you.'

'I want to go down to the morgue right away. Could I meet him there? God, I can't even think!'

'All right, I'll have him meet you, sir.'

When I arrived at the morgue, Pedro was already there. We stood out on the street for a few minutes before we went in, and I said, 'For God's sake, tell me what the hell happened!'

'It is a very sad and a very strange thing, Señor.'

The man spoke fairly good English.

'Oh, Señor, Señor,' he continued, 'it is a very bad thing to speak ill of the ancient gods.'

'What the hell do you mean?'

'One must not profane the ancient gods.'

'What are you talking about?'

'Señor, it is the ancient gods who have claimed the *señora*.'

'What kind of bullshit are you talking about? Let's go in the morgue.'

The mortician was an educated fellow and spoke perfect English.

'Oh, Mr. Cartwright,' he said, 'this is terrible.'

I took a deep breath. You can imagine my state of mind. I

just couldn't seem to get clear information. When I asked him what had happened, he said, 'Well, as I understand the story, sir—you must know that these people are very superstitious, and they see and feel all kinds of things we don't understand. These Mayans go to church all the time, but they don't necessarily believe all the Christian dogma. They have a good deal of hang-over from their own gods and still think a lot of them.'

'I understand, but what has that got to do with this?'

'Apparently, your wife was looking over the ruins with an archaeologist friend whom she met here in Mérida.'

'Where is that son of a bitch? Do you have his name?'

'He is an Englishman. His name is Dr. Charles Berkeley. He is from the British consulate. Evidently he accompanied your wife to Chichén. He said that she was standing on the altar, the stone foundation where the human sacrifices were made at the edge of the *chenote*. You know where I mean.'

'Yes, yes, I know—where they threw the sacrificial girls into the well.'

'She was standing there, and she was mocking the gods— "Oh, Chac, god of rain, take me," or something like that. I don't know why she would be doing that.'

'Sometimes Ellen liked to make fun of things that were serious,' I said.

'You know the old story was,' the mortician said, 'that the priest held the maiden up over his head waiting for the sign of whether she was to be sacrificed. If a cloud passed over the sun, that meant the sun god desired the maiden, and she was then hurled into the well. Apparently, a cloud did pass over the sun just as your wife made this statement. When it happened, the Englishman said, "You know, my dear, you've been accepted, it seems."

They were both laughing when suddenly the whole side of the altar slipped away. I understand that she screamed and fell eighty feet into the well. Getting her out of there was a terrible problem. I don't know whether she was alive at that time or not. She apparently floated for a while. The fellows finally got some ropes and went down there. When they brought her back up, she was dead. That happened yesterday, and they brought her in here last night. It is a strange thing—I could find only one broken bone at first. Her chest wasn't crushed, and there is no evidence of her head hitting a rock. But on close examination, we found that her back was broken just above the pelvic structure.'

I was shaken to the roots. I felt as if somebody had lowered a dark curtain over me. I just couldn't believe it. I asked the mortician if I could see her. She looked lovely and peaceful and had a sort of little half smile on her face, as though she had fooled everybody again. I put my hand on hers and stood looking at her for a time. Then I knelt down and put my forehead on her shoulder. Maybe I was looking for a sign, something that Ellen was trying to tell me. I waited for quite a spell, but I heard nothing. I turned my head so that my temple touched her cheek. It felt cold. Finally, I stood up and strode out of the room.

I went back to the hotel to get her things. I wanted to talk to the archaeologist. I had a feeling of animosity toward him, I guess because they said he was a good friend of Ellen's and had escorted her to the ruins. I tried to tell myself there was nothing wrong with that. But still ringing in the back of my mind was what Pedro Estaban in Mérida had said: 'It is a very bad thing to speak ill of the ancient gods.'

When I did get ahold of Berkeley, he seemed like a nice

enough fellow. He looked me straight in the eye. I had to give him credit for that.

'It is a very terrible thing, Captain Cartwright,' he said. 'Why don't we sit over here, have a whiskey, and talk about it. Your wife, I must say, sir, was a lovely, interesting girl.'

'You're telling me?'

'I know this is a terrible shock. I have studied here at Chichén for two years now and have a fair grasp of its history. I did take her around. Whenever we talked about the gods or the folklore, she would laugh and deride the idea. I once whispered to her, "Madame, I strongly suggest that you don't make fun of them where these people can hear you. Some of them still believe in the old gods."

As an Englishman with scientific training, I always look for proof, finding cause and effect only where it can be positively discerned. I am very disturbed and a little bit taken aback that there may be an occult meaning in this situation.'

I looked at him for a long time. Finally I said, 'Dr. Berkeley, I doubt if either you or I will ever know. I thank you for your information, sir. Good day.'

There was no way I could have her body shipped back on the little eight-passenger S-38, so the next day I made arrangements to take her remains back to New York on one of the regular banana boats. I accompanied her on the slow journey to Jersey City.

Her family met me at the train. They had made all the funeral arrangements. We had a slow sorrowful journey to St. Paul's Church near Oyster Bay, Long Island, where the service was held. Then my Ellen was laid to rest in the family plot.

That night, I took a train to Miami. The next morning I went to Dinner Key with the express purpose of rearranging my flight schedule. I wanted no more of flying around the Caribbean. I wanted to get as far away as possible and immediately applied for the Rio de Janeiro–Buenos Aires run."

Becky stood up for a minute and walked back and forth in front of the fire. "Steven," she said, "I am so sorry. I never knew how your wife had died."

"For many years, I simply couldn't reconcile anything," Steven continued. "I loved Ellen dearly. After five years of real happiness, I was again without a companion, without a lover, without a friend. I dared not think anymore about the occult significance, lest I go mad.

Trippe, meanwhile, had been working to establish Pacific routes. He'd chosen the Pacific over the Atlantic because of better weather conditions. He had followed his instincts with respect to the Caribbean, and he thought Pacific islands like Hawaii, Midway, Wake, and Guam were good places to start. They had smooth quiet lagoons, and if there was a typhoon in the area, you generally had about two days' notice.

In 1933, when Ellen died, work had just begun in the Pacific. I only knew vaguely that something was going on out there because I hadn't seen Trippe in maybe a year's time.

Then one day when I was in Rio, I got a call from Trippe's office asking if I would come up to New York to visit him. His invitation was a flare of light in my dark hours, and I caught the first S-42 out of Rio to Miami. I went from there in an Eastern Airlines DC-3 to Newark.

'Hello, Cowboy, how are you doing?' Trippe asked as I entered his office.

'Oh, fine, fine, Juan. How are you?'

'Steven, I heard about your wife's death from Trubee Davidson. I am very sorry.'

I simply nodded. I still couldn't talk about it very much. But right away I saw Trubee's fine hand in this summons from Trippe.

'You know, Cowboy,' Trippe went on, 'you are one of the most valuable men we have around this airline.'

'How is that, Juan? I don't fly any better than these other guys.'

'I believe you do,' Trippe said. 'Not only do you know all there is to know about flying boats, but you are also a civil engineer, and we have some big construction jobs coming up. We are going to push this China Clipper stuff, and we've got to get proper setups in Pearl Harbor, Midway, Wake, and Guam, as well as in Manila and Macao. You know we can't go directly into China. We have to land in Portuguese Macao, where our passengers will connect with China Airlines. We Occidentals are viewed with great suspicion in the Heavenly Kingdom.'

'I never thought about it,' I said.

'I'd like you to do something for me,' he said.

'What's that?'

'We need someone to coordinate that whole business out there. I would like you to go to the western Pacific as vice-president in charge of facilities construction.'

You could have bowled me over.

When he told me the salary, which was about fifty percent more than the good wages I was making as a captain, I said, 'Thank you very much, but that would take me away from flying.'

'Oh, no. Not at all,' he responded. 'I want you to keep on flying. Not the heavy schedule you have now, but I want you to go in and out of all these places. I want you to see the bases and slips from the standpoint of the pilot.'

That was one thing about Trippe. He never monkeyed around with anything theoretical. He himself was enough of a flyer that he knew, by God, that if you were going to operate an airline, you had better get advice from the guys who were doing the flying. I was impressed, and as a matter of fact, I felt a great relief. The idea of going to the western Pacific hit me as a challenge I could really sink my teeth into.

'Okay, Juan, you've got your man. When do you want me out there?'

He smiled, shook my hand, and said, 'Cowboy, just as quick as you can get on your horse.'

I laughed. 'Fine, I'll go out there, but there is one thing I'm going to do first. I want to take a couple of weeks and stop off and see my mother and dad at the ranch in Colorado.'

'Oh, yes,' he said, 'I'd forgotten about that ranch. You once asked me out there.'

'You better come,' I said. 'We'll go out there and have a hell of a time.'

'Jesus, there is nothing I would rather do, but I'm up to my ears in alligators here. I've got to keep going.'

After saying good-bye to him, I got in the elevator on the fifty-eighth floor of the Chrysler Building and didn't stop moving until I was back at Broken Bow Ranch at the foot of Lone Cone. I was in the place where the grandeur of the towering mountains and the magnificence of the land itself somehow healed the soul."

"Steven, it is wonderful," Becky said, "that opportunity came along. I'm sure you were right about Trubee Davidson's influence on Trippe."

"Yes, I can just hear him. 'Juan, the Cowboy's down, he's lost his wife, and he's wasting away down there. You ought to put him to work on your main project. Remember he has a civil engineering degree.' And Juan would have agreed. I got the story later on, and that's pretty much what happened."

"Now let's see, this was in 1933?"

"Yes. I had a lovely time with Mother and Dad. Of course, I didn't miss going up to see old Brules. He wanted to know all about this airline thing I was doing. So I told him about setting up the bases. Just being at home did me a world of good."

"When did you get home next?" Becky asked.

"Don't you remember? That was in 1938, when I got a telegram from Mom telling me that Dad was very ill."

"Oh, yes," she said, "that's the year your father died."

"It was really tough getting from Wake Island back to the ranch. They were both so remote. I caught a Clipper headed for the States and reached the Pan Am Alameda base in San Francisco harbor within two days. Then, I caught a flight to Denver on one of United Airlines' new 'luxurious' DC-3's. We made only one stop, and that was in Salt Lake.

When I got to Denver, I took a dim view of the dismal rail transportation to the western slope, which would take almost two days by narrow gauge. They told me that the railroad had given up on regular passenger cars in 1935 and that they now had a thing called the Galloping Goose, which was a bus mounted on the rails—it ran at odd intervals.

I was anxious to get home, knowing that Dad was so very ill, so I went out to a small airfield on the edge of Denver. It was not the main airport, Stapleton, but a little grass pasture on the east side of town right by the sagebrush plains. The guy there had just started a flying school at what had been Lowry Field, an old military field in the late twenties, early thirties. This guy had a bunch of Piper Cubs, and he also had a cabin biplane. It was a

YKS Waco with a single-ignition Jacobs engine. Matter of fact, it was a pretty good flying machine.

I made a deal with him to fly me to Norwood, Colorado. There was a small airstrip there, and I figured somebody from the ranch could come down in the power wagon and pick me up. I got ahold of Mom on the phone and told her my plan. She almost burst out crying when she heard my voice. She was plenty excited. I hadn't been home in over five years, and she'd never thought I could make it back from the South Pacific in time.

We got in the Waco and taxied out onto the field. There was no runway. It was all just grass. We took off north toward the power lines and the railroad tracks. I remember thinking, Jesus, this field is small, and it's at five thousand feet altitude. But when the pilot opened the throttle, that Waco biplane bounced out, and we cleared the wires by a scant thirty feet.

It flew beautifully, but it was slower than the second coming of Christ. It did about 120 miles an hour, and as usual, we bucked headwinds going west toward the mountains. But that little thing really got up and went, and it did very well when it came to crossing the 14,500-foot peaks.

We were in the air over two hours, but that beat the hell out of two days on the railroad.

That was also the time when a little freckle-faced girl, much to her distress, left the gates to the alfalfa field open again."

THE FANCIFUL JOURNEY

Becky was deep in thought as Steven went over to the packs, pulled out his old flight jacket, and wrapped it around her shoulders. As she watched him, she thought about the fascinating life he had led and how much he had told her tonight. Then her thoughts went back to the Shetland ponies and the connecting link he had found between them and the wild paints here on the ranch.

"Steven," she said, "I still don't understand how the painted horses got back to the American continent and why they ended up in the northern part."

He looked at her thoughtfully for a moment, his hand on his chin. "Well, I can tell you exactly when and where it all came to me.

I saw it very clearly on a brilliant sunny afternoon when I stood waist-deep in the icy waters of the Viðidalsá River in northwestern Iceland. I love to fly-fish, and I was casting for the elusive flash of an Atlantic salmon.

It was such a beautiful sunny afternoon, unusual in the Icelandic climate, which is misty, rainy, and swept by cold winds off the Arctic Sea most of the time.

But this day it was warm, and the midnight sun shone brightly over the land. As I looked around at the green tundra of the Icelandic hills and the snow-capped mountains, I realized that the scene was not unlike some of the wild treeless parts of Wyoming.

I thought of the times I had stood in the shining waters of the North Platte River, casting for trout and looking up at the barren hills alive with cattle, driven by hard-riding cowboys.

Just such a scene struck me as I stood in the waters of that river in Iceland, looking at a high hill to the right. The native tundra looked for all the world like purple sage. A band of cattle moved across the skyline. These were not beef cattle but Icelandic dairy cattle driven by drovers. At a distance the Icelandic lads on horseback looked for all the world like Wyoming cowboys.

And then very startlingly, I noticed that they were riding painted horses—not all of them, but most of them—and suddenly it all came together. This was where the Indian got his painted horse!

"From Iceland?" interjected Becky.

"No, go a little farther west."

"Greenland?" she asked.

"Of course! We know from the Viking sagas that these same painted horses were carried by the Vikings across to Greenland from Iceland, so why not on to North America?"

"But I don't quite understand," said Becky. "I've heard of

Lief the Lucky, the Norseman who first discovered America and called it Vinland because of the grapes they found there. In school, we were taught that Vinland was perhaps Newfoundland, Nova Scotia, or maybe Cape Cod. But those places are perhaps three thousand miles from the upper Missouri. Even if the Vikings had brought the horses, how would they have gotten through the very dense and impenetrable forests of the East to the western wilderness? No, you can't sell me on that."

"Now, don't you get all hot-headed before you know the facts. You're right. By that route, the distance and the terrain would have been impossible. But they didn't go that way!"

"Well, then, what way did they go?" she asked irritably.

"Don't you realize, it's about the same distance from Greenland to the Great Bend of the Missouri as it is from Greenland to Cape Cod?"

"You're kidding!"

"No, I'm not. The great circle course from Greenland to the Hudson Strait and through Hudson Bay to the Nelson River is a straight shot. From there, it's all waterway to Lake Winnipeg, and the Red and Assiniboine rivers and their tributaries, like the Souris, down to within fifty miles of the Mandan villages!"

"Wow!" she exclaimed. "But is the Nelson navigable as far up as Lake Winnipeg?"

"Good question. No, it is not. There are a number of big rapids."

"But if they had horses with them, those portages would have been a lot easier, wouldn't they?" Becky asked.

"Yes, and we know the Vikings learned a great deal about portages when they explored the Dneiper, Don, and Volga rivers in eastern Europe in 800 A.D.

The Volga has no rapids and flows into the Caspian Sea. But the Dneiper and the Don, which empty into the Black Sea, had very difficult portages of far greater length, and they involved treacherous cataracts as well.

So, you're right. Once they reached Lake Winnipeg, it was a cinch. They sailed the length of the lake to the Red River of the north, to the Assiniboine, then on to the Souris and to a point where there was only a fifty-mile portage across the open prairies to the Great Bend of the Missouri.

This is how the Vikings came into the middle of the North American continent, and it accounts for the connection between the towheaded, blue-eyed, fair-skinned Mandans and the Norse penetration of the territory.

You must remember that the Kutenai and the Flathead Indians of the Columbia River Basin were also mentioned by the Lewis and Clark expedition as being the 'whitest of white' Indians. And what's more, all of the nations—the Mandans, Nez Percé, Kutenai, Flatheads, and Shoshones—were the possessors of large numbers of painted horses.

It was this explosion of westward Viking exploration between 1000 and 1300 that carried the painted horse into North America and into the hands of the northern Indian tribes.

It was so clear. I wondered why I had never seen it before.

This would account for the large numbers of painted horses found by Lewis and Clark among the Dakota tribes and in the Columbia River Basin. It would also account for the sturdy paint's ability to handle the rigorous northern winters, a fact that has always mystified students of equine history who believed that all North American horses descended from the Spanish horse of the Mexican Southwest.

It is so easy to see how it must have happened.

THE LEGEND OF THE PAINTED HORSE

When the painted horse was domesticated, he traveled all over the known world under the protection of man and was bred for all sorts of purposes. Various breeds of the horse as we know them today came from the paint, which adapted to specified needs.

One can also see the very clear rainbow curve of the painted horse—how he came into history, appearing as early as thirty thousand years ago in Eurasia, how he followed the retreating lines of the glaciers to the mountainsides, and how in that environment his coloration changed to allow him to survive.

If we observe this pattern carefully, we can see that the painted horse must have taken one of his last wild stands in the high snow-blown Khingan Mountains. He was finally captured, on the northern frontiers of China and in the brown desert mountains that border Mongolia, by the Chinese or Mongols for purposes of domestication. Chinese emperors were pictured riding on painted horses, and we also find models of painted horses in their tombs.

In the Karakoram Himalayas and along what was later to be the great silk route from Sian to Damascus, the painted horses existed on the sides of the snow-covered desert mountains of Mongolia and Tibet. The Tibetan Tangum is living proof of the long snowline arc. As domesticated animals, they became the proud possessions of India rulers.

When the glaciers receded ten thousand years ago into the Elburz and Caucasus mountains, south and west of the Caspian Sea, the painted horse was domesticated by the Scythians and the Parthians. Paints later fell into the hands of the Persian kings, who rode them proudly with all the regal trappings.

These horses also survived in the Scandinavian Highlands

and on the north slopes of the Alps, where eventually they became the painted horses of the Germanic tribes and the Scandinavian peoples who inhabited this region.

The famous spotted horses of Friesland in the northern Netherlands, the Overo horses of the Danes, and the painted horses of the Swedes and Norwegians descended from the painted horses that roamed wild thousands of years before, when the last traces of the glaciers still clung to the mountainsides.

Later, the painted horse ended up in the Shetland Islands, where he existed in a domestic state for more than a thousand years. He was then brought to the Orkney and Faroe islands and on to Iceland by the Vikings. The sagas tell us of the important part he played in the life and culture of Iceland from the tenth century on.

We also know that when the Norse colonized Greenland, they took horses with them. The saga of Lief the Lucky tells that when Eric the Red rode down to the dock to join the expedition to Vinland, he was injured in a fall from his horse and, therefore, did not join the voyage. To his son, Eric said, 'It was not given to me to find other lands.'

We also know that horses stayed in Greenland from the account of Ivar Bardarsson, who, in 1340, journeyed to the Western Settlement of Greenland to see what had become of the settlers there. He found that although there were cattle and sheep on the hillside, there were no settlers around and, significantly, no horses. He reported to the Bishop of Greenland in Norway that this could only mean that the people of the Western Settlement had taken their horses with them when they left.

When Greenland's climate started to deteriorate, there seems to have been an emigration westward, which continued over a period of a hundred years or so. At the height of Viking

THE LEGEND OF THE PAINTED HORSE

colonization, there was reportedly a population of about ten thousand. So their emigration involved thousands of people, mostly headed west, either on board visiting ships, or on ships that they had constructed out of timber brought from Vinland, or in the skin boats developed by the Thule Eskimos.

So the rainbow curve of the snowline horse continued beyond Greenland across the Davis Strait. The horses traveled with their Viking masters to the New World, just as they had traveled from Norway and Sweden to Iceland and Greenland.

Paul Knutsson's voyage, launched in 1355, must have numbered many ships—ships far superior to those of the early Greenland settlers. Those ships, and ships of other expeditions, must have carried horses. There is evidence of Vikings having traveled through the Hudson Strait to the western shores of Hudson Bay, up the Nelson River to the southern prairie shores of Lake Winnipeg, then up the Red River into the lakes of Minnesota."

"Your theory sounds wonderful and logical, but is there any proof to support it?" asked Becky.

"I think so. I came upon an article in an historical magazine the other day, and it struck me as very significant. I cut it out and have it in my saddlebag. I was thinking I might study it more carefully sometime on this pack trip."

"A magazine article?"

"Yes, it's sort of a cataloging of some of the Norse expeditions that were recorded by the Church and are on file either in the Vatican or in the Bishopric of Bergen. Here, let me get it for you."

Steven stood up from the fire and walked over to the tarp that covered the saddles. Reaching into his saddlebag, he withdrew two or three folded pages. Coming back to the light of the fire, he began to read:

"'Gudlief was a Norse trader, who in 1025 rescued the Icelander Bjorn Asbrandsson, whose ship had been wrecked somewhere on the coast of North America.

There is an account of an Irish or Saxon missionary priest named John, who went to Vinland in 1059. He was apparently murdered by the Skraelings, which is what the Norsemen called the Indians.

In 1067, Adam of Bremen, the historian of Scandinavian life during that period, wrote of the existence of Vinland. That is three generations after Lief's voyage. This indicates that the Norse were familiar with the existence of Vinland and that people of their race had visited that land on many occasions.

Erik, the Bishop of Greenland, sailed for Vinland in 1121. His missionary expedition was never heard of again. In 1266, the Gardar priest of the Eastern Settlements sent an expedition into northwestern Baffin Bay to reconnoiter the Skraelings.

In 1356, the King of Norway commissioned a certain Paul Knutsson to visit Greenland and find the lost colonists of the Western Settlement who had gone over to the heathen. This expedition, which appears to have been of considerable size, continued over nine years.

Henry Sinclair, Earl of Orkney and a Scot of Norman Viking descent, accompanied by Antonio Zeno, a Venetian navigator, led an expedition of many ships to Nova Scotia in 1398. They perhaps went as far as the New England coast.'"

"Good heavens," said Becky, "I had no idea there were so many recorded Viking trips to the New World."

"That's not all," Steven replied, putting the article aside. "When I was young, I read the Icelandic Sagas in English. Then when I was on that fishing trip to Iceland, through the courtesy of an influential friend, I was able to go into the archival vault of the museum to see the ancient Icelandic Sagas themselves. Of course, I couldn't read tenth-century Norse, but the museum was kind enough to have a scholar translate as he read them. It was wonderful to see the actual ancient manuscripts and to be able to recognize the same stories I had read in English. They recounted the adventurous trips of Eric the Red, Bjornia, Leif, Thorvald, Thorstan, Karsefini, and Freyda. All seven of these expeditions took place between 982 and 1015."

"Steven, do you realize that's seven expeditions over a period of thirty-three years?"

"I know, Becky, and none of them are duplicates of the recorded trips mentioned in the magazine article. Remember too that these accounts stemmed from a relatively illiterate culture and really pertained only to matters that were considered to be of some historical importance.

There must have been scores, if not hundreds of other voyages. The Norse were a vigorous and adventurous people. They loved to sail the seas, to explore rivers, lakes, and forests. Of the thousands who lived in Greenland for over four hundred years, there must have been many who could not be contained. I'm sure many hunters, fishermen, and explorers sailed across to Baffin Island and farther—"

"Yes, but you can't prove that they took horses with them," Becky interrupted.

"Oh, yes, I can. At an excavation of a probable Viking campsite in Cape Cod, a shin bone of Equus caballus was unearthed. Upon examination by experts, the bone was pronounced to be at least a thousand years old. It was small and indicative of a horse about the size of the painted Shetland, a horse of Norse origin.

If the analysis of its age is correct, this horse was in America five hundred years before the Spanish horse, although it did not take hold in the eastern forest land.

Then there is L'Anse aux Meadows, in the northern part of Newfoundland, where there is an absolutely authenticated Norse site. And on the Nipigon River, between Lake Nipigon and Lake Superior, the so-called Beardsmore Find consisted of a Norse sword, an ax, and a piece of helmet.

Then there is the much-debated Kensington rune stone, found in Kensington, Minnesota, in 1898. The Norse inscriptions obviously specified members of a Norse expedition and described a disastrous encounter with the Skraelings. Robert Hall, Jr., a professor at Cornell University, recently pronounced the Kensington rune stone genuine, after conducting the most thorough study to date.

Many Norse artifacts, such as axes, halberds, spearheads, fire steel, and the like, have been found in northwestern Minnesota. A series of drill holes was also discovered along a chain of lakes in the same area. These drill holes look the same as the ones used in Norway to solidly anchor a ship to the shore by means of a rope and an iron peg, and they are similar to ones found on Cape Cod.

A rune stone at the junction of the Red River and the Assiniboine tells the story. For it was from this region that the Norse culture seems to have spread southwest to the Mandan village area.

Most of the few thousand Norse who left Greenland in the thirteenth and fourteenth centuries moved to the New World. They formed small, scattered settlements and eventually must have intermingled with either the Indian or Eskimo cultures there.

There are so many striking resemblances between the Mandan and the Norse cultures that the inference that they were a mixture of Norse and native Americans is overwhelming.

When the Lewis and Clark expedition came upon the Mandans, they observed that their houses were different from any they had previously seen inhabited by American Indians. Their houses, strangely enough, had the same general plan and form as Norse houses of the tenth century.

Both had a fireplace in the middle of the room and a hole in the roof. Both had entrances on either end of the structure, with benches and booths along the sides. The booths were hung with curtains, which separated the families and provided privacy.

In a Norse house, a Viking warrior hung his shield, spear, and helmet on the partition of his booth, showing that this was his place of abode. Strangely, or not so strangely, the Mandan warrior hung his buffalo-hide shield, with its evil-eye markings, his colorful feathered lance, and his buffalo-horned headdress in exactly the same manner. The display on the partitions between the booths signified that they were private quarters that belonged to him and his family.

The Lewis and Clark people also remarked on the fact that the Mandans possessed saunas, the steam or dry heat baths that are so common to Scandinavia but that were apparently unknown to other Indian tribes.

The practice of several families living together and gathering around a central fireplace was not uncommon among primitive peoples. Still, the similarities between Norse and Mandan customs are striking.

Another clue to the origin of the Mandans is their round bull-hide boats. George Catlin painted them with great fidelity because of their curious nature. They were exact replicas of the Irish coracles used by the 'west men' in their journeys overseas to Iceland, where they were found and enslaved by the Vikings. So it was the Norse that brought the Irish hide boat to America. No other Indians except the Mandans built this kind of boat. The tradition must have come from somewhere other than the North American continent.

In fact, it was the peculiar form of the bull-hide boat and its similarity to the Irish coracle that led many people to believe that the Mandans were descendants of a lost expedition. Welsh mythology said it departed Wales in 1170 under a certain Prince Madoc and never returned.

It is no wonder that this far-fetched fable was given little credence. On the other hand, there is an abundance of evidence that the Mandans were the result of the westward thrust of the Norse.

When Catlin first visited the Mandan villages, he observed that some of the ceremonies of the Mandans were conducted around the outline of a boat, indicated by stones placed on edge in the shape of a hull.

The Mandan elders told Catlin that this was symbolic of 'the great canoe,' by which the first man—in other words, the ancestor of the Mandans—arrived at the Heart River region many, many generations ago.

The Heart River is located at the southern end of the portage from the Souris to the Great Bend of the Missouri. Is it possible that the ceremonial 'great canoe' of the Mandans represented the ancestral Viking longship?

The clincher to my theory is the story of Pierre La Vérendrye. La Vérendrye visited the Mandan villages in 1738, some four hundred years after the Vikings arrived there. La Vérendrye, his son, and a band of Assiniboine Indians were exploring the west under the auspices of the King of France and the Governor of New France in Montreal.

He had been told that there were white Indians at the Great Bend of the Missouri, and quite naturally, he thought he was about to make contact with the Spanish or other whites. On his arrival at the Mandan villages, he was disappointed to find no white man, only Mandan Indians with their Caucasian features. He did, however, notice that the Indians had painted horses and kept them inside during the winter, a practice that was typical of the Norse.

There is not much difference in severity between a winter in Greenland or Iceland and a winter in the Dakota prairies, as many pioneer accounts will attest. The cold polar air that sweeps down over the ice cap and the tundra of the Hudson Bay country penetrates the Dakota prairies and can reduce the windchill factor to as low as ninety degrees below zero.

The most startling of La Vérendrye's discoveries was a rune stone placed in typical Norse fashion in a cairn, or pillar of stones, which he found somewhere 'near the Mandan villages.' The stone caused him considerable puzzlement and seemed beyond the Mandans' own comprehension.

Vérendrye carefully packed it up and carried it back to Montreal. The Jesuits there could not solve the riddle of the characters, so they shipped the stone to their more learned brethren in Paris, who declared them Tartar inscriptions.

The fact that they looked like Tartar inscriptions to the Jesuits in Paris is entirely understandable. Even though the runic script had its origins in the Greek and Latin alphabets, there is still a possibility that some Norse characters were adapted from the Tartars when the Norse raided the east side of the Caspian during their many expeditions down the Volga.

All of this evidence seems to tie the Norse to a significant penetration of North America long before Columbus.

It has always been a puzzle to horse historians and horse lovers as to how an Andalusian horse, descended from the Arab and European saddle horse and brought by the Spanish to Mexico, could possibly have roamed wild on the prairies of the Dakotas and Manitoba and survived.

The answer is that the Andalusian horse was *not* the horse that roamed these areas. Rather, it was the painted horse, the Scandinavian horse brought by the Vikings, which was inured to the harsh northern climate.

Just as only a very few Norse penetrated the inland reaches of the North American continent, so too they brought few horses. But those they did bring were mostly of the painted or appaloosa coloration and were strong enough to survive.

Years later these horses came into contact with the great horse herds that had spread out of Mexico. There were still enough paints surviving in pockets through the northern latitudes that their line extended from Lake Winnipeg westward to the Pacific shore.

When the Vikings first reached the lower end of Lake Winnipeg or ventured up the Saskatchewan or Assiniboine rivers, they must have run into the Kutenai, who at that time occupied the area of Manitoba that bordered Lake Winnipeg. This tribe, along with the Nez Percé and the Flatheads, occupied the area three or four hundred years before the coming of the white man.

The Kutenai, the Nez Percé, and the Flatheads were gradually pushed from the Winnipeg shorelines by the Blackfeet and the Cree to the area of the Rockies where the Marias River joins the Missouri. The Blackfeet roamed even farther to the west and eventually pushed these tribes, along with the Shoshones, across the Shining Mountains into the Columbia Basin. There they lived for several hundred years, raising their beloved painted and appaloosa horses.

It was here that the Lewis and Clark expedition found them and their wondrous supply of painted horses.

The expedition observed these Indians to be rather tall and fair-complected—as Sergeant Egan said in his diary, 'the whitest of white Indians.' Does it not seem possible that these characteristics were the result of contact with the Norse?

Lewis was so astounded by the size of the horse herds that he wrote in his diary, 'It is not uncommon for one individual warrior to own as many as two hundred head. They prize these horses greatly and even though in extremities of hunger they will not eat horse meat.'

It is also interesting to note that the horses that lived among these Indians in the Columbia Basin were of no real economic value. There were no buffalo in the area, and therefore the horses were not used for hunting. With the exception of the Shoshones, these tribes survived on salmon, relying on the annual runs that came up the Columbia waterway. Horses would obviously not be useful in a fish culture.

The truth of the matter is that these tribes had become attached to their horses and felt that they had spiritual significance. It was a relationship that had existed for hundreds of years and that stemmed from a long-forgotten but very real source.

The contact between the paints and the Mexican horses took place long after the first paints came into the area. Their remarkably strong genetic coding carried the paint characteristics throughout the horse herds of these northern Indians.

The paints interbred with horses stolen from the ranches far to the south and produced a horse that was known as the "wild horse" or the "Indian horse" of the cavalry days. This horse was noted for its painted coloration. It was also known for its stamina, its swiftness, and its remarkable capacity to survive the bitter cold.

The Columbia basin, with the Clearwater and Snake rivers, is the western end of that long rainbow of the snowline horse that stretched all the way from the northern Chinese border, with its snow-flecked hills, across the Mongolian Altai and the Tibetan Himalayas, the Hindu Kush, the Caucasus, the Carpathians and the Scandinavian Mountains, and then across the Iceland and Greenland ranges to Hudson Bay and the open prairies and Shining Mountains of northwestern America.

Here in the basin of the Columbia and the Palouse River Valley is the end of the rainbow trail of the painted horse—the end of thousands of years and thousands of miles of snowline wandering.

And here, my dear, is the end of . . .

The legend of the painted horse."

THE SECRET

"Steven, your theory of the trail of the painted horse makes so much sense. It is a wonder that no one else has ever thought of it."

Becky lapsed into deep thought. She had never known him to talk so much about things other than running the ranch. Was something happening between them that would bring them closer? She wanted to keep him talking.

Steven was also trying to recall things that he thought would be of interest to this beautiful woman. Suddenly he wanted her to know everything about him.

"Steven, you were with Pan Am when the Second World War broke out, weren't you?"

"Yes, I was on Wake Island because it was in the middle of the chain—Pearl, Midway, Wake, Guam and Manila—the route of Pan Am's 'China Clipper.' Because of its remote location, we often had to wait weeks before construction supplies came, and I had a lot of free time.

I had my office at the base and a lovely little cottage right on the beach on the east coast of the island. I loved the deep blue color of the sea and felt such tremendous peace as I watched the undulating waves wash and sculpt the fine white sand of the beach.

My thoughts were often filled with pictures and memories of the ranch, Mother, and my dear friend Brules. Mother had never wanted me to have anything to do with him. In fact, you'll remember that when I was young, she forbade me to go see him. I was pretty sure that she knew of the relationship that developed over the years, but neither of us ever spoke of it. I think she recognized that I had turned out to be a son of whom she could be proud. Furthermore, Brules had never caused either her or Dad any problems. I'm not sure that she ever knew that Dad saw him occasionally or about the business relationship they had with regard to Brules's property.

I thought of him rather as the grandfather I never had. He taught me so many things about living in the wild. He had led such a fabulously exciting life in the Old West. Over the years, Brules told me so many stories about his life, and I realized that they should all be written down.

I decided to do some historical research into the Indian wars, General Crook, and the Battle of the Little Bighorn. I wanted to get additional background information and substantiate some of the stories Brules had told me. I remembered his beloved wife, Wild Rose, and their little daughter, Morning Star, whom he had taken back to the Shoshone Reservation in Wyoming, as well as his adventures with his blood brother, Wesha, the son of the Shoshone chief.

I sent off letters to the Indian Agency in Wyoming and to the War Department, seeking any information they might have in their records.

The Indian Agency was actually extraordinarily helpful and sent me on a trail that I didn't expect."

"What do you mean?" asked Becky.

"Well, I asked the agency for everything that they could tell me about a scout named Brules, a Shoshone called Wesha, a baby named Morning Star, and an Indian agent by the name of Robert Irwin. And you won't believe what happened.

Among the records that Agent Irwin had left was a journal of sorts. Judging from his entries, his job was not an easy one, for it was about that time that the government, in its infinite wisdom, decided to resettle the Arapaho tribe on the legitimate reservation of the Shoshones. It was a neat scheme devised by the Bureau of Indian Affairs, but it had one severe problem. It failed to take into account that the Araphoe and the Shoshones had been blood enemies for centuries.

Naturally, the whole arrangement was very unsatisfactory to both tribes. It was particularly difficult for Irwin, who had to report a number of fatal quarrels between the Arapahoe and the Shoshones.

There were other entries written in 1881 in which he described a young five-year-old girl who was half white and half Indian. She was a very bright, beautiful little girl, and because Irwin was concerned about her future on the reservation, he had contacted his sister, Mary, about her.

It seems that she had been brought to the reservation by a certain mountain man and Indian scout by the name of Brules. He advised Irwin that the child was his by a Shoshone woman named Wild Rose, whom he had married the year before. The

223

mother was apparently closely related to the old chief of the Shoshones, Washakie. Brules said that she had been severely injured in a fall from her horse one week before the child was born. She died three weeks later.

The little eight-week-old baby was delivered into the care of one of the squaws of an Indian brave named Wesha, who was the oldest son of the Chief Washakie. She had recently given birth to a child of her own and was therefore able to serve as a wet nurse.

Brules, perhaps under the influence of his friend Wesha, had opted to join a contingent of eighty Shoshone warriors who were leaving the next day to rendezvous with General Crook at Cloud Peak Camp in Wyoming in the campaign of 1876 to subdue the Sioux.

From that time on Irwin had absolutely no record of this man Brules. He seemed to have disappeared off the face of the earth. However, five years after Brules left the baby, the Shoshone squaw, who was acting as the foster mother, died of tuberculosis, the same plague that struck down so many Indians who had no immunity to the white man's diseases.

It was then that Irwin wrote his sister in Ohio suggesting that she might be interested in adopting the child. Irwin stressed that the Shoshone Reservation was extremely volatile and that it was not an environment in which to bring up a young girl, especially one whose father had been white. From his notes, one gleans that Mary Hamilton was delighted by the whole idea.

There appears to have been some difficulty finding a way to transport the young girl from Wyoming to Ohio. But it was finally accomplished under the kind auspices of two gentle nuns from the Convent of St Albans, who were traveling eastward to visit relatives. For a reasonable stipend, paid to the convent, they delivered the child to the adoptive parents.

The actual execution of the adoption procedure was not complicated. Irwin had to provide the girl with some sort of Anglo-Saxon name to satisfy the court. The girl's Indian name was Morning Star, hardly suitable for white civilization. Irwin decided to use the last part of the girl's mother's name, Wild Rose, and the name of the girl's Indian foster father, Wesha. The adoption papers in the court house at Rock Springs, Wyoming, state that the baby, Rose Wesha, was adopted by Richard and Mary Hamilton of Granville, Ohio.

"Wait a minute!" Becky cried out. "Rose Wesha Hamilton—that was your mother's name!"

"I cannot tell you what a jolt it was for me. My beloved friend Brules, with whom I had always felt such a kinship, was in fact my grandfather!"

"Did you write your mother immediately?"

"No, how could I? She had always thought him a murderous good-for-nothing. How could I put this bombshell in a letter? I didn't know what to do."

"But how and when did you finally tell her?"

"I didn't tell her until fate forced my hand."

"What do you mean?" she asked.

"When Pearl Harbor was bombed, Pan Am evacuated all civilian personnel from the islands. I went out on the last Clipper from Wake. I will never forget looking down on that Marine garrison as we took off. Those poor devils faced either certain death or years in a Japanese prison camp. It was a wrenching experience, I can tell you. And when later I saw the terrible damage at Pearl, it filled me with an iron resolve.

As soon as I arrived at Oakland, I went to the nearest

Naval Recruiting Station and offered my services. With my background as a Pan Am captain, my civil engineering degree, and my previous military service, it didn't take them long to offer me the rank of lieutenant commander with naval aviator wings and assign me to Naval Air Transport. I went right back in to the action in the southwestern Pacific."

"Where were you stationed most of the time?"

"Henderson Field in Guadalcanal in the Solomons. I had command of a Naval Air Transport station there. It was really a big job. It covered most of the South Pacific. I was not, of course, in charge of any troops, only of the Naval Air Transport.

By that time, we had gotten away from the converted B-24's for transport. We had a marvelous new airplane, the Douglas DC-4, which was then the state of the art. The army called it the C-54, and we called it an R5D. It was a wonderful airplane. The cockpit was way forward of the engines so that you didn't get that constant roar. Both the B-24 and the B-17 had engines outside the window, right by your ear. A long flight in a B-24 could make you half deaf, at least temporarily.

But in the R4D, you could look back from the cockpit and see twenty or thirty feet behind you. Those beautiful full-feathering, hydromatic silver-domed whirling props glistening in the moonlight are a sight I'll never forget. It was a marvelous airplane to fly. There were bunks in the forward part of the cabin ahead of the wing, where crew members could rest on long flights.

Using these new airplanes, we set up a very good air transport system. I think I visited almost every base we had, and God knows I tried my best to keep the morale high and the work efficient.

It was while I was in Guadalcanal that I received the letter from Mother that brought me home.

She wrote to say that some of the cowboys had been up looking for strays in the snow near Brules's cabin and that they'd stopped by to see him. They were shocked at what they found. The old man was still alive, but the stove had gone out, and he was unable to rise and feed himself. By rights, he should have been dead long before, but he had hidden strength and somehow managed to survive.

Although the cabin temperature went down to well below zero at night, those heavy buffalo robes must have kept him alive. The men cooked him a big pot of soup and stayed with him for a while.

'I must say, it is a very sad thing,' Mother wrote. 'I'm sorry to know that this man is lying up there dying alone. It must be a terrible thing to face death by yourself. But I have heard that he lived the life of an outlaw who committed many terrible crimes, so I am afraid he is meeting a just fate.

'I hope, son, that you are getting on with your job in the Pacific. I pray for you morning, noon, and night and think of you always. Your loving Mother.'

Needless to say, when I received the letter, I was filled with rage at her lack of understanding. She knew nothing of the true nature of this man whom I loved so dearly. I decided that I would have to reveal the secret, which even Brules did not know. I knew it would come as a terrible shock to her and decided to tell her when I saw her instead of trying to do it in a cable.

I sent her a short message immediately: 'Dearest Mother, I am shocked by the news of Brules's sinking condition. Even more, I am saddened by your harsh judgment of the man. You don't know whereof you speak. The time has come for me to give you the facts as I know them. I will do that when I see you. It is very difficult for any military personnel to pull out of an active war zone, but I shall try to return home as soon as possible.

'Meanwhile, you cannot allow Brules to die up there alone in his cabin. He is not what you think. There is a strong connection between us which I will explain when I see you. In addition, Dad had business dealings with him, and we will inherit his land. Please, you must bring him down to the ranch immediately. For God's sake, dearest Mother, don't delay.'

About four hours later I received her reply.

'Dear son, I received your cable. I don't understand why you have always cared about that wicked old mountain man, but out of respect for your father and you, I will follow your instructions. We will do everything to save Brules. Please come as quickly as possible. We want to see you so much! Your loving mother.' "

Steven paused. Then Becky asked, "You were able to get back here, weren't you?"

"Yes. I think I made the fastest trip on record up to that time from the South Pacific to the Rocky Mountains. I had to do some fancy footwork because we were preparing for the Battle of the Bismarck Sea at the time, and the demands on our transport unit were enormous. Fortunately, I had a very good adjutant and was able to delegate some of the planning operations. As a Captain I was able to cut my own orders and caught the next R5D leaving Guadalcanal. I was fortunate in knowing the crew, and since they considered it quite a privilege to have me aboard, they made every effort to make things comfortable.

I slept a good deal of the time, knowing that I had a long

and grueling passage. It was about seven hours to Kwajalein, and from there to Johnson Island was about six more. Then it was four to Honolulu, and fourteen more from Pearl Harbor to Oakland. The whole flight took around thirty hours.

When I arrived in Oakland, I immediately made my way to Naval Air Transport Headquarters, where I was fortunate to find one of my friends. I told him of my dire need for transportation to southwestern Colorado, knowing that the transport squadron there kept two or three fighters on hand for proficiency checks.

'Cowboy,' he said without hesitation, 'we've got three F6F's here. You're welcome to one of them. Bring it back in due time.'

My heart leaped. You couldn't beat that. This little airplane would eliminate a long ride from San Francisco on a United Airline DC3, and then two days on the railroad to Rico. I knew that with gas rationing, there was no chance of renting a car in Denver. This would save three days' travel time. Perhaps I had a chance to make it home before Brules died.

The F6F was a hell of an airplane. It had a Pratt and Whitney 2800 double row WASP, eighteen-cylinder radial, two-thousand-horsepower engine. This was the first propeller-driven fighter to break four hundred miles per hour, and it was capable of staying with any of the fighters of the war, including the P38, P51, and Spitfire.

The little airstrip at Norwood that I had used at the time of Father's death was way too short for a fighter. But I recalled a gravel strip down in Cortez, Colorado, that was better than four thousand feet long. If I could just get in there, I thought, it would be great.

Unfortunately, there was no naval aviation fuel there, but I hit upon the idea of stopping at the Naval Air Station in Salt Lake City and refueling there.

229

I knew Rollin Usher, who ran the Cortez airport, and his wife, Polly. He was the president of the bank as well as a flight instructor and manager of the airport, so he had plenty of local influence. I called him from San Francisco and told him of my wild plans to fly into Cortez.

He seemed excited to hear from me. 'Don't bother your mother, Steven,' he said. 'Polly and I will run you up to the ranch.'

When I told him I was coming in with an F6F fighter, he about tore the telephone off the wall. His operation was all Piper Cubs. 'Oh, God,' he yelled, 'I'll clear all the aircraft in the vicinity.'

That's how I made it from one of the farthest outposts in the South Pacific to Colorado in under forty hours.

I had telephoned the ranch from California and spoken to Mother. She almost screamed over the phone when she heard my voice. After all, it had been about five years since we had seen each other. She told me that Brules had been brought down from the mountain and was in bed at the house. It had been a tough trip through four feet of snow and deep timber. But he was clinging to life and constantly asking for me. I told her I would fly a fighter to Cortez that afternoon and that Rollin and Polly had offered to drive me up to the ranch.

I came whistling in to that gravel strip, catching the awe of the Piper pilots and the other locals at the airport. Rollin and Polly quickly packed me into their car and drove the sixty miles up to the ranch in jig time. It started to get dark and was snowing when we arrived.

Mother had seen the lights of the car coming up the road and was waiting in the open doorway. I jumped out and raced over to her. I hugged her tightly as tears of joy and relief flowed down our cheeks.

We turned to Rollin and Polly and begged them to stay the night or at least have some coffee, but they tactfully declined.

I stood there for a moment, hugging her in that glorious big living room with its cathedral ceiling and towering fireplace. There, high on the wall, hung Brules's trophy from our last hunt, the third largest bull elk ever killed. The roaring fire cast a warm glow on the rich patina of the worn leather furniture. The well-read books and familiar paintings welcomed me into what I felt was the greatest home in the world. I knew that through the big window on the south side of the room in daylight we had a magnificent view of Lone Cone Peak.

When Mother quieted, I slipped out of her grasp and said, 'I must go see Brules.'

'Yes,' she said, 'go right away. He may not have long to live.'

I shot up the stairs to the guest room and opened the door. The lamp on the table cast a low light on the bed. Brules opened his eyes when he heard me come in. He finally recognized me and raised himself up on his arm, calling out, 'Oh, my boy, my boy, you dun come back!'

His eyes shone in the light. Those strange eyes that I had watched so many times thrilled me through and through. Eyes that had seen the Old West when it was young, that searched far horizons with snow-clad mountain peaks, eyes that spoke of the prairie wind and the thunder of the buffalo herds, the eagle's scream, the crack of rifle fire, and the wild shrill cry of the Comanche charge. In a flashing second it was all there. Old Brules was the man I had always remembered. There he was. I had come halfway around the world to see him.

I dashed over and threw my arms around him and he kept saying, 'My boy, my boy! My flyin' man. So you are back to see me before I go. Oh, my boy. Look at ya now in that great-lookin' uniform. Boy, you must be something. You got lots of braid and stuff. What kind of rank ya got? How ya been doin'?'

'Well, Mr. Brules, I'm a Navy captain.'

'Hell, a captain, is that all you is? You ought to be a colonel.'

'Yes, but, Mr. Brules, the Navy doesn't grade people that way. A Navy captain is the equivalent of a colonel.'

'Oh,' he said, 'well, that's better. That's the way it ought to be. You bet, or else you oughta be a general.'

'Well the Navy doesn't have generals, Mr. Brules, they have admirals.'

'Well, hell, you ought to be the first admiral.'

I laughed and said, 'Oh, I'm a long ways from anything like that. But it is so wonderful to see you, sir. I'm so glad I was able to get here. How are you feeling?'

'Well, I don't feel too good, son, and I'm kind of slippin' a stirrup here and there. The last few weeks have been a little cold and tough. I ran out of heat and almost froze to death. I curled up in them buffalo robes and just decided I was gonna die. But, by Jove, the next thing I knowed, them cowboys from the ranch come and cooked me some soup and that helped a lot. I tell you I had been about a week with nothin' to eat. And then there come that wonderful lady. Boy, she is a magnificent woman. She's your mother, ain't she?'

'Yes, sir, she is,' I replied.

'Well, I want to tell you she is wonderful. You should have heard her givin' orders and movin' them guys around and the first thing you knowed they had me on kind of a toboggan thing

232

and they pulled me down off the mountain. It was a nice ride, I enjoyed it. The sun was out and the sky bright blue. The snow was just starting to drop from the white-covered pine trees. It was just beautiful. We come down that trail—a pretty tough trail too. And say, that lady was riding a stallion just like she was part of the horse. The strange thing is that she had some look about her that was real familiar.'

'What do you mean?'

'Well, you know, she had a look about her that reminded me in a way of Wild Rose. She's a much older woman, but I thought, well, you know, that might be the way Wild Rose would look when she was old. 'Course, when she always come to me in my dreams she's a young girl. But you know, your ma, even with her gray hair and all, kinda looks like her.

Isn't this the greatest house? I seen it from a distance lots of times but I ain't never been in it.'

'Yes, and, Mr. Brules, did you see what was up above the fireplace?'

He said, 'I seen a great big bull elk. My God, he was big! He was probably as big as the one that you and I dun killed. How many years ago was that?'

'Well, sir, that was back in 1928.'

'Yeh, I remember. That's just as big as that elk.'

'That is that elk,' I replied.

'You got to be kidding! How did that get here?'

'I told you what I was going to do. I was going to have it mounted and put up above the fireplace. That elk has been there fifteen years. He wouldn't have lived that long. But he's down there now giving everybody a lot of pleasure. Everyone remarks about it.'

'Well, they ought to, I guess. It is a pretty big old animal. I never knowed you could stuff anything like that. Well, how about you anyway? How did you get here? They tole me you were down there in the South Pacific Ocean somewhere.'

'Yes, sir, I was. I was down in the Solomon Islands, halfway around the world.'

'How did you get here?'

'Well, when Mom wired me about you, I just grabbed some airplanes and took one after the other and finally got here.'

'Oh, ain't that wonderful. I'm so glad you're here. I ain't feelin' too good, but I'm tough. Hell, I may go back up on the mountain again soon.'

'Yeh, you just might, Mr. Brules.'

'I sure like that wonderful lady, your ma, and I'd like to know somethin' about her.'

'Mr. Brules, remember the story you told me about your wife and baby daughter, Morning Star? Do you know what happened to Morning Star after you took her back to the Shoshone reservation?'

'No, but I always wondered what the hell happened to her. I left her with my buddy Wesha, the son of the chief. He gave her to one of his wives, who was gonna take care of her. I was so heartsick 'bout Wild Rose's dyin' that the next day Wesha and I went out on an expedition to join General Crook at Cloud Peak Camp to go against the Sioux, their blood enemies.'

'Yes, I remember that, sir. You fought at the Battle of the Rosebud and the Little Big Horn. But did you ever try to find your little daughter?'

'Yes, I did. I was down at the San Carlos Indian Reservation in Arizona, in '85, after the Geronimo wars and I was fixin' to go back and see her. I figured she was about ten years old and I ought to go back to the Shoshone Reservation and see her. I

got one of them clerks at San Carlos to write a letter to that
fella, Irwin, who was the agent up there and tell him I was a
comin'. I sent her a little pair of Indian boots all braided and
pretty. I got a letter back saying that she'd been shipped out of
that reservation five years before. She was living in Ohio or
someplace like that. She had been adopted by a bank president
and his wife. They loved her and was givin' her a fine education.
They said she was doing real well and it was much better than
living with an old mountain man. Irwin wrote that it would be
awful for me to go back there and present myself. I checked with
a few friends and they all said the same thing, "For God's sake, it
would be too much of a shock for her. You stay right where you
are and leave her alone." So I dun it. It was hard 'cuz I woulda
loved to see her again.'

'Well, Mr. Brules, you did see her again.'

'I did? When the hell was that?'

'She was the lady that brought you down off the mountain
five days ago.'

'Oh, come on, what the hell are you talkin' about?'

'Yes, that lady is my mother and she is your daughter,
Morning Star. She was adopted by the Hamiltons in Granville,
Ohio. She was educated and went to Oberlin College. And then
my dad, George Cartwright, stopped at the National Bank there
in 1896 on a cattle-buying trip. Mr. Hamilton asked him to
come to dinner that night. Mom took one look at him and
decided that none of those eastern fellows could come close to
having what she wanted and that he was the man for her. They
were married that summer and he brought her out to this ranch
in 1897.'

Old Brules's mouth was open. Then he kept saying, 'I don't

think you know what the hell you're talkin' about. Come on, now, say that all over again.'

I repeated it and he said, 'Well, I'll be goddamned, wait a minute, I got to think about it.'

For a minute Brules sank down and went into deep thought.

He said, 'Did she ever get them boots?'

'I don't know,' I replied.

'Well, you know,' he said, shaking his head, 'that's the damnedest thing. That's a wonderful woman, damned right. She's my daughter, ain't she? That's what you are saying.'

'Yes, that's what I'm saying. And you know what that makes me, Mr. Brules?'

He thought a minute and he said, 'God damn, you're my grandson!'

I said, 'That's exactly right, sir. And one more thing, Mr. Brules, I'm never going to call you Mr. Brules again. You're Granddad now?'

He said, 'You bet yer damned right I am. Don't ever call me Mr. Brules. You're my grandson. I don't call you boy no longer, I call you Grandson and you call me Granddad.'

We got to laughing a little bit and hugged each other again. I noticed the old man was getting tired, so I said, 'You ought to get a little rest. I've got the hardest job in the world now.'

'What's that, son?'

'I got to go down and tell that lady that you are her dad.'

He said, 'Oh, my God, you better get out the whiskey before you tell her that. She is liable to faint away. To think a smelly old mountain man like me is her father. Please take it easy with her. She's a real nice lady.'

'I will, Granddad. Now, you ease back on the pillows and have a little sleep. I'll come back and we'll tell some wonderful lies about our hunting days.'

'I'm so glad you come, son. I'm so glad you come,' he said.

I went down to the living room and found Mother sitting in the rocking chair near the fire. She had been knitting but had apparently dozed off. I went over and kissed her cheek. She opened her eyes and said, 'Oh, my wonderful son. I am so glad you're here. This terrible, terrible war is causing so much grief. But we are making progress, aren't we?'

'Yes,' I said, 'it looks like things may turn out all right. But it still looks like there are years of fighting ahead.'

She nodded and said, 'Yes, that's the horror of it. Such a waste of all those fine young men. What a terrible thing modern warfare is. How's the old man now?'

'He is not ready to indulge in anything very vigorous, but I think he is holding his own for the moment. By the way, he thinks you are pretty wonderful. Mother, tell me something— where were you born?'

'Why do you ask? You know where I was born, son. I was born in Lander, Wyoming, on the Shoshone Reservation.'

'Do you remember the trip you made as a little girl when the two nuns from the Convent of St. Albans took you to Ohio to meet your adoptive parents?'

'Yes,' she said, 'I do. I remember quite a bit about that. You know I was five years old.'

'Tell me what you remember about it.'

'Well, I remember Mr. Irwin, the agent, took me in a buggy down to the railroad station to meet the nuns. I remember the train coming in. I had never seen a train before, and it was very exciting. It came chugging in with ringing bells and blowing whistles. It stopped and the engine sat there just sort of breathing, huffing and puffing.

We scrambled on board and got into our seats. I was rather scared and shy, but the nuns were very kind to me. They offered me some candy, which broke the ice immediately. I don't remember their names now, but they were very nice to me. I'll never forget how fast and thrilling the train ride was.

We stopped in Chicago and had to go over to another station to change trains. The other station was near the lake, Lake Michigan. I was so excited, as I had never seen a body of water that big. It took a couple of days to make the whole trip. I remember when we arrived at the station in Granville, Mother and Daddy Hamilton were standing on the platform, waiting for me. We got off the train and they gave me a big hug and kiss when the nuns said, "This is Rose."

The nuns said some nice things about my good behavior on the trip. I don't remember anything about the rest of the conversation because I was so busy looking around everywhere. There were so many beautiful trees, and Ohio was so green compared to where I had been in Wyoming.

It was in 1881 when I took that carriage ride out to the Hamilton mansion. The mansion was something I could never have dreamed of. I had never seen anything like that on the Indian reservation. My heavens, there were three stories. The many rooms seemed large to me and were airy and well decorated. The house was located on grounds that looked like a park.

Mother and Daddy Hamilton seemed to take to me immediately. The Indian agent had said that my name was Rose Wesha, and now I was to be called Rose Wesha Hamilton. I thought that was a very nice-sounding name.

I had a wonderful childhood. Daddy Hamilton gave me a

little pony which I loved to ride. Once in a while Mother and I would go down to the bank to visit Daddy. I thought the bank was a wonderful place. Everyone paid lots of attention to us since Daddy Hamilton was the president.'

'You went to Oberlin College, didn't you?' I asked.

'Yes, I did. I majored in music and was an honor student.'

'Then there was a big change in your life, wasn't there?'

'There certainly was! When I was twenty-one years old, Daddy brought a magnificent man home for dinner. I had never seen anyone like your father. He was so tall, handsome, strong, and rugged-looking. He was full of life and had piercing blue eyes.'

She smiled a little and continued. 'When I first saw him, my heart started to beat wildly and I knew that I was looking at somebody that really was somebody. He didn't look anything like the young men that I had been going around with. This man came like thunder out of the West.'

'You saw him that one night, and then—well, tell me about it, Mother.'

'Well,' she said, 'when he left I wondered if I would ever see him again. I felt very apprehensive about it. He was very polite, and as he left said, 'I hope I have the pleasure of seeing you again, Miss Hamilton.'

'Well, I certainly hope so,' I said.

'He had come east to buy cattle. He was changing over from the longhorn breed, which he had driven up from New Mexico the year before, to white-face Herefords. They were a lot less wild than those longhorns and the meat was better. There was more meat on the bones. He was always at the advance point of the industry and thought he ought to be running Hereford cattle instead of longhorns. Ohio was known for its

Hereford cattle and he bought numbers of them in different parts of the state. I don't know at that time exactly how many thousand head he was running at the ranch, but I would give a guess that it was something around four or five thousand. We ran more than that later, but that's about what it was at that time. He never made a trip into town but what he didn't come to see me.'

I began to smile a little bit and said, 'You really got taken with this fellow, didn't you?'

'Oh, I was wildly in love with him, and each time he came to see me, I couldn't bear to see him leave. Finally he asked me to marry him and I couldn't say yes fast enough.'

'That's wonderful, Mother. He was a tremendous man. You came out west and lived a great life, didn't you?'

She said, 'Yes, I have, yes, I have. I've lived an incredible life in this beautiful country.'

'Mother, are you sure that you were born on the Shoshone Indian Reservation in Lander?'

'Yes, where else would I be born? That is all I remember from the very beginning. Of course I was born there.'

'Do you remember a famous warrior named Wesha?'

'Oh, yes, I remember him. He was my father.'

I said, 'No, I think he was your foster father.'

'What do you mean? What are you trying to say?'

'Remember when I lived on Wake Island building the Pan Am base there? I decided to research Brules's life and wrote many places for information. I received information from the army, the Shoshone Indian Reservation, and St. Albans. And I am absolutely sure of what I am going to tell you.'

'What are you talking about?'

'Mother, you were not born on the Shoshone Indian Reservation.'

'I wasn't? Well, where was I born?'

'You were born in that cabin up on the mountain.'

'I never heard of anything so outrageous in all my life. Where did you get such an incredible idea?'

'I'm telling you where I got it. The records prove it all. This man, Brules, whom you have disdained for all these years, actually saved your life by a magnificent piece of horsemanship. Your mother, a Shoshone girl named Wild Rose, was terribly injured in a somersault fall off a horse high up on the mountain. You were born prematurely and she died three weeks later. Brules tied you, a tiny naked baby, to his bare back and covered you both with a bearskin coat and rode from that cabin on Lone Cone Peak to Mexican Hat. He rode one hundred twenty-four miles, as the crow flies, in twenty-four straight hours without stopping in order to find a wet nurse for you. The ride almost killed the magnificent painted stallion that Brules rode, and I guess in a way it almost killed Brules.

He told me that when he got off the stallion, the paint took two steps and fell to the ground. Several squaws came running when they heard a baby cry. They took you off his back and he knew you were being fed when you stopped crying. He was so tired he just fell down, put his head on the neck of the horse, and fell asleep on that dirt street with all the pigs and chickens running around him. No one bothered him until the next afternoon.

Then Brules engaged the services of a Navajo warrior and his squaw, who had a newborn child. He persuaded them at the cost of many painted ponies to accompany him back to the Shoshone Reservation at Lander to deliver you into the hands of Wesha's family. You were only about three weeks old at the time of the journey.'

'I don't understand,' she said. 'You mean my mother was a Shoshone girl named Wild Rose? I was never told anything about her. What was she doing up in that cabin up there and how did Brules find her there?'

'She was married to Brules. He brought her down here from the Shoshone Reservation in the fall of 1875 and they built that cabin together. You were born in that cabin in the spring of 1876.'

'Are you telling me that that mountain man, Brules, is my father?'

'Yes, Mother, I am telling you just that. And I am telling you that he is my grandfather. And I am damned proud of it. He was probably the greatest scout and marksman on the western frontier. White men called him Cat Brules. The Indians called him To-ye-ro-co, the big cat of the mountains—the panther. He was highly respected by many famous generals in the U.S. Army.

Brules captured a hundred horses from the Blackfeet in a daring raid to get the bride price for your mother, Wild Rose. She was absolutely crazy about him and he about her. And when she died it was a hellish tragedy. He didn't know what to do. He took you back to the Shoshone Reservation, put you in the care of Wesha's family, and then went off with Wesha to the wars with the Sioux and later Geronimo. He was gone for ten years.

There is no doubt about it. I have all the proof and I have pieced it together with Brules's life story that he has told me over the years. I for one am so proud that Brules is your father and my grandfather. He is the greatest man I have ever known.'

Slowly, very, very slowly Mother slid from the chair in which she was sitting, down onto her knees, bent her head forward almost to the floor, put her hands to her face, and gave a loud cry, 'Oh, God in heaven, what have I done.'

She broke into uncontrollable sobs. I sat down beside her and tried my best to comfort her.

'It is all right, Mother, it has all turned out all right.'

'What have I done?' she said. 'What have I done? For forty years my father has been up on that mountain and I have ignored him. May God forgive me. How could I have done such a terrible thing. I even had you punished for going to see your own grandfather. I thought he was a criminal, an outlaw, and I was afraid of him. I saw him in the meadow once and I ran away.'

I could do nothing except hold her in my arms and comfort her.

Soon dawn began to break and the snow on the mountain turned red and gold with the promise of a beautiful day. I looked into Mother's tired, tear-stained face and said, 'Shall we go see if Brules is awake?'

She nodded slowly and we went upstairs. Mother sat down on the chair next to the bed. Brules opened his eyes when she tenderly took his gnarled old hand in hers and said, 'I never dreamed. I had heard such awful tales of the old man on the mountain. How could I possibly know you were my father? I am so sorry. We have wasted so many years!'

'My sweet Morning Star, your life has been good. I couldn't have dun nothing for you, and you dun give me a wonderful boy, a grandson. We sure dun some huntin' and ridin' and swapping stories, haven't we, son?'

'We sure have, Granddad. And you taught me a lot.'

243

'I told you, son,' Brules said, 'I thought I saw a young girl in the meadow many years ago that looked just like my Wild Rose, 'cept she were wearing white man's clothes, not Indian ones. I even hollered out, "Wild Rose," but the girl run off on her horse.'

'I remember that,' said Mother. 'That was me. I'm so sorry I ran away.'

'Hell, girl, I never blamed you. There I was a grizzly old mountain man hollering at a beautiful young woman wearing fancy clothes.'

'Did you ever try to come back to the reservation for me?'

'Yes, child, I did. By the time the wars was over, you was about ten years old. A fella wrote a letter to Irwin for me to tell him I was coming for ya. I sent him some Indian moccasins to give to you. But he wrote back and tole me you'd been adopted by some rich folks back east and that I should leave well enough alone.'

Mother got a strange look on her face. 'I received a pair of beautiful moccasins when I was little,' she said quietly. 'I wore them all the time until I outgrew them. My mother said they were a gift from someone out west.'

They looked at each other, eyes bright with tears, and I left them alone. I thought they had a lot of years to catch up on."

Becky's own eyes were glistening as she walked over to where Steven sat staring into the flames. She put her hands on his shoulders. "Oh, Steven, what a moment in your life! What a sad yet joyous moment. I can see it all. Aunt Rose must have been beside herself."

"She was, but more important, she was beside her dad. That was something that had been missing all her life.

Old Grandfather Brules lasted four more days. I stayed

there, stretching my leave, determined to see all I could of him before he passed away.

Just before he died, he told me, 'Son, you are the pride of my life and I want to give ya the things that I prize most. That 1873 Winchester that dun me so good for so long and took care of me and Wesha in lots of scrapes is yers. And so is that Buffalo Sharps that old General Crook give me when I left his command back there in 1885 in Arizona. They're yers, son, and I hope ya get some use from em.'

There was no treasure that I would rather have had than the two guns that had meant so much to Granddad Brules. He died late that night. Mother and I were with him until the last. After he was gone, Mother broke down in a way that I had never seen before.

The next morning we made a coffin for Brules and buried him in the frozen ground near the house, where he could look up at his beloved mountain. We promised ourselves that when summer came we would take him from that grave and carry him back up and lay him beside his Wild Rose. We could do no more.

Mother and I bade our sad farewell. She sobbed her heart out, saying she'd lost her husband and her father, and now she was losing her son. I told her that I would be all right and would be home as soon as I could.

About five days later I reported back to the squadron and we continued our terrible war in the South Pacific."

NAVY CROSS

The embers of the fire were low, and the stars shone brilliantly. Becky was so caught up in Steven's story, she couldn't wait for him to continue.

"When you went back out to the Pacific, after Brules's death, how long was it before the war was over?" she asked.

"About a year and a half. It ended maybe three months after I saw action in Iwo Jima."

"The capture of that island played a great part in the delivery of the atomic bomb to Hiroshima, didn't it?" Becky asked.

"Yes, indeed it did."

"Were you surprised when you heard about the bomb?"

"I and a hundred million other people! No one had any idea that anything like that was going on."

"It stopped the war," she said.

"It sure did! Think what it would have been like if we

hadn't had that bomb. Instead of facing years of bloodshed, we were now free to go home. I'll tell you, I was pretty well worn out mentally and physically by the time I came back to the ranch."

"I didn't notice that you were worn out," Becky said. "You seemed the same, but I guess a man can be exhausted emotionally without showing it."

"I suppose you're right."

"You got the Navy Cross, didn't you?"

"Yes."

"That's the highest honor you can receive, isn't it?"

"Well, not quite. The Congressional Medal of Honor is considered a bit better, I think."

"Yes, but didn't you get that too?"

"Now, how did you know that?"

"Aunt Rose told me. She was so proud."

"Well, yes, I got both medals for the same action—one from the Navy, and one from the President of the United States."

"That's wonderful! Please tell me about it."

"I don't like to talk about it. It brings back bad memories."

As they sat in the warmth of the fire, she reached over and took his hand. "Please, Steven, I really want to know all about you. I've heard about some of your war experiences, but I would like to know how you won the Navy Cross and the Congressional Medal of Honor."

She gave him a squeeze. Every time she did something like that, it stirred him in a very strange way. My, how he loved this girl. She was so lovely, so beautiful.

"You remember something about Iwo Jima, don't you?" he began.

"Was that the island halfway between Saipan and Japan?"

"Yes. The U.S. Army Air Force Bombing Command felt it was absolutely essential to control Iwo Jima in order to make bombing raids on Japan practical. It was just a little too far to carry a decent bomb load from Saipan to Japan and back, but a lot could be done if we could move another eight hundred miles closer to the target.

The island was a cone made mostly of black volcanic rock. When the Marines invaded the island and attacked the Japanese garrison, their shell fire would strike the rock, and it would explode like shrapnel in every direction. Many young men lost their lives not from the shells but from the cutting edges of the black obsidianlike rock.

The Japanese garrison was fanatical about holding on to Iwo. They fought our men inch by inch.

The fighting was so prolonged and intense that the marines were in danger of running out of ammunition. After all the lives and bloody sacrifice that had gone into gaining a little territory at the base of that volcano, it would have been hell to back off because they didn't have the ammunition.

The Naval Air Transport Command was suddenly called to the rescue. We were needed to bring ammunition to the marines who were in such dire straits.

At the time, there were no airstrips on Iwo Jima available to us. There was only a flat-top ridge that ran about halfway up the volcano in a steep incline. It had been observed and surveyed by Marine engineers, who had come to the conclusion that it would be possible to land one of our R4D's there. If we could successfully land one of those cargo aircraft full of ammunition, we could save the day.

My command had serviced almost all the landings in the

South Pacific, including the one at Leyte in the Philippines. We knew nothing about an atomic bomb and thought the war might last another ten to twenty years. I believed that it was vital to get close enough to the islands of Japan to be able to hammer them properly. Taking Iwo Jima, where we could build a base, would make that possible. I thought we should do it at all costs. In any case, I volunteered.

They took the seats out and loaded my R4D with nothing but ammunition. The Marines themselves would take care of unloading the ammunition if we made it.

The commercial weight of a DC-3, when fully loaded with passengers, was around 21,000 pounds, but we were flying military loads of 27,000. I prayed that we wouldn't lose an engine because with that kind of gross weight, we wouldn't be able to hold our altitude if one engine quit.

It was about seven hundred miles from Saipan to Iwo. We left with enough fuel to do the round trip of fourteen hundred miles. Generally, the weather in the Pacific was very good, and you could see for hundreds of miles. But this time we had to go through a tropical front. It was a little bumpy and our visibility was low, but when we came out on the north side of that front, we saw the cone of Iwo Jima. We kept craning our necks looking for Japanese fighters, but we didn't see any. Our carrier fighters had apparently done a great job.

We came in close to the island. We had been flying at about six thousand feet, and I began to drop down to scan the situation. I knew I wasn't going to be able to circle the island. If we were spotted, we'd be shot down in a minute, and since we were full of ammunition, we'd be blown all to hell. I knew where the ridge was since I had been completely briefed on the topography. From the movement of the wind on the waves, it looked as if we were going to be landing upwind and taking off downwind and downhill.

The long ridge of volcanic rock that ran maybe a mile out to the extremity of the island was exactly where it was supposed to be. If they ever had time to develop it, it would make a good emergency field. But at the moment, not very much had been done except for smoothing it out a little. We had a relay command communication setup so that we could talk to an offshore cruiser and get a message relayed from some marines who were on the spot. They gave me a wind speed coming in of about twelve to fifteen knots on the trail, so it had to be a fast landing. I asked for the length of the runway and was given an estimate of twenty-eight hundred feet. Holy smokes, that was just a few feet more than a half a mile, I thought. Even landing uphill, it wasn't enough, but that was all we had.

I knew one damn thing. We sure as hell weren't going to turn around and fly back to Saipan without leaving some ammunition even if I had to crash that crate right there. If it didn't blow up, they would have the ammo. I thought about putting it in on its belly, but figured that those rough rocks would probably tear the fuselage open. Then first thing you knew, a fire would start, and we'd lose the whole load. So I made up my mind, it would have to be a straight landing. And we had one shot.

We had finally established direct communication with a Marine battalion commander on the radio by using a relay from one of the Navy ships far offshore.

'Come on in, boy,' he said. 'We are desperate for you.'

'You bet I'm coming. Whether we go out again is not important. We'll put that load there for you. Get your boys ready. I'm coming in on the roll on the uphill side. Give me some of the gradients.'

'The grade is about one in five.'

That meant for about every five hundred feet of runway, you had a hundred feet increase in elevation. That was pretty steep, and I thought that it would stop my roll awful fast. But then, what was I going to do once we turned around? We weren't going to be able to hold the brakes with the propellers going. We could hold the brakes at idle or a little higher than idle going up the hill, but if we shut down, we would coast back downhill and pile up.

I told the commander I was going to keep my engines running and hold my position on the hill until his boys got all the ammunition that they could out of there.

'That's great,' he said. 'We've got a hundred Marines here to unload you. Then we'll swing that tail of yours around, and you can take right off.'

'Fine, that's fine,' I said. But I wasn't very hopeful.

I turned to Jack Harris, my copilot. 'Jack, maybe we ain't coming out of here.'

'I know, skipper. But by God, we're going in, ain't we?'

'You better believe it!' I said.

Anyway, I tried to come in just a little below the ridge with the idea that I'd stall the airplane and kind of flop her down on what was supposed to be a runway. It was a hell-of-a-looking runway, I can tell you that. But it was the best the fellows could do. I lifted her up and cut my throttles real quick, and we hit with a kind of a bump and a bang.

'That ain't no grease job!' Harris said.

'It wasn't supposed to be,' I said, romping on the brakes as hard as I could.

I could see Marines lying on the ground all around us. By

God, they were watching this airplane as though it were something sent from heaven. And I guess it was.

Actually, the plane didn't roll very far because it was so steep. When we stopped, she started to roll back. I opened the throttles to about a quarter throttle and held it at about eight hundred RPM, just enough to keep her from rolling down the hill. Jack jumped up and worked his way around the load. When he got back to the big cargo door, he cut it loose and opened it up. Jesus, the Marines just poured in there.

Meanwhile, the Japanese gunners were working on us. I don't know what kind of artillery they had, but it was pretty good stuff. It was banging around the slopes below us, and shells were whistling overhead. But those Marines formed lines, and they did a damn fast job of unloading that ammunition. The only time they even faltered slightly was when some Japanese machine gun would start working on the Marines who were passing the ammunition.

The Japanese machine gunners put a few holes in my airplane but nothing fatal. What I was really worried about was the heavy artillery that they had up on the mountain. They were getting a pretty good range on where we were, and they were lobbing shells closer and closer. I knew that if they ever got a direct hit, it would be all over. But we had to get the ammunition off so the guys could use it. It didn't make any difference if we got blown to hell."

"Oh, Steven, how can you say such a thing?" Becky interjected.

"Let me tell you. When you get in a jam like that and you see fifty thousand men in the same jam you are, you don't spend any time figuring how you're going to sneak out of the deal.

I kept the throttles running, and it made hard work for the

fellows because the slipstream from the props was blowing them all over the place. But they sure did it! Boy, those Marines cleaned us out. 'You're empty! You're empty!' one of them shouted. 'We're turning you around.'

I could see forty or fifty of them on the fuselage swinging me around, and then I cut the engines way down because I was headed downhill, and I just stayed on the brakes as hard as I could. We were just barely holding on the hill. I didn't dare shut down the engines because if I did, I might never get them going again. Artillery shells were getting closer and closer.

One Marine major opened the door and yelled, 'You're all set now, God damn it! Get the hell out of here while you can!'

'We're not leaving yet!' I yelled back.

'Well, why the hell not?'

'By God, I'm not going empty! Put some wounded on board here.'

'We hadn't thought of that,' he said. 'That's a hell of an idea.'

He began snapping out commands, and those guys were quick as hell to get on top of what was going on. A lot of them were under fire. Their ring of defense fighters was pouring the stuff to the Japanese too. They were giving them hell.

Anyway, they began passing these poor wounded fellows up into the plane. You should have seen the condition of some of them. They were all shot to hell. They also put a couple of medics in with them. They just loaded up that goddamn airplane.

'Hurry up!' they kept shouting. 'Get out of here! Go on!'

I kept hollering for them to put some more guys on until they shouted, 'You're smothering what you've got!'

'Okay, close the door, we're going!'

Boy, when I opened the throttles and poured the coal to that thing, we went roaring down the runway, bouncing and banging over the rocks. Finally, we sailed out of there just as smooth as silk.

When I went to haul the gear up, old Harris said, 'Oh, hell. The hydraulic line is busted. The fluid is all gone. You've got to try to make it back to Saipan with the gear down. I'll try to hand-crank it.'

'Yeah,' I said, 'but we've got a lot lighter load now. These guys don't amount to the same load as we had coming in. Get out your calculator and see what we can do here. I'm going to pull this bitch down to the lowest goddamn RPM I can and hold altitude, and I'm going to put her in high pitch and put as much manifold pressure as I can. I'm going to lean on this thing and either blow those heads, or we're going to make it.'

Well, we made it all right, but there wasn't much left of the airplane. As I understand it, we had something like thirty-two wounded fellows on board, and only two of them died on the way back. So it was worth it. It was worth the try."

"Oh, Steven, that must have been hair-raising! And they gave you the Navy Cross?"

"Yes."

"And the Congressional Medal of Honor?"

"Yes," he said softly. "President Truman gave it to me at a special ceremony in Washington in the fall of 1945."

"Why don't you wear it or at least display it?" she asked.

"The only time I'd wear it would be for those boys that did that job. Boy, when you talk about heroes. Incidentally, we had just barely gotten off the ground when the artillery shells began smashing the hell out of the area where we'd been parked. We could have been shot to pieces. The Marines ran like hell and got out of the way. That's all there was to it. I didn't earn it—those boys did."

"You're the one who made the decision to pick up the wounded. That was a noble gesture."

"What else was I going to do? You couldn't leave those guys there if you could possibly take them out! God knows as pilots we used to pity those ground troops and think how we were so damn lucky to be flying. We might get shot down all right, but if we made it back, we got a square meal, a decent place to sleep, and medical attention if we needed it. Those poor devils lying out on the hillside, they got nothing."

Becky gazed out into the distance. In the east the thin rosy light of dawn streaked the sky, and the black outline of the mountains was etched in stark relief. She felt so complete, so in tune with the new day and the world. It was as though knowing Steven made her whole and the new day exciting. She looked intently at him through lowered lashes and watched as he got up, stretched, and walked over to the water bucket. He took a dipperful and raised the cool delicious spring water to his lips.

He drained the contents of the dipper, then hung it on a nail in the tree above the bucket.

"Would you like to get some sleep while I round up the horses? We can put off packing till about noon if you'd like." He turned toward the trail.

"Steven," she called softly.

He stopped quickly.

"Yes?"

"Steven, please come here for just a moment."

He drew closer, thinking once again that this young woman was absolutely the most beautiful thing he had ever seen. Her features were tinted slightly by the pale light of the new day. Her eyes sparkled, and a tender smile played upon her lips. He stood in front of her, his heart beating wildly.

"Steven, there is something I want you to know. You are the finest man I have ever known. You have such heart. You are the bravest, most handsome, charming man in this whole world. There is no other man like you. I love you, Steven. I have loved you all my life ever since I first saw you when I was a little girl.

I know you may think that the age difference is important, but you're wrong. Please believe me, Steven, I love you so much. I love and adore you with all my heart and soul. If you want me, I will be your woman. I will live with you and love you as long as the breath of life is within me. I want to have your children. I want to be with you in all the glory of this great world as long as we both shall live. Please, Steven, we belong together."

With a pounding heart, Steven took one step forward and gathered this glorious girl in his arms, looked into her eyes, and pressed his lips to hers. Slowly, as the light of the early dawn fingered the eastern sky, they sank gently together onto the soft green moss beneath the pines. Somehow he felt as though he was dreaming. It was as if he was young again, and with the rising sun, the whole world lay before him. They held each other breathlessly as the red dawn rose like thunder behind the snow-clad peaks of the San Juan Mountains.

Author's Note

Rebecca Stuart and Steven Cartwright were married the summer of 1950. They had four children, three boys and one girl.

The last I heard from the Cartwright family was in 1992. At that time old Steven Cartwright was ninety-four years old. But I was told he still rides up the mountain once every two weeks to check the high range and see how the cattle are doing and to visit his grandparents' grave. He has a gentle horse and takes one of the young cowboys with him. Mrs. Becky Cartwright, now sixty-six, supervises the Broken Bow Ranch with her oldest son, George.

The second son, Wesha Cartwright, is a heart surgeon practicing at Massachusetts General Hospital in Boston.

The daughter, Diana Rose, lives in California with her husband and two children. She is an accomplished concert musician.

The youngest son, nicknamed B after his great-grandfather, Brules, was an F16 fighter pilot in the Gulf War.